CHAPTER
ONE

✔ KU-754-863

Valentina stifled a yawn and waited for Phil and the rest of the band to unload the van. They had just finished their third gig in a week and, having attended them all as wardrobe mistress and publicity girl-cum-cheerleader, she was tired. Getting home late and rising early to go to work was hard enough but this time, following a late-night performance a long way from home, they had been forced to drive through the night. Dozing and coming to with a jerk when the van stopped or swerved was not conducive to relaxed sleep and she was determined not to do this overnight thing again. This uncomfortable trip would be the last one, whatever Phil had to say. She was tired of living like this, behaving like a young teenager, but telling Phil of her decision wouldn't be easy.

Phil and the boys had promised to arrange their bookings more reasonably but when a booking was offered they accepted without asking her. The trouble was, Phil Blackwood, the lead singer of The Shoremen, couldn't manage without her. They had been friends since he had walked her home from her first day at school and for Phil she was more than someone to look after their stage clothes: she was their talisman, their good-luck charm.

The reason for the all-night drive was an appointment in London where they were to audition for a spot in one of London's favourite venues. Unknown outside their small area of South Wales, they would not be accepted on trust but had to play and convince the manager that he wouldn't lose custom because of their performance.

Freshening herself in the washroom of a service station as well as she could, Valentina looked at her face in the mirror. Long, dark hair pulled untidily back in a bunch, small nose and wide-apart brown eyes that looked bleary and larger than normal in the early hours. She wore one of Phil's jumpers, over her own, which came down to her knees, and jeans that stopped at her shapely ankles, revealed slippers of black suede on her dainty size-three feet. She cleaned her teeth and washed her face with cold water then went out to re-join the boys. Phil was waiting near the door, looking anxiously at everyone who came out.

"It's all right, Phil," she teased. "I can hardly get lost in there!"

"You were a long time," he said gruffly. "I worry about you."

"I'm twenty-one, not five. I've been going to the lavatory on my own for ages!" As usual, he couldn't be teased out of his almost obsessional concern for her safety.

"Come on, love," he said, taking her arm, "the boys are already in the van."

Staffordshire Library and Information Services

Please return or renew by the last date shown

2 6 AUG 2015		
BURTON LIBRARY TEL: 239556		
Edwards	1 8 SEP 2015	

EAMERS

If not required by other readers, this item may may be renewed in person, by post or telephone, online or by email.
To renew, either the book or ticket are required

24 Hour Renewal Line
0845 33 00 740

Staffordshire
County Council

STAFFORDSHIRE LIBRARIES

3 8014 04557 4024

PITY THE LONELY DREAMERS

Grace Thompson

ISIS
LARGE PRINT
Oxford

STAFFORDSHIRE
LIBRARIE
AND ARCHIVES

04567 4024

ULVERSCROFT   1 3 FEB 2015

F   £15.95

Copyright © Grace Thompson, 2013

First published in Great Britain 2013
by
Robert Hale Ltd.

Published in Large Print 2014 by ISIS Publishing Ltd.,
7 Centremead, Osney Mead, Oxford OX2 0ES
by arrangement with
The Author
c/o Johnson & Alcock Ltd.

All rights reserved

The moral right of the author has been asserted

CIP data is available for this title from the British Library

ISBN 978–0–7531–9244–3 (hb)
ISBN 978–0–7531–9245–0 (pb)

Printed and bound in Great Britain by
T. J. International Ltd., Padstow, Cornwall

Five of them in a van with only two seats did not spell comfort and, as it was her turn to sit in the back, Valentina piled up coats and bags and tried to make a bed of sorts before settling to doze away the last few miles.

Their audition was on the outskirts of London at a public house where bands performed for an audience that frequently included agents searching for fresh talent. The Shoremen had only been together for a few months but Phil was already aiming high. He had very few favourable reviews with which to "sell" the band so he had phoned with promises to send others on, implying they had dozens. Sometimes that approach worked, as with their present appointment, although they still had to audition.

They reached their destination with two hours to spare and members of the group wanted to stretch their legs and find coffee and food.

"We stay together," Phil said firmly. "And we leave here in plenty of time for the appointment. Right? Come on, Valentina." He helped her out of her cramped position. "We'll all go and find a cafe and we can go through the sequence again to make sure we get it right. No pauses as though we don't know what we're doing. This is the closest I've been to a big London booking and I don't want you to mess it up."

"Go over the sequence?" Valentina laughed. "Just you and me?"

Phil looked around and saw the others had vanished. "They'd better not be late," he growled. They found a cafe and Phil ordered eggs on toast for them both. He glanced around frequently, waiting for the other three to appear.

Phil was slightly less than average height and broad in the shoulders. He wore a cowboy-style shirt and a black leather jacket, heavily fringed, cowboy boots also fringed and a wide leather belt to support jeans over his slim hips. His eyes were dark and solemn. He was brooding over the next few hours and dreaming of where they might lead. His face was dark too. "Gypsy" had been his nickname at school. His hair was long and wavy, covering his ears and bushing out where he had encouraged long sideburns.

Valentina wanted to tell him then that she wouldn't be taking part in future trips but knew from his expression that now was not the time. Today he had to concentrate on pleasing the manager of the pub and hopefully opening the door on better things. She mustn't spoil his chances by worrying him about her decision, but she determined to tell him on the way home.

Two members of the band were waiting at the van when they got back. Of the drummer there was no sign. They were within fifteen minutes of their time when he came running up explaining that he had fallen asleep in a cafe.

"If we'd lost this chance because of you . . ." Phil threatened.

"You'd better thank the cafe owner then," Henry said, unrepentant. "He threw me out because I was snoring!"

4

Perhaps because they were over-anxious, they played badly. Phil pleaded and explained they had travelled overnight and had given up two days of their holidays and the man grudgingly offered them the first spot that evening, which they knew would be disrupted by people arriving and drinks being ordered and the scuffling of feet and chairs. Phil accepted gratefully, even though they were all exhausted by the overnight travel.

"In fact," Phil told Valentina later, "our bodies were in a state similar to a hangover." Their performance hadn't improved from their audition.

They were driving home, another late journey in the cramped van, and Valentina talked to Phil when he was driving as she was in the much-coveted passenger seat.

"I won't be coming with you on any more trips," she said quietly. "This one is the last."

"Don't say that, Valentina!" The van swerved as he turned to her in dismay. "You haven't found someone else, have you?" It was his response to every disagreement, his fear that she was leaving him.

"I'm tired of all the travelling and the late nights, Phil. I want to do something else with my time."

"Sounds good to me," muttered the drummer's sleepy voice from the back.

"Shut up, Henry," Phil snapped.

"He's right though," another sleepy voice added. "I don't think we're going anywhere with this outfit and I think we should call it a day."

"Me too an' all," another said over a yawn.

"Fine by me!" Phil increased speed and the van shook as he aimed it at South Wales.

He was silent for a while and Valentina imagined the glittering anger showing in his dark eyes. "Why not give it a rest for a while and start again when you have more songs written and rehearsed?" she suggested quietly.

"I've got a better idea," he said later when they had stopped for coffee and were sitting apart from the others. "I'm going to move to London and show this lot how it's done. They're a lot of losers and I don't know why I've pretended different. I don't need them. I can sing and play the guitar and I look the part. I can't fail, can I?"

She stared at him, about to shake her head and discourage him from giving up everything for a dream, but something stopped her. There was a warning look in his eyes, a scowl breaking out around his full-lipped mouth. He was expecting her to answer in a negative way and was preparing for an argument. Instead she said, "Phil, love, you can't fail." She reached out and touched his hand. "Why don't you call yourself Gypsy?"

"Then you'll come?"

"What?"

"You and me, heading for the capital city where anything can happen. Valentina, please don't let me down. You're so enthusiastic about the music scene, you'll find it easy to get a job in the business. Your memory and your amazing knowledge of the music from the fifties, sixties and seventies, you'll be offered

6

work straightaway. We make a wonderful team. We could be married if you like."

She turned to stare at him. "This is a night for surprises! But I'm saying no to both offers!"

"All right, we needn't get married but we could share a flat. It's bound to be too expensive to live separately — until I start making big money."

"This is crazy. I can't uproot myself and leave Mam and Dad and Michael just like that."

"Why not?"

"I'd need to think about it for longer than it takes to drink a cup of coffee for one thing." The other, she thought, was the casualness of his proposal. "We could get married if you like" was not how she had imagined it. "Actually, no, I won't go with you, Phil."

"You said you needed time to think about it."

"I was wrong. No, Phil. Count me out of your fantasies."

"You're saying you don't want to share my future? You're letting me down? It's been a bad weekend, that's all. It'll be different when we get to London."

"I won't be going with you, and that is definite."

Although Valentina knew she had made the right decision in not going to London with Phil, a seed had been planted and the idea of going there, but without him, began to grow. Over the next few days she bought magazines dealing with the entertainment world and answered a few advertisements for staff in various businesses, including one for a record distribution company. Hearing her brother Michael strumming on his guitar in the next room — another dreamer — she almost didn't send that one. Perhaps she'd be better giving the music scene a miss, but she popped it into the postbox with the others.

A few days later there were three replies asking for more details and one from the record distribution company asking her to go to London for an interview. The moment she read the letter, she knew it was what she wanted.

Her heart was racing when she reached her destination. She was met by a secretary called Gillian Lever, who sat with her until the boss called her in and whispered good luck as she went through the door. The interview was brief and at the end of it she was offered the job.

Travelling home on the train, remembering the uncomfortable journeys in Phil's van, she was smiling. Unlike Phil, she wasn't a dreamer, she hadn't longed for impossible things, yet here was a dream she hadn't really wished for coming true. She would be working in the world of music.

She had told no one of her plans; had been avoiding Phil, said nothing to her parents. They would have to be told but it wasn't a happy prospect. Her parents wouldn't approve; they never did approve of anything she did. Sometimes she wondered why.

She waited until they were eating supper and said casually, "Mam, Dad, I'm going to work in London. It's for a company selling records and —"

"Don't tell your brother about this," was Valerie Robbins' harshly whispered reply. "I don't want you filling his head with such stupid ideas."

The reaction wasn't the one she had hoped for. "I went for an interview and I'll be given a trial to see how well I do."

"A trial? That's that, then. Next week you'll be back here shamefaced and asking for your old job back!"

"Don't you think I might do well? It's a company selling records and I know a lot about the music scene."

"London, is it? Your own family and home aren't good enough, then?"

"Mam, it isn't like that, I just want to get away and try something new. London must be the most exciting place to work and live." She didn't try to explain that the main reason was to get away from Phil Blackwood, her constant companion for years but who was possessive and demanding with no thought for her own abilities. Love didn't come into it. Sadly she realized it never had.

Phil had been trying for years to find a backer, get a record contract, and Valentina knew that in an overcrowded profession he simply wasn't good enough. All her suggestions on ways to increase his chances were laughed away. What could she possibly know? Now she needed to get away before she was swamped completely. If only her mother understood, wished her well, but in her heart she had known that wouldn't happen.

"I met a girl who works for the company called Gillian Lever. She's offered to help me find a room to rent. I'll be fine," she added sadly; a pretence that her mother was concerned. All Valerie Robbins worried about was her son, Valentina's younger brother, Michael, on whom all her loving was spent.

"Don't encourage your brother to go with you. Too young to leave us, he is. And what about Phil? Don't think I'm stupid, he'll be going with you, won't he?"

"No, Mam. I'm going on my own."

"Oh, go, then," her mother said irritably, "but no talking about how wonderful it is. D'you understand? I don't want your brother upset. I want Michael to have something better than leaving home and living among strangers. He's got talent and doesn't need to leave us to prove it, to make a grand gesture."

"Is that what you think I'm doing, making a grand gesture?"

"What else?" She said nothing of Michael's pleading to let him go or his assurances that Valentine would look after him and help him to "make it".

The Robbins family lived in a small town in South Wales. Dewi worked as a storeman in a grocery wholesalers. His wife Valerie worked in a bookshop. Their son Michael was unemployed, drifting through life dreaming of a career in the music world.

Breakfast in the Robbins' home was never a social affair and the next day was no exception.

"These days it's more like a stand-up cafe," Valerie moaned, putting extra toast onto her son's plate. Dewi and Michael ran down the stairs, grabbed some toast and ran back upstairs to finish dressing as they ate.

10

Valentina sat and ate in silence before putting on her coat to leave for the job she would only have for a few days more. Behind her she heard an argument between her parents, something that regularly began their day.

"You've driven her away with your criticisms, Valerie," she heard her father accuse.

"*I've* driven her away? You did that! You never wanted her!"

Valentina sighed and closed the door quietly. I must have been a difficult baby, she decided. Crying all the time and driving them crazy. That was the only explanation she could come up with for her mother's anger and her father's indifference and the arguments about her father not wanting her.

Setting off for London was both a relief and a worry for Valentina. Telling Phil had not been easy and his anger had alarmed her, so she caught an earlier train than planned, thankful not to see his face among the crowd. Setting off with no idea where she would be sleeping that night was scary but walking away from the possessive Phil was like shedding shoes that were too tight. She wished her father had been there to see her off, but he and her mother had stood silently as she gathered her suitcase and given only a slight, disapproving nod as a farewell.

Although she had done the journey before, she still found Paddington station rather terrifying, with people dashing about oblivious of others, oblivious of everything, all focused on getting to their destination. The sounds were like nothing she had heard before, voices and machinery a discordant symphony. She wished someone would stand still long enough for her to ask for help but it seemed impossible. She had forgotten previous instructions, her head empty of clear thought, and eventually found an information office and was given directions to go via the underground. She found the offices of Music Round and was met by the secretary, Gillian Lever, who offered tea and a few minutes to calm herself before she was taken to see her new boss, Ray Everett. The company supplied records to many small outlets all over London and beyond, he explained. Small customers valued the service they offered, as Music Round bought from all the recording companies and were then able to accept small orders. It was a huge advantage for small and new businesses. Instead of having to have accounts with dozens of publishing companies, Music Round supplied them from their own stock and enabled them to avoid minimal limitations with several companies which small outlets would not have been able to afford.

Ray Everett interviewed her for a second time and he was impressed. She was able to recite the names of every recording made by the names he mentioned and in most instances the dates as well. She had a rare gift and one he knew would be a valuable addition to his business. He was delighted with his find and showed her around the offices, explaining the role of each member of staff.

Gillian Lever took her out for a coffee after the meeting and Valentina told her of her urgent need to find somewhere to live.

"I'll have to check with my friend but we're looking for a third to share and you'd be welcome, at least until you find something better."

"Thank you. I — I've broken up with my boyfriend, you see," she explained. "Phil was so possessive he was stifling me, I had to get away. I only hope he will accept we're finished and not become a problem. Leaving Phil was one of my most sensible decisions."

"I've left my husband," Gillian said sadly and tears reddened her eyelids. Her fair skin was mottled a rosy pink, showing her deep distress. "He's in the music business too. A songwriter."

"Successful?"

"Very. I didn't understand the stresses of what he did, fool that I am."

Newly met but with something in common, they shared confidences and put down the foundations of friendship. Valentina told her new friend something of the difficulties she had with her mother. "Michael is the beloved son, and I'm nothing but a nuisance," she said sadly. "I'm not jealous of him — in fact I love him too, but it makes me sad that whatever I do, Mam will still consider me a failure."

They found her a room in a small bed and breakfast and a few days after starting her exciting new job, Gillian invited her to be a third share in the flat where she lived with another girl called Beth. The flat was in Ealing and a short walk from the flat led them to the underground station which took them to the office. A bus along the main road and they were in the shops of

West Ealing, where they could obtain most of their needs.

Valentina and Gillian worked together at Music Round but their jobs were not similar. Valentina had presumed she would be in the room with the other typists but soon found herself involved with the ordering alongside her boss. Ray Everett had quickly realized she was capable of working at the centre of the business. Her remarkable memory, which enabled her to read the list of the new top fifty recordings when they appeared on Tuesdays and immediately be able to repeat it, was something he wasn't about to waste. And besides this, and even more valuable, she had a flair for spotting potential successes.

First she studied the office routine, asked endless questions, and even made a few suggestions for improvement. This was a very busy organization where recordings were bought in their thousands and sold to hundreds of outlets. Yesterday was forgotten; today was all that mattered; everything was immediate and fast. She quickly learned the way the system worked. She was pushed along at an alarming pace and began to see some of the reps from the record companies, first with Ray Everett then on her own. It was scary but a newly discovered confidence emerged and she knew she had found her niche. Being so busy and with so much to learn helped her cope with the loss of her family. Leaving Phil should have saddened her but it hadn't. It had led her to this, and "this" was a job she could do extremely well and thoroughly enjoy. With a fascinating job and money in her pocket, Valentina was introduced to the joys of working and living in London.

She met several recording artists and a large number of young hopefuls. Most were charming, anxious to please in the hope of her one day being able to help them on their way. The most irritating was an overconfident young man called Tony Switch, who had an ego far greater than his singing abilities. Valentina quickly realized that he could become a nuisance. He invited her out several times, implying that he was doing her a favour by offering to spare time for her and give her the pleasure of his company. Pre-warned by Gillian, she declined.

With Gillian her enthusiastic guide, she wandered the streets and lanes, admiring the historic buildings great and small. She explored a different area each day and gradually the whole city came together so she could move from one area to another without cheating and darting down into the underground whenever she got lost.

She found her way to the galleries and began to enjoy the cultural side of the city. With Gillian pointing the way at first, she began absorbing the magic of secret places revealed in long walks and short bus rides. Neal's Yard was a place they frequently visited on their days off, Camden Lock and Portobello Road their favourite markets where they searched for bargains. Carnaby Street was still a venue for the smart, the outrageous and the trendsetters, and with a good wage Valentina experimented with fashion and found she had a flair for it. Phil, she missed not at all. She had heard nothing from him, which made her relax more with every day that passed. She had been so afraid of difficulties, of him begging her to return — but, she thought wryly, her vanity had been misplaced!

It was after midnight, a month after moving into the flat, and the night was typical of November: gloomy with fog and temperatures dropping to freezing. Valentina had just returned from the cinema with Gillian and Beth. They made hot drinks and were settling into their beds when the crash came. A nervous investigation showed a broken window in the living room. Warily looking out, Valentina saw a very drunken Phil standing, or rather staggering about, on the pavement below, shouting abuse.

Grabbing a coat, she went down to talk to him and he began pleading with her, tearfully, to come back to him. She realized there was no way to pacify him other than to agree — and that was something she couldn't do. So she left him there and returned to the flat.

When he disturbed them three times in the following week, she discussed moving out to leave Gillian and Beth in peace. "It's no use, he isn't going to stop until I move away," she told them sadly. "I don't want to go, and I feel it's wrong to allow him to drive me away, but I can't let you two suffer this any longer and I don't want to call the police."

Beth looked thoughtful but added little to the discussion. A few days later she told them she was leaving London, going back to her parents and the boyfriend she had left behind.

16

"I don't fancy looking for two new people to share," Gillian said to Valentina. "It's always a risk, fitting in with someone new and so often it doesn't work. What d'you say we look for a smaller place together?"

"And this time I'll ask Mam not to give Phil our address!" Valentina added.

It seemed the perfect solution. They got on well and they could afford a reasonable rent between them.

They moved just before Christmas. Not far, just around the corner and still convenient for the underground and the shopping centre. The flat was an improvement and Valentina felt at last that her life was perfect. There were a few things needed, including a fridge that worked and more comfortable chairs. A second-hand shop provided the chairs and a few items like cushions and pictures and a rug to make the place their own but they decided to wait for the sales before buying a new fridge.

It wasn't long, though, before Phil found her, and again he begged her to go back to him. At first he pleaded and promised her anything she wanted, then he threatened violence. Another time he knocked at their door and calmly offered them tickets for a gig he'd been given.

"No, thank you, Phil," Valentina replied, equally calmly. "Now please excuse me, I'm rather busy."

"I've been the only constant in Phil's life," she explained to Gillian later. "His father left when he was a baby and his mother left him when he was only three. Since then he has lived with a long list of foster parents and in between them with a grandmother who was constantly punishing him for imaginary bad behaviour. One of her favourite punishments, if he didn't do exactly what she asked, was to lock him in the coal shed. She proudly told everyone that it was the quickest way of making him behave." She shuddered. "He used to be terrified as she sometimes left him there overnight. And worse still, some of the foster parents followed the same method of making him behave as they thought he should. He still has a phobia about dark and closed-in places."

"It must have been terrifying for him." Gillian's face became blotchy and tears reddened her blue eyes as she imagined the child's torment.

"I've known for a long time that I'm not the one to help him," Valentina mused. "I hope he'll find someone to help him sort himself out, but it won't be me."

There was a knock on their door and a very excited Phil stood there. "It's over, Valentina. Our separation is ended and you can come back to me."

"What?"

"I've got a job! I start on 13 January as a clerk in —"

"I don't care if you have a dozen jobs, Phil," she interrupted. "I have no intention of coming back to you. We're finished. I hope you'll stop all this nonsense about my belonging to you then we can be friends. Nothing more than that. Not ever."

His anger seemed to fill the room. For a moment Valentina felt it like a blow. Gillian came and stood beside her, offering tacit support. In a voice that trembled, Valentina told him to leave.

"I'll go but I won't forget this. You used me! You used me to get your knowledge of the music scene, used me for a chance to get away from your family, give you the chance of a better life. Now you think you can push me aside."

"Maybe that's true and I'm sorry but I'd have left home anyway."

"Good job, smart flat, new friends. I don't fit into your new life, do I?"

"No, you don't, Phil. I like the freedom of not belonging to anyone."

"You belong to me and don't forget it!" He glared at them both then stormed out.

"It looks as if we might have to move again," Gillian sighed.

"Not pygmalion likely!" was Valentina's response.

CHAPTER
TWO

Valentina left the flat and walked slowly to the station, nervously looking out for Phil. They still hadn't bought a new fridge and the margarine had looked suspiciously green that morning and the milk had gone sour. With these things, plus the unwelcome letters delivered in the morning mail, the day could only get better.

Increasing her pace a little, she followed after Gillian, who had gone ahead to buy a morning paper and some magazines. Valentina usually hurried through the busy streets to begin her day working at the business she loved but the two letters wouldn't allow her mind to be free. Both were in her pocket, burning her flesh, demanding something of her that she couldn't deliver.

The first was from her mother, and she put it aside to read later. The other was from Phil, pleading with her to meet him and talk things through. What a stupid phrase! How many times had she and Phil talked things through? And how far had it got them? His jealousy and possessiveness had ruined any chance they'd had of a good, loving relationship.

For as long as she could remember it had been presumed she and Phil would marry one day. Leaving the sleepy South Wales town only a few miles from the sea to live in seventies London had changed everything for her. It had shown Phil up for the small-minded person he was. For that revelation she was grateful. Ridiculous jealousy and resentment of her achievements had bitten into his ego.

"The trouble between us is mainly because I've been more successful and I no longer look up to him, trust him, follow wherever he goes," she told Gillian as they stepped onto the crowded early-morning train. "Moving on, out of our safe home environment, showed our differences in several ways and caused a rift that I'm exceedingly glad to perpetuate."

"Your relationship must have been precarious before you left for it to fail as soon as you got to London?"

"I was tolerating his selfishness, believing it to be a normal part of life. Coming here has opened my mind to what I was getting into: a life of submission to Phil's dreams and ambitions, without a life of my own. I was a shadow, Gillian, and I've just come out into the sun," she said with a laugh.

"You had a lot in common, though? The music?"

"D'you know, he tells people back home that he's the successful one and he's keeping me. Oh yes, and they believe we are living together!"

"If he's so macho he must find it difficult to cope with your success. In such a short time you've been promoted twice and you now have the grand title of singles buyer. How he must hate that."

Valentina's boss had soon realized that with her flair for the business and her remarkable memory she was a very valuable addition to the team. He had given her the role of assistant to the singles buyer and then the buyer had resigned and he had promoted her to that coveted position. There had been resentment: Phil wasn't the only man to declare that the job was too important to be given to a woman. Her days were frantically busy, exciting and completely fulfilling. With Phil Blackwood out of her life, everything would be perfect.

"He'll soon get fed up," Gillian assured her. "With an ego the size of the polar ice cap, he'll have to get away from you. You're a reminder that he isn't as good as he'd hoped. He won't stand that for long!"

Valentina was doubtful but hoped her friend was right.

Phil had lied and cheated his way into a temporary and rather menial job in a company which employed pluggers. Although only dealing mainly with message-taking, he proudly and untruthfully called himself a plugger and described incidents during interviews with top producers — that in fact had happened to others, stories he had overheard or had learned second or third hand.

The job he described and pretended was his own involved phoning and visiting radio and television stations begging air time for new recordings. A thick skin plus a relentless determination being the necessary requisites for the job, he convinced himself he would do well if only he was given the chance.

His opportunity came when Carl Stevens, one of the company's top men, became ill. He offered to take the man's place and argued his case so successfully his boss agreed. Sickness had depleted the staff and it would only be for a few days.

A lot of the contacts were by telephone, repeating the calls, persisting, ignoring the irritation he engendered, laughing at put-downs, being a nuisance, until air time was offered.

There were a few personal appointments, most of which had been set up by the absent Carl Stevens, so with no one else available, the sales promotion manager knew there was little to lose by sending a relatively untried person. He had realized fairly soon that besides being keen, Phil seemed to know Carl's job well. He didn't know how closely Phil had watched Carl and how carefully he had listened to his every word, drawing on the man's experience, attitude and knowledge like an insect sucking blood. Phil had learned the jargon and talked as though he had been in the business for years instead of on the sidelines for weeks.

Once it was agreed that he kept Carl Stevens' appointments for the remainder of the man's sick leave, Phil got on the phone and managed to arrange others. Worming his way in to see the top people came easily to him. He felt he was established, and planned how he would tell Valentina.

Once Carl was back he reluctantly handed the job over but when opportunity came he enthusiastically lied and bluffed to be given other chances to prove his worth. He was presently standing in for the third time for an absent employee.

"You can come back to me now, Valentina," he said condescendingly one morning when he called at her office with news of a new singer called Claire, who, talented and mysterious, was issuing a record that month.

"Can I? How kind you are!" Instead of looking up to him in admiration, she told him "goodbye" and refused to discuss the singer.

Valentina knew from the gossip that filtered through that Phil wouldn't get a permanent position. Rumours spread about his methods, and more and more people who mattered were seeing through his dishonesty. But he had a few bursts of success, and he worked hard and long and earned a reasonable wage. He boasted about how smart he was and how he was teaching the experts how it should be done. Valentina knew he saw no end to it all and believed he was set up for life.

Valentina's thoughts went over all this as she and Gillian travelled to work that morning with Phil's letter in her pocket alongside one from her mother. Determinedly pushing worries of Phil and her family aside, she braced herself for the hectic day ahead.

The racy atmosphere when they reached the road after the short train journey was like a breath of life to Valentina; people pushing their way to work through the crowds on the pavement, many with their necks craned forward as if to reach there sooner. Cars and taxis and buses were blundering along carrying more people to their myriad destinations in the exciting city. All in a hurry, all filled with the need to be somewhere fast. People with blank faces already wrapped up in the work they had yet to reach. Taxi drivers threading their highly manoeuvrable vehicles in and out, saving a second here, two seconds there. Cyclists working their way along the edge of the chaos with disregard for the danger close at hand.

Risking the edge of the pavement, Valentina grabbed Gillian's hand as she stopped to look in a shop window and pulled her along. "Come on, slow coach! It's Tuesday, remember, and there's lots to do," she reminded her.

"All right, but not before we've eaten. I'm starving."

"So what's new? We'll have to do something about that fridge. Milk we can cut with a knife, green margarine. Not a good start to the day, specially Tuesdays."

Worries about the letter from home and the pleading of Phil were forgotten as she drank in the excitement of living and working in the capital city. The music industry stimulated and thrilled her. How lucky she was to have found a place in this magical world.

She took out Phil's letter and, tearing it into as many pieces as she could manage, threw it into a litter bin. Shaking off once more the irritation his letter had caused, she followed Gillian into Charlie's to drink coffee and eat the large bun that awaited her. The second letter she would open after the coffee had revived her sufficiently to cope with whatever her mother had to say. It was never anything she wanted to hear.

They were early, having allowed time to eat breakfast at Charlie's snack bar, which was run by Charlie's parents, Mary and Joe Trapp. There was time to relax and savour the coffee and read the morning paper. Valentina smiled as Gillian rubbed her blonde curly hair in a gesture she knew well, seeing her friend's eyes threatening tears, her face blotchy, revealing her distress about something she was reading.

Glancing at the page, she saw a piece about a family reunion. Definitely not that. Further down she saw an item about the death of a child. She saw Gillian shiver. "How does a family ever recover from such a terrible thing?" Gillian asked as they waved goodbye to Mary and Joe.

"They don't. They live with it for the rest of their lives." Valentina sharpened her voice after a silent moment and said firmly, "Now, Gillian, forget it or you'll be crying and making your face a mess."

Gillian was soft-hearted and made everyone's troubles her own. Being exceptionally fair and with the palest of blue eyes, she showed her distress easily.

In contrast Valentina was small and dark, now wearing her thick, shiny hair cut in a short, bouncy bob, with a fringe across her brown eyes. Both girls wore slim-fitting-style dresses and high-fashion boots. The sharpness of the April breezes had not persuaded them to add a coat and spoil the appearance of long, slender legs under short skirts.

It was still early when the girls entered the office and began to sort through the mail. In Valentina's pocket the letter from her mother remained, unopened. Plenty of time for that. She could guess what it contained. More abuse about her unwillingness to help her brother

Michael — or Moke as he now preferred to be called — to start his career as a vocalist and guitarist and set him on the path to becoming a top recording artist. He had finally persuaded his mother that London was the place for him to be, even though Valentina told her he hadn't the talent.

Tuesday was the day on which the new top fifty recordings were announced. Gillian began updating the chart on the wall, where the names of titles and artists were written. On one side of the wall the board showed the top fifty and another chart showed the five special choices which Valentina had "hotshotted" previously. Being chosen for hotshotting — giving it on a sale or return agreement to as many outlets as the reps could cover — gave them a much better chance of success.

As singles buyer, the selection of these five recordings was Valentina's responsibility. Although she could check her decisions with her boss if she had doubts, she rarely did. This time her choices had moved up the chart and she was satisfied her selection had been well chosen.

She and Gillian saw with undisguised pleasure that last week's twenty-three had slipped right off the chart. With a bit of luck Tony Switch, a man they disliked intensely, was on his way out. Tony was an irritation to everyone who worked at Music Round. His vanity and disregard for others, his lack of interest in anyone's success except his own, made him few friends. She nodded approval as she touched the name of one of her favourites. Mobile Nubile were at number fifteen. Their record was one she hotshotted some time ago and they had been moving up the charts ever since.

With her remarkable memory, by concentrating on the chart for only a few minutes Valentina knew the listing completely, with former places and the relevant details of the group or artist. She was an important cog in the ever-changing wheels of Britain's music business in 1975, and she loved it.

"Now for this week's hopefuls," she said, smiling at Gillian.

In an hour she had the first of her four appointments for the day. Reps from record companies would call and persuade her to listen to new recordings, which they hoped to persuade her to hotshot the following week. There would sometimes be as many as five of these sessions and her enthusiasm for her work was the reason she never became too bored or too tired to listen to "just one more". She loved listening for that special sound and everything else her job entailed.

That evening she and Gillian were going to a gig at which Danny Fortune was appearing. Danny was an Irish singer/songwriter who accompanied himself on guitar. He had made two recordings but neither had climbed into the top fifty. The girls liked him and his music and always supported him when he played at a venue they could reach.

Considering the career he was determined to follow, Danny Fortune was a surprisingly shy and self-effacing young man. He played guitar like a dream and sang with his eyes on Valentina, a wistful song about a boy leaving town having lost his love, with touching appeal.

28

She thought his was a performance that needed to be seen as well as heard. It didn't work on records.

She liked Danny and wanted to like his latest offering but when the song came to an end and he came over and asked for her honest opinion, she shook her head. "Sorry, Danny, I really am. But it just isn't commercial. I didn't get that special buzz when I closed my eyes and just listened. I'm sorry to disappoint you but if it's any consolation I'm disappointed too. I really wanted to like it. Perhaps the next one, eh?"

She doubted whether the recording company would give him another chance if this one failed and she guessed it would. Danny had something, she sensed that. All he needed was a good song. His own were sweet but without hope in a world where sweetness wasn't enough. The seventies were more aggressive than the sixties, which was where Danny's music belonged, she thought sadly.

If only Gillian's estranged husband Bob Lever would write for him. But with Gillian and Bob separated and perhaps considering divorce, now was not the time to ask. Such a pity, she thought, as she took the drink Danny had brought. If only Bob Lever could be persuaded to write just one song for him, Danny's luck would change. But life wasn't that simple. She couldn't risk hurting Gillian by contacting Bob.

Later, Danny found them a taxi and Valentina turned to see him standing watching until they were swallowed up in the traffic. There was something appealing about the thought of helping Danny to succeed, but she had no illusions about her lack of influence when it came to record companies choosing who to select.

Gillian was only twenty but had been married to Bob Lever for two years. Although they were living apart, with Bob sharing a house with four others in Chiswick, Valentina believed they still loved each other. It had been the constant rows as Bob worked long hours to make a name for himself as a songwriter that had taken the gilt off their previously happy marriage.

Gillian had once confided in her that she had laughed at Bob's disappointment at the cancellation of a tour on which he had been songwriter and arranger. She had teased him and accused him of overreacting. He had been exhausted, having worked through the night, and the disappointment as all his efforts had collapsed, followed by her lack of sympathy, had made him hit out at her. He had caught her a glancing blow at the side of her face and she had walked straight out and sworn never to forgive him.

His genuine regret and apologies went unheard and now pride, and an unwillingness to admit to their true feelings, were keeping them apart. On the few occasions she had seen them together, Valentina saw the pain in Bob's eyes as he looked at Gillian and the tell-tale blotchiness and red eyes on her friend's face.

The next day as usual, at lunchtime the girls ate at Charlie's. Going there at 12.30 between Valentina's third and fourth appointments, they bought salad rolls and coffee and sat to discuss the newest arrivals on the chart wall. They had taken their first bite when the door opened and Phil Blackwood entered.

"Oh no!" Valentina picked up a newspaper left by a previous diner and tried to hide. Joe Trapp saw her dilemma and hurriedly placed his large frame between her and the newcomer.

"Slip out through the kitchens, Valentina," Joe whispered. Using the large man as a shield, Valentina went through the staff entrance and along the back of the buildings to her office, where a few minutes later she was joined by Gillian, laughing and carrying their lunch.

"Did he see you?" Valentina asked her.

"Afraid so. He asked where you were and I said I had no idea but I don't think he believed me."

When Valentina left the office at 5.45, Phil was leaning against the wall, waiting with what was for him a surprisingly patient expression on his face.

"Hello, love. Come and have a bite to eat and we'll talk about where we go from here," he said, smiling that special smile that many girls found irresistible.

Phil was a thick-set young man, with the habit of standing in a sort of crouch and looking out of dark eyes that smouldered as if with a burning passion for the object of his gaze. His hair was wild and jet black, grown fashionably long and with coarsely curling sideburns down cheeks that always looked in need of a shave.

He dressed in smart and fashionable clothes while working: suits with flared trousers and a narrow-shouldered jacket, worn with large collars and very large ties. Now he wore tight jeans tucked into long boots sporting spurs, and a wide leather belt with a brass buckle slung casually around his hips. His stage name of Gypsy, suggested by Valentina and now accepted, suited him and Valentina couldn't resist a smile, seeing him putting on the act for her.

"I don't have time for a meal and neither do I have the inclination. Goodbye, Phil," she said, turning away.

He grabbed her arm and turned her to face him, looking into her eyes and trying to persuade her to soften her attitude. She picked his hand off her arm as if it were an unpleasant insect, and glared at him.

"How can I make it clearer? Goodbye, Phil. I have nothing to say to you."

"Please, Valentina. Just ten minutes."

Impatient to be rid of him, she abandoned her intention of using the underground and hailed a taxi that was fortuitously passing.

His expression changed from gentle pleading to smouldering anger as she was driven away and a shiver of apprehension disturbed her satisfaction of her neat escape. It was a pity he knew where she lived. Phil Blackwood was becoming a nuisance.

There was a function at a hotel that evening and later, as she ran quickly from the flat into the waiting taxi, Valentina was nervous and at the same time angry with herself for imagining Phil standing in the shadows and following her moves with anger-filled eyes. What if he did follow her around wearing a sad spaniel expression? Surely, with his ego, he will become tired of her rejection and find someone else?

32

The evening was boring, with Tony Switch trying to take over from the compere and run the entertainment. She had to admit he did well. Several times he was pushed aside but back he came, making condescending remarks but being modest when there was applause for his constant interruptions.

She was late home and Gillian was already asleep. As she was getting ready for bed she remembered her mother's letter and reluctantly opened it. As she had guessed, it was like the others: repeated criticism of her, followed more recently by demands for her to do something to help Michael. The letter contained the usual stories about his continuing success locally and her mother's presumption that, as his sister, she should do what she could to help him onto the wider stage of the London scene.

She almost threw the letter away but at that point some masochistic urge made her read on. Michael — whom she must now call Moke — was coming to London to further his career and was expecting her to accommodate him until he was established.

Late as it was, she replied immediately, explaining that for him to stay in the flat was impossible. Anxious to stop him coming, she redressed and ran to post it. Thank goodness she hadn't thrown the letter away unread!

It was a long time before she slept. Her mother managed to upset her even with more than 150 miles between them. Looking back, she couldn't remember a time when she and her mother had been friends. There had always been resentment there. Even as a very young child she remembered trying to do things to please her — and failing. Strong disapproval was shown towards her every day of her childhood and even now, at the age of twenty-one, nothing had changed.

She had tried to understand why, and had approached other members of the family, but no one offered even the slightest clue. "It's all in your head, girl," her mother had insisted, adding that she shouldn't be so self-centred or expect more attention than her younger brother. Her father just sighed and told her that her mother was bitter that she hadn't married someone more successful instead of tying herself to a failure like him.

Although he took the blame on his own shoulders, Valentina knew it wasn't her father but she who had caused her mother's bitterness, but no one would explain just how. Drifting into sleep, she saw the figure of her mother: small, slim, dark-haired and with such a look of anger on her face that she gave a sob of dismay.

On Saturday Valentina and Gillian went shopping but they still didn't buy a fridge. They felt in the mood for more frivolous things so they bought clothes instead, trying on some of the more outrageous selections with much laughter. High heels, platform soles, trousers wide enough to make their feet disappear. Skirts so mini they shocked people. Jackets made of leather and highly coloured suede and some outrageous fun furs. Around them were more daring exhibitions of hairstyles as hair was becoming more and more a fashion item, coloured to match an outfit, worn in many ways from long and loose to tightly stiffened with gel.

"Don't you just love living here?" Valentina said with a smile, doing a twirl in a red sequinned dress. There was no reply and she turned to see that Gillian had sobered up and was watching a couple kissing without restraint against the corner of the fitting room. Valentina knew she was thinking of Bob, her estranged husband.

Euphoria dissolved on their way back to the flat. Gillian was pining for Bob, whom she refused to meet, except by accident, and Valentina was still trying to think of ways to escape Phil's determined pursuit of her as well as cope with her mother's disapproval. Returning to the flat with the fridge problem still unsolved but loaded with fashion shop carriers, before they could drop their shopping there was a knock at the door. It was Phil.

"I'm not going before we have our talk." He looked dangerous, his dark eyes glittering below thick eyebrows, and there was a tightness around the mouth that made Valentina think he had been drinking and working himself into a rage.

"Go now, Phil, and I'll meet you at Charlie's restaurant at eight."

"Was that wise?" Gillian asked when Phil had gone.

"Probably not. But he can't stay drunk all day. And with some food inside him he might stay calm enough to listen to some sense. I have to get this sorted."

"Perhaps. Anyway, Charlie will keep an eye on him. He's fond of you, isn't he?"

"Charlie? Yes, I suppose he is, in a big brother kind of way."

Charlie's was the restaurant on the other side of the building in which Mary and Joe Trapp ran the snack bar the girls frequently used. The whole place belonged to Charlie Trapp, and he ran the restaurant that attracted people in search of good food at reasonable prices, leaving the running of the cafe to his parents.

Valentina had chosen Charlie's as a rendezvous as the presence of Charlie and possibly Mary and Joe too gave her some reassurance. Phil had never hurt her and, until recently, had never shown a tendency towards violence. However, he was occasionally roused to argumentative behaviour, an embarrassment she could do without.

Phil was waiting for her when she arrived, again in his stage clothes. His shirt was pale mauve and his hair stood in tufts high above his scalp with each tuft edged with purple dye. Punk rock was the style and although amused by the fashion on others, it embarrassed Valentina a little as she sat beside him. Charlie raised an eyebrow questioningly from his position near the coffee machine and made her smile.

Phil looked morose and she began asking questions, making comments but without receiving any response apart from sad looks. He looked up at the waiter standing near the kitchen door and he came to take their order. "Fish?" she asked Phil in growing irritation. He gave a slight shrug which she decided was agreement and ordered a seafood platter for them both.

Waiting for the meal to arrive, she tried again to start a conversation but he was still disinclined to speak and she wondered if the evening was to be a monologue. He finished one bottle of wine and called for another. Her brown eyes glittered with increasing exasperation as the meal arrived and all he had done was drink and look at her with sad, moist eyes.

"Stop this poor-hard-done-by-me act, Phil, or I'm going home now this minute. I gave up an arrangement to go out with Gillian and some friends this evening. I didn't expect to spend the time you begged me to give you in silence."

"Beg, is it? Now there's a thing!" His Welsh accent was becoming more pronounced as anger burned off the pretence. "Me? Beg you to spare some of your oh-so-valuable time, is it? There'll come a time when you'll be begging me, Valentina Robbins! You won't last long in that fancy job of yours, they'll soon see through you and your pretence. You haven't got what it takes to hold down a job like that. A fluke, that's all it was, you getting it. Who did you sleep with to get it, then, eh?"

Valentina stood to leave, throwing her napkin in his face and wishing it had been a well-filled glass. "Don't come near me again or I'll seek advice; use the law if necessary to stop you pestering me."

"It's your mam I'll be talking to next. She'll listen when I tell her about you and that boss of yours, and the way you're blocking your brother's prospects because you can't face anyone being better than yourself."

He was talking rubbish. Utter rubbish. Too late she realized that rather than sobering up, he had begun the evening with a large amount of drink already inside him to which he'd added copious quantities of wine. Why hadn't she recognized the signs? Self-pity, jealousy plus too much alcohol all made a troublesome cocktail.

She walked to where Charlie stood, large and comfortingly strong like his father, Joe. "Sorry, Charlie, but I have to leave. I'll come in on Monday and settle what we owe. All right?"

"Wait in the kitchen, I'll ring for a taxi. It'll be safer than a bus or train with him about."

Seeing them talking together, Phil stood up without moving his chair back and tilted the table, depositing the contents onto the floor with a satisfyingly loud crash. He moved towards them. "You're coming with me." He stepped over the debris and grabbed her. She pulled away with a squeal of alarm and Charlie pushed Phil to one side. Phil aimed a lunging swipe at Charlie and lost his balance, stumbling against the nearest table, where three people were dining. Charlie held him, twisting his arm behind his back, then nodded to one of the startled waiters to call the police.

"On Monday morning," Charlie told his father later, "I'll make sure his boss knows how he behaved. He can explain to him as well as the police."

Two days later Phil was out of a job. The fight didn't really concern his employers — they would overlook a lot worse — but they had other reasons for sacking him. The truth had come out about the way he had lied his way in, and how he had cheated others on the team to improve his position. There had been complaints from other people who'd had to deal with him too.

The smile that had flattered and enabled him to inveigle his way in had lost its charm. In his determination to be accepted as a valued member of the firm he had shown a condescending attitude towards the rest of the sales team that had quickly begun to annoy. As his success weakened, they had seen his anger strengthen and he was no longer a charming young man with a future.

Phil's strongest emotion was fear, mainly of having no money with which to impress Valentina and others. For the short time he had been employed he had earned what was to him a large amount of money and he had enjoyed spending it. Largesse bought him friends and the feeling of being an important man in an important place. He had been shocked at the way those same friends had disappeared once he could no longer afford to entertain them. He had to get a job. He'd convinced himself that it was Charlie who was to blame for him losing the one he had. He must have reported his behaviour. He had to earn some money. But how?

Valentina sighed with relief as she prepared to go out the following Saturday. A week without a sign of Phil and no response to her letter to her mother explaining that she couldn't provide a bed for her brother. She and Gillian had an appointment that evening with a singer, to discuss his newest recording. And she had a new outfit to wear, a red two-piece, with trousers that clung to her thighs and flared out below the knee. The outfit included a scarf which she hung from her wrist, tucked into a bracelet, and with gold shoes and a gold evening bag across her shoulders she felt good. It seemed that her life was on track at last.

Then she groaned as she opened the cupboard and took out dried milk to add to her coffee. Life would be just perfect if only they had done something about that fridge!

CHAPTER
THREE

The reception at which Valentina was to make an appearance was at a hotel not far from the office and she hurried through the chill of the evening, past Charlie's restaurant. As she entered the hotel she immediately began to look for familiar faces. Several people she knew would be there but it was with genuine pleasure that she spotted Danny Fortune first.

Danny was very slim, and together with his light complexion this made him look younger than his twenty-five years. He was standing at the bar talking to a girl he knew from the BBC. He wore his light brown hair in a Beatles style low on his forehead above greeny eyes. Fashionably dressed in flares and a colourful shirt, he avoided the excesses of seventies fashion yet still looked part of the scene.

As if sensing her presence, he looked up and, smiling in a way that warmed her, walked across to greet her. "Valentina, me darlin'. What a good start to the evening," he said. Walking back to the bar, he ordered her a drink then left her as others came to talk to her. She caught his eye before she lost herself in business chatter and smiled her thanks. He was so thoughtful, never pushing himself. It was such a comfortable feeling that her being in demand on occasions like this didn't worry Danny. He would wait until she had a moment to talk to him, something Phil would never do.

Or Tony Switch, she thought with a groan as she saw the unpopular man making his way towards her. There was an air of confidence about Tony Switch that brought out the worst in her. He always wore a condescending smile as though the recipient should feel honoured to be given a few moments of his precious time. She tried to turn away but his voice stopped her.

"My dear Valentina, how lovely you look."

She smiled and offered a polite thank you then pointed across the room to where someone was waving. "Look, I think one of your fans needs you." Quickly she moved away as he turned and waved back. Although she hadn't been long in the job, she recognized a few people to whom she had helped to give a start, one reason why many people wanted to talk to her and encourage her to take an interest in their business or someone's career.

Valentina mixed with the guests, stopping to talk to those she knew, avoiding Tony and others who would try to monopolize her time and pressure her to listen to their sales patter. Danny unobtrusively helped out, weaning away those she preferred not to meet or were staying too long.

Several young men, and some not so young, invited her out but she declined them all. Most only wanted to get her ear and persuade her to consider their particular offerings. It was Danny who gathered

42

together her papers, walked her to the taxi and waved her off when the function ended at 11.30.

Gillian was waiting for her when she unlocked the door and stepped inside. Surprised, she asked, "What's up, Gillian? Why aren't you asleep?"

Gillian gestured towards the kitchen. "Your brother arrived at ten and he's snoring like a good 'un in there."

"What?" Valentina opened the door to the small kitchen and groaned. Michael was in a sleeping bag, his head and shoulders tucked inside an open cupboard to allow room for him to stretch out across the floor.

"Michael! This won't do!" Valentina shook him. "We can't have a third person in this flat. I explained to Mam clearly there isn't room for you here!" There was no response and she shook him again. "Wake up and listen to me! Michael!"

"Call me Moke," he said sleepily and, turning on his side, relaxed again into sleep.

On Sundays, Valentina and Gillian usually allowed themselves a lazy day, often walking along the path beside the Thames to Strand on the Green. There they joined friends for a lunchtime drink at The Bull. When they set off a few days after Michael's arrival, he was still with them and fast asleep in their kitchen.

Two friends who were always waiting for them were John Ellis and Peter Philby, who owned and ran a successful estate agency. Friends since their childhood in Surrey, John and Peter shared a flat and occupation, working together in complete harmony.

They had started their agency from an empty shop and had built the business up as far as they wanted to go. Unwilling to expand further and have to take on new premises and extra staff, with all the problems that might entail, they were satisfied with what they had.

They were Valentina's self-appointed minders for the Sunday lunchtimes and today they did their usual trick of discouraging one or two who had found out about the arrangement and hoped to influence Valentina in her choices for the following week. These hopefuls were swiftly elbowed out by John and Peter with a stiff smile through gritted teeth, which made them reluctant to try again. When Phil Blackwood walked in, they looked at each other and shrugged. This one was down to Valentina herself.

"Your Moke turned up yet?" Phil asked, pushing his way to the bar to be served.

"You knew he was coming? Even though I wrote to tell Mam he couldn't stay with us?"

"He's your brother. How can you expect your mother to understand you didn't want him there?"

"You told him to come, didn't you!" Valentina stared at him in disbelief.

"I explained that your refusal to have him stay was an impulse you later regretted, yes."

"Keep out of my life, Phil. Just stay away from me and my family."

"I know a few people who'd help him find a place. I'll call round later and take him out for a drink, introduce him to a few friends."

44

"NO! I don't want you near the flat, d'you understand?"

"Don't worry, it won't be to see you. But a young boy so far from home, someone has to help him."

All this was exchanged in an undertone and John and Peter stood as close as they could, trying to listen but without success.

"All right, Valentina?" John called. "Time we were on our way if we're to be on time for the meeting at two."

The meeting was a pretence but it had the required effect of making Phil leave. "Catch you later," he called defiantly as he banged his empty glass down on the bar.

"I have to get a place for Michael to stay — and fast!" Valentina said as they went back into the flat where Michael was still sleeping. "I don't want him here as an excuse for Phil to call."

"Better to put him on the Swansea train," Gillian said, and at once Valentina realized it was the solution.

"Come on, Moke," she said as she pushed and pulled her brother to rouse him. "Your train goes in an hour and I want you on it."

Valentina's parents didn't have a phone; her father considered it an unnecessary expense. Not wanting to worry a neighbour and let them know more than her mother would wish, she didn't phone to tell them Michael was on his way home. They'd learn that soon enough.

On Tuesday evening, her mother phoned to ask if Moke was all right.

"What d'you mean? He left here on the Swansea train on Sunday afternoon!"

"I haven't heard from him since he called Mrs Francis to tell me he'd arrived at your flat and you'd made him welcome. Oh, my boy! Where is he? You've let him loose in London on his own! Anything could have happened. You're wicked, that's what you are. Wicked and uncaring."

Gillian's eyes filled up as Valentina repeated her mother's words. "What have you done to make her treat you like this? I was a pain to my parents, I know I was, but they soon forgave me, realizing it was a part of growing up, asserting my personality and all that. But your mother, she's one on her own!"

Valentina forced a smile, although she was shaking with hurt and the injustice of her mother's attack. "Come on, Gillian. It's me who should be crying, not you." She spoke briskly, hiding her own distress and coaxing Gillian out of hers. "Come on, stir your stumps and get us a cup of coffee. Help me forget what she thinks of me — if I can."

By Friday, Michael had still not been in touch.

"I'll have to go home for the weekend," Valentina told Gillian as they ate their lunch in Charlie's snack bar. "Our plans for the weekend will have to be abandoned. Mam's so worried."

"How is your Michael? Got a job yet?" Mary Trapp asked as they were leaving.

"We put him on the train to go back home." Valentina frowned. "I didn't think you knew him?"

"He came in on Monday and introduced himself. Phil Blackwood was with him. They said he was intending to stay with you but that Phil had more room."

"He got off the train and he's staying with Phil?"

"I don't know about any train but he was definitely in here on Monday and again yesterday."

"I don't want to talk to Phil, so I'll phone Mam's neighbour, leave a message telling her he's staying with Phil. Then I'll leave it for them to sort out."

"At least you won't have to drive to Wales this weekend," said Gillian.

"Oh, I think I will. It'll be nice not to be in the same town as Phil for a day or so!"

"Even when he isn't visible, you have a feeling he's around, don't you." Gillian twisted her fingers in her pale blonde hair.

"Now, Gillian, don't get all psychic on me!"

"It is eerie though. He does seem to know your every move. How did he get in touch with Michael after we'd put him on the train? We actually saw him get on, remember."

"I don't know and I don't care. I have some figures to go through and I don't want to think about Phil Blackwood for another ten years."

"Perhaps you ought to phone him, just to make sure Moke is really there. Then you can reassure your parents and relax. Didn't he write the number on the calendar?"

Valentina dialled Phil's number and handed the phone to Gillian. "You speak to him," she urged.

Gillian listened then replaced the receiver, looking puzzled. "Phil doesn't live there. He moved out several weeks ago."

"Then where is he? And where's Michael? I don't like not knowing where my brother is, pain though he might be."

She didn't go home to Wales. With so little to tell them, she thought it wiser to wait.

As Valentina listened to the music and sales talk of her last appointment of the day later that week, her mind was not on her work. She had chosen her five hotshots and this audition was a favour for one of the reps. Ashamed of her poor attention, she asked the rep and the singer who had accompanied him, a lovely young woman called Claire, to come back the following week and made a firm appointment to spend time with her. Even in her inattentive state, she knew there was something special about the sound and the looks. This young woman could be a fast-rise performer.

"Who wrote the music?" she asked as the girl was about to leave.

"Bob Lever," she was told.

"It's good. It's very good," Valentina said thoughtfully. "What is your other name?" she asked, adding a few words to her notebook.

"Claire. Just Claire."

Again Valentina's thoughts drifted and she decided she would contact Gillian's husband and ask if he would meet Danny Fortune and maybe write something for him. Danny's way of putting over a song plus the skill of Bob's music was something she would like to hear.

Charlie's snack bar was a relic of the sixties: chrome tables with red and white check cloths, potted plants and a balcony. There was a huge chrome coffee machine and glass domes covering sandwiches and rolls and cakes. The restaurant on the other side of the building had a smart, modern décor in blue and grey with touches of green. With subdued lighting and fish tanks — not part of the menu — lining one wall, the place had an air of tranquillity. As well as the excellent food, many customers became regular diners simply because of its peaceful atmosphere.

Charlie stood in the shadow of the restaurant doorway looking towards the office door through which Valentina would soon appear. He knew about Moke being missing, and of the boy's apparent involvement with Phil Blackwood, from his parents. He waited for her to come, wanting to offer his help should she need it. Large, dark and looking older than his thirty-two years, he had been running Charlie's for five years. It gave him a good living but his social life had suffered because of his concentration on its success.

He couldn't remember when he had last taken a girl out. Valentina reminded him it was time to revive those pleasant times. He had been attracted to her the first time she had entered his door. He had hesitated, hoping that by timing his approach correctly she would look at him with more than the casual interest of a valued customer towards the maitre d'.

He had found out where Phil now lived and the knowledge worried him a little. Phil had taken a small flat, little more than a bedsit, very close to where Valentina and Gillian lived. Charlie couldn't be certain but he suspected that from his window, Phil would be able to watch the comings and goings of Valentina and Gillian with ease. The flat Phil had left had been an expensive one but, beside the reduced rent, Charlie wondered if Phil had chosen it because of its close proximity to the girls, and if so why.

That evening, leaving the restaurant in the hands of his parents for an hour, he drove to where the girls lived. He saw Phil knock at their door and watched him walk away having been refused entrance. Following him, he saw him go back to his own place, climb the stairs to the top floor and bang impatiently on the door. Hiding at the bend of the stairs, he saw the door being opened by Michael. Sharing with Phil must be a temporary arrangement, surely? The place would be too small for two people. From the brief glance he'd been allowed, it was no more than a box room. He returned to the restaurant, phoned Valentina and told her where her brother was living.

"I knew you were worried so I followed him," he explained. "I hope you don't think I'm interfering. I only wanted to help."

"Thanks, Charlie, I really appreciate it. I can tell Mam where he is and leave it at that."

"Valentina, if you're free on Sunday, would you like to come out for lunch?"

"The restaurant will be closed, won't it?"

"I didn't mean eating at Charlie's. I'm inviting you to come somewhere and have lunch with me. Will you?"

Valentina had fully understood but had needed a moment to overcome her surprise. "Charlie, I'd love to come. Thank you."

"I'll book somewhere on the river and call for you at twelve."

"Perfect."

He sensed her smile through the mouthpiece and sat for a long time waiting for his heart to settle before going to relieve his parents in the restaurant.

On the following Friday, Valentina and Gillian went to a gig in a very large pub and while the performers prepared for their acts the two of them sat in a smaller bar and drank martini. Others arrived and looked around, unsettled, waiting for something, obviously there for the music. Valentina saw a few people she knew including Carl Stevens, the plugger, whose job Phil had tried to steal. Her boss Ray Everett had told her that Carl had once made a record but it hadn't reached the charts.

Tony Switch arrived but fortunately didn't notice them. He didn't wait to be called into the room where the performance would take place, he just went straight in and could soon be heard advising the acts, his voice loud and confident. The two girls pulled a face of disapproval. The man really was a pain.

When the musicians were ready, they walked through the passageway to the larger room with its stage. The lights were low but as the last of the audience pushed into the crowded room, stage lights burst into brilliance and at once the music began. After some shuffling as people found places near friends and with a view of the small stage, both girls relaxed and began to enjoy the evening. The first band, Square Clock, a glam rock group, were new to Valentina. It wasn't until they were halfway through their first number that Valentina gasped and said, "Gillian! Look at the second guitarist!" It was her brother, Moke. The five members of Square Clock were dressed in smart clothes but wore eye make-up in garish colours and Moke had attempted to grow a beard. His sparse hair had been dyed green to match the rest of the group's wild colouring, designed as a contrast to the black set. It was as he had leaned back and lifted his guitar for a brief solo and smiled his thanks for applause as it ended that she had recognized him.

During the interval the lights went up and the musicians drifted off to find a drink. Valentina pushed her way through the noisy, chattering mass to find her brother, but by the time she had struggled to the door he had slipped out. She went back to the other bar but Moke was nowhere to be seen. Had he known she'd be there? Her boss had suggested they come and he wouldn't have known about Square Clock. Unbelievable coincidence, though.

The first of the interval performers was now singing and she recognized the strong voice of Claire. She moved through the crowd to congratulate her when her song was done and missed seeing the second act walk onto the stage. As soon as he began singing, she forgot

52

Claire and turned to listen to Danny. This must be why Ray had suggested she came. When she saw Ray standing in a corner listening to Claire's second number, she went across and thanked him.

Danny carried his equipment around in a small van and when the evening ended he drove Valentina and Gillian home and stayed for a coffee and an inquest on the evening.

"It'll have to be dried milk," Valentina warned. "And the grounds are a bit stale."

"Lord help us, I've drunk coffee in so many places I wouldn't recognize a good cup if you gave me one," he said in his soft Irish voice. "Hot, cold, warmed up a couple of times, if it's wet and warm it'll be grand."

Several times Valentina had tried to bring up the subject of Bob Lever writing for Danny but then stopped, afraid she might upset Gillian. Then, as Danny stood to leave and break up the small party, she decided it was now or never. "Gillian, would you mind if I met Bob and asked him to write a song for Danny?"

"Bob Lever?" Danny frowned. "He wrote that raunchy number for Claire. She's wonderful. She sings like an angel and is bound to succeed."

"A bit of a mystery though," Gillian said. "Strange, isn't it, that in the gossipy world of music no one knows who she is, where she comes from?"

"I can't find out anything about her," Valentina added. "She appears to perform then vanishes. Once she's really well known the news reporters will get the story."

"I couldn't sing that kind of music though," Danny said. "I like what I do, I don't look for anything more."

"Bob can write for anyone. He's very talented," Gillian defended.

"He'd listen to you and then think about what you need," Valentina encouraged, glancing at Gillian for her approval. "Would you meet him if I can arrange it?"

"Of course I will, me darlin', and thanks for taking an interest. That's really grand." He kissed her lightly and the touch of his lips on her cheek had a startling effect. She looked at him with new eyes as he walked back to his van in the calm, quiet night. Tall, slim and with that delightful hint of an Irish accent, he was suddenly very appealing. She wanted to please Danny Fortune more than she had realized.

On Saturday morning the girls went to buy a fridge. "At least we can offer decent coffee to our visitors," Valentina said, and she surprised herself again by hoping Danny would be one of the first.

Sunday was one of those early May mornings that seemed freshly painted. Even in the quiet of the London streets there was a feeling of spring, of summer just around the corner. As she went to get the morning papers, Valentina smelled the air with delight. The slight breeze seemed scented. There were no trees in the road she walked along but she just knew that close by trees were in bloom; it was that sort of morning.

People walked slowly, savouring the newness. Customers in the newsagent shop relaxed and seemed over-polite. No one pushed their way through and demanded, everyone seemed willing to wait their turn

54

or even offered others their place in the queue. Excitement was in the air, something like birthday mornings she remembered as a child, with the promise of something wonderful to come.

Was it lunch with Charlie making the day feel special? Was that prospect making her feel so invigorated and full of happiness? No, not lunch with Charlie, she admitted, with a shiver of excitement. It was thoughts of Danny sitting in their flat drinking awful coffee that warmed her as nothing had for a very long time. She strolled in a leisurely fashion back to the flat, aware that her life was about to turn a corner. Anger towards Phil had faded and life was urging her back to live it to the full.

Charlie called for her at twelve and she was glowing when she answered the door to him. Gillian stayed in the flat, looking upset, Valentina having persuaded her to keep the appointment she had made with Bob to discuss Danny Fortune.

"Now don't read the sad bits in the paper — remember how red your eyes will be if you get upset," she teased. "Here." She handed her the comic section. "Read this and have a good laugh instead."

Valentina and Charlie ate at a restaurant where, from their window seat, they looked down at the Thames. They watched people feeding the gulls that used the river as a substitute for the distant sea, and admired the powerful young men pulling a narrow craft through the water and being kept in order by the shouted commands of the coxswain. The meal was excellent and Valentina found Charlie amusing company. He talked about the restaurant trade and asked pertinent questions about the world of popular music.

It is usual at the beginning of a friendship for the questions asked of each other to be about background and events of previous years, but Valentina and Charlie only spoke of today and tomorrow. Neither complained about their lot but shared with each other the joys of their particular occupation. The result was a greater understanding than could have been expected after so few hours in each other's company and Valentina let herself back into the flat feeling refreshed.

Gillian's lunch had been a solitary one and she had been nervous and had eaten very little. At 2.30 she had travelled by underground to meet her ex-husband. She and Bob Lever hadn't met for several weeks and that meeting, like so many others, had ended in a row. This was the first time he had asked her to come to the flat he had just bought. Her stomach churned as if it were an appointment with the dentist rather than the optimistic hope they might hold a civilized conversation and part as friends.

Bob was thirty-two, twelve years older than Gillian, but in appearance the age difference wasn't apparent. Bob wore his age well, being small, slim and youthful in manner and dress. They were similar in colouring, both unusually fair, but Bob's beard already had touches of grey and his hair looked as though it would change from gold to silver without darkening. Gillian treated her hair regularly, to keep it as light as it had been for twenty years.

56

There was the usual hesitant, prickly greeting as if they were eyeing each other up, preparing for battle. Then he threw his head back and gave that roar of a laugh she had once found so enjoyable to share. Now, she was suspicious.

"What's funny?" she asked, frowning, wondering if she had been the unwilling cause.

"I was just thinking that if we were a pair of dogs, we'd be circling around each other waiting for the first move in a fight. Gilly, I'm glad to see you!"

"Me too."

Going into his flat, of which she had no memories, was painful. Many of the small items they had bought together were there. A few clothes were spread around and from the piles of papers in the corners, she guessed an attempt had been made to tidy it up.

The room which had been a second bedroom was soundproofed to enable Bob to work on his recordings without upsetting neighbours. She smiled when he showed her and reminded him of how they had started with a shed, "soundproofed" with egg cases and old mattresses nailed to the walls. The room was cluttered with tapes and recording equipment and yet more piles of papers.

"You're sharing with someone?" she asked. "All this mess of paper can't be all down to you, can it?"

"Afraid so. Coffee?" he asked. "I'm not good at shopping so it'll have to be dried milk."

It was her turn to laugh and explain about their lack of a fridge. Gillian could feel the atmosphere ease and she almost embarrassed herself by crying with relief.

It was some time before they reached the reason for her visit and when Gillian asked him if he would write a song for Danny, Bob shook his head. "I'm committed for the next few weeks at least. I'm going on tour again, not as a performer, just as manager and song arranger. Most of the songs are written but I'll be needed on tour — in case there's a chance of other bookings, for one thing. I'm so sorry, Gilly, I can't fit anything in for a while."

"When are you leaving?

"Friday 16th May."

"Can't you spare an hour, please, Bob?"

He looked at her quizzically. "Someone special, is he, this Danny Fortune?"

"Not to me. But he might be to Valentina."

"Hmmph, whoever he is he's bound to be an improvement on Phil Blackwood." He thought for a moment then smiled at her. "All right. For you, I'll find an hour to listen, but I can't promise to write for him. It'll depend on more than how much time I have. If I like what I hear and think I can do something, well, we'll see."

"Thanks, Bob." She smiled at him and he winked a large blue eye. How, she wondered, can a wink be so sexy? Her feet dragged as she left the untidy flat. Women's Lib, eat your heart out, she muttered to herself. I'd love to stay and create order out of his chaos.

The girls arranged for Danny to come to the offices of Music Round and Bob arrived early for the two o'clock appointment and went with them for lunch. Mary Trapp came over and fussed over them as if they were special friends. Valentina guessed she knew about her date with Charlie, which made her feel a little uneasy; she found the friendly smile on Mary's face a bit threatening. She had just the slightest sensation of being pushed in a direction in which she was not sure she wanted to go.

Joe came over and offered them a drink on the house but at once Valentina refused. "Thank you, Joe, but I have to work this afternoon. Two reps with endless tapes to listen to and a pile of paperwork."

"Another time then?" he asked and she felt ashamed, her words echoing in the air around her, sounding sharper than she'd intended. Joe and Mary were such nice people. The Sunday lunch was making her edgy.

"Yes, please, Joe. When I don't have such a busy afternoon ahead of me, right?"

"Any time," he replied amiably.

She had arranged for Danny to sing a new song, one he had written since the recording he had performed for her recently. Again it was a plaintive melody, about a lovelorn boy watching his girl marrying another.

Bob listened attentively as Danny sang it twice more, then nodded. "I'll be in touch when I've had a think," was all he said and, collecting the recording Valentina had made, he walked off without another word to any of them.

"Head in the clouds," Gillian explained.

"He didn't like me," Danny said.

★ ★ ★

"I think Bob did like what he heard," Gillian said later to Valentina. "He gets lost in another world like that when something interests him. His funny moods, as I called them, took some getting used to. I got angry at first and put them down to bad temper and sulks, but I know now that it isn't that. He gets so wrapped up in what he's doing, he isn't aware of what's going on around him. I didn't fully understand then."

"But you do now?"

"Yes, I understand now."

"Have you told him?"

"What's the point?"

A few days later Bob phoned and told them he had something for Danny. He invited them to come and listen and they eagerly agreed. They met at a rehearsal studio, rented for a few hours. There had been previous sessions at Bob's flat, early morning, late evening, whenever two busy people could get together. A representative of the recording company Danny had sold to before arrived at the same time as Valentina and Gillian, with his assistant.

It was due to Valentina that he had agreed to come, although Valentina tried to stay right out of it as she didn't want to lose her job by being accused of unfair support for a friend. News had seeped through that Danny was of special interest to her and as she worked for Music Round she was important enough for the record company to want to please their singles buyer. She had checked with her boss as usual when she was in doubt and Ray Everett agreed that it would do no harm for her to go along.

At first, Danny hadn't been too pleased with the new song. It had a lilting rhythm that was different from his usual quiet melodies but as he began to rehearse it, encouraged by Bob, he began to realize that the treatment had lifted the song and given it a lightness he had failed to achieve. They had previously spent two evenings in Bob's makeshift studio working on the accompaniment, and with Danny still unconvinced, Bob had introduced drums, keyboard and a second guitar. Now, as the small group listened to the finished recording and applauded, Danny admitted that it worked. He thanked Bob for his tireless efforts to bring about the remarkable change in the way he put over a number.

"Now to convince the recording company," he said, looking at the man anxiously.

"I've changed him, but it's still Danny," Bob told Valentina. "He won't lose friends but will make new ones. D'you approve?"

Valentina smiled her thanks and, predictably, Gillian burst into tears.

A week later, after Bob had left on his tour with a group calling themselves Pebbles On A Beach, Danny rang to tell Valentina the recording company had accepted the new song and hoped to get it out by the summer.

Valentina and Gillian hugged each other. Danny Fortune was on his way.

CHAPTER
FOUR

Coming straight from a gig in Oxford, Bob Lever went back to his flat for a brief stay. Travelling through the night, he reached London at about 4a.m. and slept for six hours. He had arranged to eat with Gillian, Valentina and Danny that evening. Gillian had booked a table at Charlie's, and until it was time to leave, he worked with his eight-track, making sure he was completely satisfied with the new song he'd written for Claire.

He made copies of the cassette and posted one to Claire and to each member of the backing group so they could start rehearsing and adding their own accompaniment. They would all meet later in a rehearsal room and go over the new song until they were satisfied that the sound was what he and the producer wanted. He never knew exactly what it was he wanted, he just knew when they'd got it.

Charlie waited until Valentina, Gillian, Bob and Danny had been served with coffee and went to greet them. He offered them a drink on the house then returned to his place and waited for them to leave. It was raining and as Valentina put a scarf over her dark hair, he said,

"I have an umbrella if you'd like to borrow one. There are always several in the stand, left by customers."

"I'll be all right, thanks. Bob has brought the van."

"A van? With seats bolted in and no leg room? I can run you and Gillian home if you'd prefer?"

"Thanks, Charlie, but we'll be fine, it isn't far."

"What about Sunday? D'you fancy another riverside lunch? Or there's a place I know of that's right out in the country."

"Sorry, but I really do have to go home this weekend. I'm going to a party on Friday and I'm leaving early Saturday — if I can rouse myself sufficiently to drive, that is!" She smiled, aware of his disappointment, and added, "Please keep the following Sunday free if you can. I'd love to have lunch with you again."

Sitting in the van, crouched on a seat that, as Charlie had guessed, had been fixed to the van floor allowing no depth for their feet, she wondered if Charlie wanted more than friendship. He had never even held her hand, he was formal in an old-fashioned way, but something in the expression in his eyes made her wonder if he wanted more. Perhaps she ought to avoid a lunch date for a while, at least until she knew whether it was what she wanted too. She had the impression that Charlie would expect her to belong to him completely and after the problems with the possessive Phil, she was cautious. She wanted to be a person in her own right, not live in the shadow of someone else.

In their small, neat living room, Valerie and Dewi Robbins were waiting for Valentina and arguing. As usual it was about their son, Michael. Dewi was tired of the boy's idle hope of becoming a success in a career that was so overcrowded, even exceptionally talented performers couldn't make it. Like their daughter Valentina, he knew Michael was not in the category of the highly talented and calling himself Moke didn't change anything. He was a no-hoper and always would be, unless he forgot this fantasy of being a pop star dressed like Gary Glitter and being idolized by millions of young kids. Then, he might get started on a career with some prospect of solvency.

He had dreams of his son being a top businessman, wearing a smart suit, but Valerie's encouragement had the boy idling his time, lolling about in scruffy denim. God 'elp, the last time they'd seen him he'd had blue hair and was wearing an earring! His wife spending their savings, doling out money every week, giving him the means of staying in London and hanging on to hope when hope was dead, was making Dewi more and more angry. On impulse, he had sent a cheque to Valentina. Why should only Michael have money to waste on impossible dreams?

Valerie knew he hadn't seen the letter that had arrived that morning. He had actually watched it fall on to the mat but hadn't read it; Valerie had whipped it away before he could do that. But he hadn't needed to take it out of its envelope to know what it said: it would be a repeat of all the others. Michael was on the brink of success and it only needed a few pounds to keep him until the record hit the shops, or the gig attended by top agents and all the names from Fleet Street took

64

place. Michael's explanations weren't even plausible, yet Valerie believed every word.

He didn't see Valerie slip two fivers into an envelope and address it to their son, who was still at Phil's flat, but guessed she had. She insisted that Phil would look after him and the money would help keep him until that elusive but certain success was achieved.

"Won't be long, Dewi," she called. "Just popping out to post a letter then I'll serve lunch."

"We'll wait for Valentina, won't we?"

"No point. There's no telling when she'll arrive. Too important for her own good, that one." She put on her coat and tried to hide the envelope.

"How much this time?" he called, but if she heard she didn't reply. He looked at the clock. A couple of hours before Valentina was expected. Damnation, Valerie could at least have prepared. If it had been Michael she'd have been cooking for days. And he would have expected her to wait for him, no matter how late he was. Why couldn't she see how she was spoiling the boy? He went out to look in the kitchen to see whether anything had been prepared.

A headline on the pile of old newspapers caught his eye. Riots at a Bay City Rollers concert. The world was going mad. There hadn't been that sort of trouble with Bing Crosby and Frank Sinatra, and they could really sing!

Driving along quiet roads in a Jaguar borrowed from Ray Everett, having left the motorway Valentina relaxed and began to think of the day to be spent at home. It would be good to walk by the sea again, and to stand on the highest point on Gower and feel the fresh, clean air. As a child the seasons had seemed so long, there had been real excitement at the first sight of a celandine, then daffodils then bluebells and the gradual clothing of the trees in rich new greens. Now, it hardly seemed more than days since she had been travelling along these same lanes to spend Christmas with her family. She put aside the thrill of driving through the countryside, remembering how miserable that occasion had been.

Her parents bickered most of their waking hours, smarting at small irritations and responding to real and imagined insults like small children. She guessed they stayed together because of a faded memory of a love once shared. That, plus convention and fear of what people might say if they separated.

She slowed down, the powerful car murmuring lazily at a fraction of its power. She was in no hurry to arrive. She diverted from her route and stopped a few miles from the end of her journey to stand for a moment on a lonely headland and look across the sea. A wind was ruffling the surface into white horses and turning to look along the cliff path she saw the slopes were bright with clumps of yellow gorse. There were always patches of gorse in bloom, which explained the saying that when the gorse was in flower it was kissing time. Not in our house, she thought sadly.

It was two o'clock when she pulled up outside her parents' house and, opening the back door, she called a greeting. For a few seconds they seemed not to have heard, they were sniping at each other as though they hadn't stopped since her previous visit. "Oh," she whispered, "why did I think I needed to come?"

"Your mother insisted on starting without you. Yours is in the oven keeping warm with mine," her father announced after brief greetings had passed between them.

"In that case, I think we should go out and eat. What about The Curlew, do they still do lunches? Or are we too late?"

"I won't come, I've already eaten," her mother said, not even looking at her.

"All right, then. Come on, Dad, we'll eat and I'll unpack later." She knew it was wrong to start taking sides the moment she arrived but irritation felt like a huge knot in her stomach and she knew that if she didn't go away and calm down she'd say something hasty and face driving straight back to London. The prospect was already very tempting.

She listened patiently with hardly a word needed to keep her father talking and complaining about his life. They ordered a simple ploughman's and before it arrived, her father began on the subject of Michael. Why, she asked herself again, why did I think I needed to come? All I do is add fuel to their arguments.

When she and her father walked back into the house, on the table was spread samples of Square Clock's T-shirts and other paraphernalia.

"Look at all this," Valerie said proudly. "Our Michael's getting real success and without your help, mind. Did it on his own. Fans clamber to buy these mementoes. We're so proud of him, aren't we, Dewi?"

"Thrilled," Dewi muttered.

Valentina's case was still standing just inside the back door; no one seemed in a hurry to make her even remotely welcome. She went up to her room, realizing that the whole weekend would be more of the same. Going downstairs again, she tried to calm things down, saying, "I've had an exciting week, Mam." She named some of the radio and television names she had met and hoped they would be impressed enough to forget her brother for a few minutes, but then her father turned on her.

"This nonsense with Michael is all your fault — you with your fancy job and your boastful name-dropping. It turned his head. Who d'you think you are? Can't you forget what you do for five minutes?"

"And you won't even use your highfalutin position to help your only brother," her mother added.

"Mam, I haven't helped because I can't. I don't think he has what it takes to succeed in a very overcrowded business. But if he does succeed, I'll be thrilled for him, I really will."

"Sure to be," her mother said icily.

Valentina looked from one face to the other, each unhappy, each looking for someone on whom to heap the blame. Picking up her case that still stood near the door, she walked out.

She was tired and angry and the meal she had eaten was like a lump of concrete in her stomach. Why had she come? "Well," she muttered as she threw her case into the Jaguar, "it'll be a long time before I come again."

In need of friendly, undemanding support, she rang Charlie and asked if it was too late to change her mind about lunch the following day. Assured he would be pleased to see her, she then started the drive back to London. Wanting to salvage something out of the miserable day, she avoided the busy roads and drove instead through some of the pretty villages. Perhaps she'd head for Gloucester and maybe find a place to stay the night.

Leaving Barry and heading towards Penarth, she drove slowly along narrow lanes she hadn't explored before and found herself in a small bay, with a few buildings in a huddle near the middle of the thin strip of beach. She stopped for coffee and drove on. Less than an hour later she came across a most charming village. It was far from the main thoroughfares, in a sleepy backwater, where a river meandered without hindrance between houses, alongside the very walls in some instances and in others out of sight, the only evidence of its presence crossing a field being an untidy parting in the hair-like grass. She stopped and found an inn where she could stay and, like a child on a first holiday, she abandoned the car and began to explore.

She liked what she saw and vowed one day to return. It would be her secret place about which she would tell no one. A place to come and recover from her disappointments and lick wounds in privacy, and a place to celebrate all the good things.

After dinner, her body felt heavy and her eyes struggled ineffectively to stay open. Before nine o'clock, she indulged herself in a languorous soak in the widest, deepest bath she had ever seen, and went to bed. She woke eleven solid hours later and after the biggest breakfast she had eaten since her teenage years, drove at a leisurely pace back to London.

Some devil in her made her phone her parents' neighbour and ask her to tell her mother she had arrived safely. "In case she was worried," she added, with a twist of pain.

During lunch with Charlie, it was tempting to talk about the village where she had spent the previous night but she resisted. One day she might be glad to have a bolthole, a place to run to where no one would find her.

When she left Charlie and returned to the flat for the second time that day, Gillian was still out. She had left a note telling Gillian about the lunch with Charlie and put it on the unit but a gust of wind as she opened the window had lifted it and deposited it inside a half-open drawer filled with old receipts. Already her mind was on the following day, going through the appointments in her mind, looking forward to some, apprehensive about others.

Over recent weeks the name of Tony Switch had failed to appear and she wondered vaguely and with little real interest what had happened to him. People came and went; shone for a while then sank back into oblivion, probably to bore their friends with stories about the time they were one of the greats.

It was at a party in June when she had surprising news of him. He had been given a radio programme. His new venture had been well advertised, some of his earlier records used for publicity. The programme had been initially offered for a two-week trial but there were hints that a contract for a longer series was already in the offing.

"That Tony Switch show is doing surprisingly well," Gillian said one morning when the programme had been given its second airing. "We'll have to listen to it. Everyone's talking about it. Apparently he's very funny."

Valentina was surprised when she was told later that day that Tony had phoned her office and wanted to see her. "What can he want? Surely he isn't trying to make a comeback?"

"Too soon!" Gillian laughed. "The ripples haven't settled from his dive yet!"

"Did he give a clue?"

"No, he just said that in his new position he might be able to help you."

"Heaven forbid that I ever have to be grateful to Tony Switch!"

The appointment was for later that day. "Best we get it over with," Gillian said with a groan.

When he arrived, the girls hardly recognized him. The crimson tufted hair of the punk rocker had been replaced with a carefully styled look. The outrageous clothes and appearance with which he had tried to hide his lack of talent were out, and in was the neat, wide lapelled, long jacketed and obviously expensive suit.

Complete transformation was avoided by the long-fringed "Afghan" coat he carried over his arm, but that was probably for their benefit, Valentina decided. He was still pretending to be the young rebel although he was in his thirties.

"Fancy him wearing a smart suit. I couldn't have been more surprised if he'd been wearing a frock," Gillian confided later.

The failed singer had quickly achieved success with his first programmes. "And," he told them, "I've just signed a six-week contract."

That it had gone to his head was not difficult to surmise from the look on his face and the over-confident attitude.

"I'm having a party tomorrow night and as many of the recording companies will be sending representatives and the pluggers will be out in force, I knew you'd want to be there."

He looked deeply into Valentina's eyes and he was looking at her as though they shared a sweet secret. "Both of us?" she asked, gesturing towards Gillian.

There was a moment of doubt in the lightly made-up eyes before he shrugged and said, "Well, the numbers are getting a bit out of hand —"

"You can count me out if it will help," Valentina said sweetly.

He shrugged grudgingly and turned to Gillian. "Of course you can come, if you wish."

"Now why don't I feel excited by his invitation?" Valentina asked after he had made his dramatic exit, blowing kisses and waiting until someone opened the

72

door for him to stride out. "And why am I glad you're coming too?"

"You think the 'party' might have been just you and him?"

"Not likely, I'm not good for his ego."

"Me neither! Remember that parody of a children's song he wrote about Andy Pandy for that charity do? I called him Loopy Lou and it got into the papers. He wasn't best pleased."

"But you'll come?"

"I wouldn't miss it. Pity it's a Tuesday though."

Tuesday was a busy day for the girls, with the wall to be updated with the latest chart listings and reps bringing recordings they hoped would be chosen for hotshotting. It wasn't the best evening to dash home, change and be out again by eight.

Ordering new releases after considering their chances was a nervous time and exhaustion showed on Valentina's face when they got back to the flat just after seven. Her slinky summer dress was still at the cleaners; there was no time to wash and dry her thick hair. There was no milk for a reviving cup of coffee. With a groan, she flopped on her bed and said to Gillian, "How I wish we'd refused to go."

"Come on, Valentina, you wouldn't miss seeing Tony making a fool of himself, would you? That's what he'll do. Inviting all those important people, pretending he's someone special, he's sure to fall on his face."

"At least if there's a crowd there'll be plenty of choice and we won't be stuck with him all evening."

"Tell you what," Gillian suggested, "if we've had enough in an hour, we'll sneak out and go to a pub somewhere on the river. It's too nice an evening to waste on Tony."

"That's more tempting than listening to Tony telling us how wonderful he is."

The hotel room was hardly full. When they walked in, Valentina wearing wide trousers and a tunic in crimson crushed velvet, and Gillian in pink pedal-pushers and a soft green and pink top, they were surprised to see only seven people.

"So much for his crowd of admiring friends!"

"Riverside pub, here we come!"

They prepared a polite smile and went forward to greet acquaintances and be introduced to those they didn't know. Several of the guests worked at BBC radio but, as secretaries, stock managers or equipment distributors, they were tucked well into the background of the medium. The only broadcaster was Tony himself. He had made certain he was the important one, Valentina thought cynically.

The girls sat and talked amiably with one or two and wondered why they were there, checking their watches regularly, anxious to be gone. As more people arrived and the room filled, Tony was very attentive towards Valentina, practically ignoring Gillian. Some of the new arrivals were known to the girls, being on the production side of music programmes, and she talked to them, trying to avoid Tony's obvious and unwanted attentions. It seemed the more she was rude to him, the more he was flattered, and he made sure everyone saw him as he went between the newly arriving guests and the two girls.

"He's putting on a show," Gillian whispered. "Pretending you and he are together in something."

"But why?" Valentina frowned but a few minutes later, she knew.

A band walked in and set up their instruments. More people strolled in, chattering and laughing, and at last the room felt like a party might be happening. "It'll be easier now to slip away," she confided in Gillian.

Then Gillian pointed to the band. The name was written on the drum stand: Square Clock. Moke was there, smiling at the crowd.

Before the situation had sunk in, Tony was on the small stage waving his hands for silence. He introduced the band and gestured proudly towards Valentina, telling everyone the second guitarist was her brother, Moke Robbins. "Surprise, surprise," he added above applause. "Valentina didn't think her young brother would make it," he scolded, waving an admonishing finger, "but here he is, playing at a party given by Tony Switch!"

"Tony's done this on purpose," Valentina whispered angrily. "Michael is telling everyone I've refused to help him. This will look as if they're right!"

"Of course people won't think that. Specially if you go across and give him a sisterly kiss."

Valentina ignored her advice and went on, "What do they think I am? I'm not some powerful impresario. I work for record distributors. Tony is deliberately trying to make me look guilty of ignoring my own brother."

Angered by what she saw as Tony making her look foolish by having her brother as a guest musician, Valentina nodded to Gillian and then towards the door.

Tony spotted this immediately. "Come on, Valentina, I thought you'd be pleased, me being a supporter of your brother." He held her forearms and, trying to get away, she gripped his in a similar way, but he didn't let go. Standing face to face, unheard above the music, it could have been mistaken for a lovers' quarrel. She was only half aware of the flash of several cameras recording the scene.

"How did you know about Michael?" she demanded.

Putting his head closer as though to hear, he replied, "Phil told me how much you wanted to help him. I booked them to please you, Valentina. I so much want to please you."

Relaxing her struggle, she allowed him to pull her closer. "Phil was lying! As usual."

"You haven't heard? About their contract?"

"What contract?" she asked in disbelief. "That's probably another of Phil's lies."

Tony patted his pockets. "I have a copy of it here." Then he sighed. "Sorry, I must have left the paperwork in my room." He looked around. "They're all enjoying the music. Pop up with me and we'll look at it."

Valentina saw that Gillian was laughing at one of the guests who was offering her another drink. Moke and his group were playing a mundane rendering of one of the Beatles' numbers and the mood seemed easy. "All

76

right, but it will have to be quick. We have to go on somewhere after this," she said, stating their prepared lie.

"Not *too* quick," he said and she looked at him and presumed from his smile he was joking. He took her hand as they left the room and as soon as they were through the doorway she snatched it back as if his flesh had scalded her. She followed him to his room, calming down, thinking about the possibility of a contract for Square Clock, however unlikely that was. It would please her mother especially as she hadn't helped him get it!

Going into the room, she was startled out of her reverie by hearing Tony lock the door. Turning, she was even more shocked to see him beginning to remove his clothes.

"Open this door!"

"Come on, darling, you can cut out the act and show your appreciation in the usual way. You don't think I did this for Moke, do you? It was for you, for us. I've known for ages that you want me, but you needed an excuse, didn't you? Silly girl. I'm yours."

"Open this door at once!"

Oblivious of her rage he went on, "I saw through that pretence of hating me. It's an act lots of girls use when they're afraid of their love not being returned. Wanting me so badly you can't sleep, so you tell yourself you hate me. Love it you will — I know how to give a girl a good time."

She was so shocked she was rooted to the spot. "Open the door. Now!" she demanded in a voice that shook.

"Come on, baby," he coaxed, kicking off his stack-heeled boots, stepping out of his flares and moving towards her. "Look at me. This is Tony Switch and I'm all yours."

Ignoring what he didn't expect to hear, he flicked off his brightly patterned underwear, smiling at her scowling face, unaware of her growing anger and fear.

"One kick and you'll be nobody's for a long time," she warned. Gathering her scattered wits, she moved a step towards him with her hand raised. Blissfully confident that she was pretending to fight him off while filled with desire, he came close enough to receive a sound blow to his ear.

"You fool!" he shouted, shocked by the pain. "You don't know what you're doing! This is Tony Switch you're dealing with and I'm not used to being treated like this. Thousands of girls would love to be where you are now." He was so busy holding his head, he didn't feel the kick that landed on his knee for a few seconds, then he threw the key at her. "Go on, you bitch! Get out!"

She fumbled anxiously with the key but as she pulled the door open, he grabbed her shoulder and pulled her back into the room.

"Don't think I'll forget this, bitch. Pretending to be so virtuous and all the time sleeping with whoever it takes to improve your chances!"

"I've never used sex to further my career. I've never needed to. I'm good at my job. Don't you wish you could say the same? Now get some clothes on. One sight of that offering and you'll lose the few friends you do have."

Too late, Tony turned from her and saw, framed in the doorway, a wide-eyed Gillian and the giggling radio producer with whom he was hoping to arrange an extended contract, plus two people he didn't know. They stared, a frozen tableau, wide eyed.

"I'll never forgive you, Valentina Robbins," he hissed, grabbing belatedly for a bed cover. "You'll regret it, I promise you!"

As she walked off between Gillian and the radio producer, Valentina was shivering. Not so much for her narrow escape but the look on Tony's face as he'd threatened her. She had made a dangerous enemy. Phil Blackwood and now Tony Switch. What was wrong with her that she had such a disastrous effect on two such different men?

Gillian had seen Tony wink and make a suggestive gesture at one of his friends as he and Valentina left the room and it had caused her to feel a bit anxious. Valentina could take care of herself, she was quite experienced at shrugging off unwanted attention, but Tony was a big man, built more like a wrestler than a singer of love songs. The thought entered her mind that he might have been drinking, or taking something else to build his confidence.

Seeing the door open on that bizarre scene was something Gillian would never forget. Yet, walking off down the corridor, laughing at the man's humiliation, she experienced feelings of guilt, as if she had been responsible for his embarrassment. Always concerned for the underdog, even though he had brought this on himself with his vanity and stupidity, she wanted to go back and help him through the aftermath. Whether he was drunk or not, it would still be painful for him.

Valentina left straightaway, even forgetting to speak to her brother, but Gillian waited. The music from Square Clock was dull but managed to keep the party going, with people huddled together sharing the story of Tony's disaster. It wasn't until people began to drift off that Tony reappeared. He had sobered up and when he saw Gillian, he glared and asked her to leave.

"I waited to tell you I'm very sorry it happened," she said calmly.

"Sorry? Best laugh you've had all year and you're sorry? Now why don't I believe you!"

She felt her throat and face colouring but she stayed with him. "Whether you believe me or not, I am sorry. I waited to tell you, and now I've told you, I'll go."

"You led him there! The man I'm supposed to work with. You probably set it up between you. She was giving me all the signals, you know. I don't need to force a girl to come to bed with me, I've never been that desperate. She encouraged me then set about humiliating me. That's what happened."

"What happened was that you were drunk and thought you were some sex god. Stop pretending, Tony."

His shoulders sagged then and he said, "Stay a while, will you? Just let me get rid of this lot and we'll have a coffee." He gave her a sulky look like a naughty child and she softened further as he added, "You needn't worry . . ."

"I won't," Gillian said with a cautious smile. "I think you've been put off women, for tonight at least. I'll book a taxi for an hour's time."

"Thanks."

"And Tony, the best way to deal with ridicule is to join in the laughter, share the joke. That way they'll be laughing with you and not at you. You're clever enough to make something positive out of this."

"You're right," he said thoughtfully. "Yes, I believe you're right."

Talking to Tony that night, Gillian thought she saw a sensitive and unhappy man. Putting on an act for crowds was like snapping on the switch he had chosen for his name. Tony Switch, turning himself into a performer, then switching himself off to become a shy, uncertain young man.

He wasn't the only one to hide, scared, behind a façade of confidence, to suffer the agonies of the Pagliacci syndrome, playing the hearty, fun-loving clown, while crying beneath the garish make-up. How much of the bizarre punk-rock fashion had been based on something similar? She wondered why Tony did it. What was it within people like Tony that made them choose something that necessitated such a dramatic change of personality?

The papers the following day were full of the story about the drunken Tony Switch. There were photographs, too, of what appeared to be an intimate moment between Tony and Valentina. Embarrassing for Valentina as they gave support to Tony's insistence she had misled him.

Rumours about Tony and Valentina getting together were hotly denied but for a while refused to die and it was Gillian, that champion of lame dogs, who helped Tony through the following days, backing up his story about him having been drunk. They met in out-of-the-way places, being careful not to be seen, and she allowed him to talk his way through the situation, coaxing him out of his humiliation, encouraging him to treat the publicity as an advantage.

She seemed oblivious to the distress caused to her friend, having decided that Valentina was better able to cope than Tony, who was on the brink of a radio career. A career that could be over before it began.

It was only their boss, Ray Everett, and Charlie and Danny who offered comfort to Valentina. Valentina was puzzled by her friend's apparent indifference but presumed it was the distraction of a new boyfriend.

Gillian said nothing to her about the meetings with Tony. He had asked her to meet him in secret, explaining that he didn't want to appear weak and in need of someone to prop him up while he waited for the press to tire of their fun.

Gillian's frequent and unexplained absences, Valentina had decided, were dates with the producer they had met at Tony's party. She asked obliquely if he was the one and Gillian said nothing to alter her misconception.

CHAPTER
FIVE

London was hot and crowded. Dust seemed to rise from the pavements and hover in the air together with petrol fumes and the smell of stale food. Besides the tourists from overseas, lured to London by its fashion, its theatres and its air of excitement, young people poured in, in their hundreds, from every part of Britain, also feeling the powerful pull of the capital city.

In their various uniform attempts at originality, many filled the streets and parks, with their aggressive clothes, hair and attitudes intending to shock. Girls in short leather skirts and fishnet stockings walked beside boys wearing black leather shorts and big boots, their heavy jackets covered with swastikas and union flags and chains and studs and more zips than they could possibly find a use for. Their bare legs looked skinny and too frail to support all the leather and metal.

The punk rockers were in the minority during that summer but Valentina found their blatant sexual antics and their semi-nude state in the parks irritating, and together with the heat and staleness of the air, she felt the need to get away. On a whim, realizing she had a free weekend, she went again to the pretty village and stayed at the inn for two nights. She walked and ate and slept and on Sunday she set off back to London feeling refreshed.

Enjoying the freedom, she stayed later than intended on the Sunday and it was almost midnight when she reached the end of her journey and approached the flat. Without warning, a woman stepped out in front of her, causing her to jump on the clutch and brake. Tired as she was after the long drive, she reacted quickly enough to prevent a collision but it gave her a fright. Although she hadn't actually touched the woman, she got out of the car and ran to where the woman was standing.

"Are you all right?" she asked anxiously. The woman nodded and Valentina's voice changed to anger. "Glad I am, but you weren't thinking about what you were doing, were you? I'd have hit you if I'd been a second later on the brake! It wouldn't have been my fault but I'd have had the blame, I'd have had to live with it if you'd been hurt!" She shivered as she realized how easily she could have been involved in an accident.

The woman didn't speak but as she moved the hood of her dark duffle coat, which had made it difficult to see in the poor light, Valentina recognized Claire, the singer.

"Claire? Is everything all right?"

"Yes. I wasn't hurt. Just frightened. I'm sorry, and you were right, I wasn't thinking about the danger. Sorry." She was about to move off but Valentina touched her arm.

"Can I give you a lift somewhere? It's late to be wandering around the streets."

"No, it's all right."

"Please. I'm shaking and I wasn't the one about to be hit!"

Claire got into the car beside her and as Valentina slipped it into gear and began to move off, waiting for directions, she asked, "Can we go somewhere and talk?"

Valentina groaned inwardly — it was already very late and she had driven a long way after a day walking in the fields. She smiled and suggested an all-night cafe where several of her friends went when the moment demanded sustenance and a need to talk, like now.

Since Friday's journey that had taken her to "her" village, she had hardly sat down. Exploring the area had been an obsession as new and fresh delights drove her further and further, in a series of semi-circles, from the inn. She stretched her aching limbs and forced herself to listen to Claire's limited comments and reply with what she hoped sounded like interest.

They ordered coffee and Valentina wondered how to begin a conversation with this strange girl. Trivial remarks about the coincidence of their meeting and the lateness of the hour were all she offered, yet Valentina felt there was something Claire needed to say. Although they had met on several occasions, Claire had never been very forthcoming and she knew little about her apart from a talent as a performer and the fact that she shunned all publicity.

"Where d'you live?" she asked, choosing what she considered a safe question.

"At the moment I have a flat in Maida Vale, but I'll be moving soon."

"You don't like living there?"

Claire turned to her then and said in an urgent whisper, "If I tell you something, you will keep it to yourself?"

"As long as it's legal," Valentina joked.

"I move around a lot because I don't want my parents to find me. That's why I colour my light brown hair black, and use coloured lenses to change my eyes from blue to brown." She looked quizzically at Valentina and added, "You had guessed, about the disguise, hadn't you?"

Valentina shrugged. "Lots of people change their appearance for lots of reasons, especially in our business."

"My reason is fear of my family finding me."

"I'm sorry you have problems and, no, I won't mention this to anyone."

"Thanks. It's difficult, you see."

That appeared to be the end of Claire's confidences and after allowing her response to hover in the air for a few moments, Valentina explained about the uneasy situation between and her mother.

"My father is all right, I suppose. At least he doesn't always agree with Mam when she has a go at me for some vague failure on my part." She frowned as she concentrated on the best way to explain. "I have to say that my mother has never done anything to make me desperately want to run away. But she has never shown affection towards me as most mothers do. I don't ever remember being hugged, even when I fell over and hurt myself as a child."

86

"Perhaps it's simply that she's a cold woman."

"I don't think so. She's different with my brother."

"That's Moke, isn't it?"

"That's Moke," Valentina said with a sigh. "Mam hugs him, glories in his successes — few real, most imagined — and boasts to everyone who will listen about how wonderful he is. But she disapproves of what I've achieved."

"Born first, were you?"

"Yes, and they're usually the most favoured, aren't they?"

"Sometimes. But what if you were the innocent cause of your mother marrying your father because he was the man who got her pregnant, and he was someone she wouldn't have otherwise married?"

"Surely not?"

"Sneak a look at their marriage certificate and do the maths. Mulling over a few dates might solve the mystery for you."

"Is it because of your success that you don't want your family to contact you?" Valentina asked. She wondered if Claire's family was perhaps criminal or embarrassing in some other way.

"Something like that," Claire said noncommittally.

Their conversation moved to safer ground then as they talked about the newest recordings and successes and failures. Claire's favourites included Suzi Quatro, and they both liked Slade and Status Quo. It was two o'clock before Valentina finally drove Claire to a smart block of flats in Maida Vale.

She waited while Claire opened the door with her key but she didn't see anyone there to greet her. Staying out so late with no one to feel anxious about her, she must live alone. It seemed her private life was well hidden, separate from her career, and she wondered again how she had achieved that. News reporters were clever and determined when they wanted to find out about someone in the public eye.

In the flat Valentina and Gillian shared, four people were sitting, looking worried. Gillian was twisting her hair into tangled knots that would defy a comb, and her blue eyes were startlingly bright, surrounded as they were with reddened rims. Gillian and Bob, who had come to see Valentina, had been joined by Danny Fortune, who had popped in on the chance of Valentina being free to go with him to a gig in Fulham, but he had found Gillian and Bob anxiously wondering where she had gone.

"I wanted to talk to her about a party I'm planning to celebrate a new album, and when I rang the flat, Gillian told me about a note she had found on the floor," Bob had explained. "It says she was going to lunch with Charlie but when Gillian checked, he hadn't made any such arrangement."

"It's unusual for her not to tell me if she's going away," Gillian said. She pointed at the calendar. "We always write down our social arrangements. She didn't tell me where she was going on Friday and I presumed she was going home. Now I'm beginning to think she's been kidnapped."

"Come on, Gilly," Bob said with a laugh. "That's a bit over the top, even for your wild imagination. She's probably got a new man in her life and doesn't want gossip to frighten him off."

"It happens! These things might sound way out but they do happen. You only have to look at the newspaper," Gillian defended.

She and Valentina had seen less of each other in recent weeks, apart from at work. Since she had been dating Tony Switch, the uneasiness about her secret had developed into a less friendly atmosphere, a lack of communication.

In spite of this, Gillian was genuinely concerned. If her friend would only open the door and walk in unharmed, she'd forget their differences and run to show her how relieved she was. How marvellous it would be to return to the close, happy relationship they had once enjoyed.

Danny performed at the gig and returned to find them still wondering what had happened to Valentina. Charlie Trapp had telephoned several times during the evening and, on being told Valentina had still not appeared, he joined the others in the vigil. They tried all the places she might be but without success, and decided that if there was no word by eight o'clock the next morning they would inform the police.

Across the street, Phil couldn't sleep. He watched with interest as first Bob Lever arrived, then Danny, who left and then returned. Then, last of all, Charlie Trapp. What could be happening? Sleep drifted further from his mind as the hours passed and a strange car had taken her parking slot.

Stopping the car outside the flat after finally parting from Claire, Valentina saw to her irritation that all the parking places were full. The car purred around the corner, where she found room to squeeze it in. When she shut off the engine and allowed the silence to settle, she was achingly tired. It was so tempting just to sit there and doze till morning. It was warm, and the seat so comfortable once she had eased herself back from the controls and lifted her feet from the pedals. So nice to just sit and relax. To get out and walk the few yards to the flat seemed such a chore.

Phil recognized the sound of the Jaguar when Valentina passed his window and, puzzled, he slipped out wearing a thick anorak and a hastily dragged-on pair of jeans and saw the car with her still inside.

He didn't knock on the window but went close enough to see that her eyes were closed and guessed she had relaxed too soon at the end of her journey. He was irritated by not knowing where that journey had begun. One day he'd find out. A car cruised past, music playing for its solitary occupant. The sound disturbed her slightly and afraid of her waking and seeing him, he hurried back to his flat.

In a nearby church a clock chimed the hour of 4 a.m. and still Valentina didn't move. It was a policeman who woke her at twenty minutes past, to ask if she was all right. Smiling reassurance, before groaning and forcing her weary body out of the car, she explained that all was well and she had simply fallen asleep. Heavy eyed, her voice slightly thickened by her sudden wakening, she thanked him and unlocked her door.

Phil saw the policeman arrive and watched as Valentina left the car and entered her door. He looked at his watch and smiled. She couldn't do a thing without him knowing, no matter how she might try.

Valentina was surprised to see the lights on and the living room filled with people, which eventually settled to become just four.

"What's going on?" she asked and as Gillian ran to tell her how relieved she was to know she was safe, Valentina stepped aside, avoiding the gesture, and again demanded to know what they were doing there.

Gillian was shocked and hurt by her reaction. "We've been so worried, not knowing where you were!" Gillian explained, still smiling her relief and holding back a tear. "We had no idea where you were and the note saying you were meeting Charlie wasn't true, and —"

"Note? What note? When did I start having to tell you all where I go and who I meet?"

"As far as we all knew, you were missing," Charlie said quietly. "We were going to contact the police if you hadn't turned up by eight o'clock."

"You what?" Startled by their words and more than a little guilty at her inability to explain, Valentina resorted to attack rather than apology. "It isn't anyone's business, but I decided on the spur of the moment to go away for the weekend. I have a rather exhausting job, in case you aren't aware of it, and I need a break now and then. Now, unless there are any more questions, may I go to bed?"

She snatched the note Gillian had offered as explanation and, as she went to her room, she heard the subdued murmurs as Charlie, Bob and Danny left. Ashamed of her outburst towards friends who had been genuinely concerned for her, she excused herself on the grounds of the briefly snatched sleep that had been broken by the constable and so disorientated her. Tomorrow she would explain and apologize, she promised herself. She should have told Gillian she was going away. Her childish resentment because of Gillian's unexplained absences had made her inconsiderate. Then she read the note, written some time before, and realized what had happened. When she tried to explain to Gillian the following morning, Gillian refused to listen.

Apart from when they were going to functions connected with work, Valentina and Gillian rarely went out together during the weeks that followed. Still hurt by Valentina's reaction when she found them all waiting for her, Gillian hadn't confided to her that she had been seeing Tony, and Valentina never found out, even though they had mutual friends who were part of the same scene. Gillian developed an increasing resentment towards her one-time friend, telling herself that Valentina had changed from the kind person she had once been due to the important position she now held. She half believed Tony's insistence that she had been the cause of his embarrassment too and, talking less and less, they no longer told one another where they were going. Their social lives became completely separate. Valentina was aware of the growing rift, regretted it, but said nothing.

Tony Switch's contract with the producer who had seen him in his hotel room that evening had almost been called off by Tony himself. But then he remembered Gillian's words and knew they made sense. He faced the situation squarely and told himself that if he could cope with the aggravation for a few weeks it would be forgotten and it might even win him a few more friends. His popularity was low on the business side of the microphone and he could do with a few more. So he had gone to the appointment previously made and, after giving as good as he got when the jokes were flying around and even adding a few of his own, he had concentrated on winning audiences for his radio show for the remaining days of his present contract.

On one of the early programmes he had asked a question of an imaginary friend, Marlene, and although the audience never heard from Marlene, she had quickly become a part of the show. Tony and Marlene, his imaginary friend, became established as a show not to be missed, with guests asking to come on instead of the production team having to beg people to take part. Tony Switch was on the verge of becoming a household name, and he loved it.

If he pressed a wrong button, he blamed Marlene for being in his way. He used her to react to his jokes, scolded her for seeing double entendres when he swore he had intended none. "Oh, Mar-LENE," he would complain. "You naugh-ty girl." Those expressions became catchwords almost overnight. He even described her outfits and hairstyles, all of which were outrageous. If you hadn't listened to Tony and Marlene, you were out of touch. As his confidence grew, Tony's talent for humour also improved and came easier, and he thrived on his fame.

He still insisted to Gillian that he was angry with Valentina for what she had done and believed the fault had been hers for leading him on, but to himself he admitted that she had done him the most enormous favour by giving him the reputation of being a man who could take it as well as hand it out, and this reflected in his programme, by his reading out criticisms as well as accepting praise — which he treated as a joke.

Gillian had been there to help him while he licked his wounds and repaired his damaged ego. He smiled happily. He'd been clever facing the ridicule instead of hiding from it and keeping his involvement with Gillian a secret, so he could ease away from her now he was building a new career. That had been his wisest move. Gillian wasn't the one to rise with him. She thought too small for a prodigious talent like his.

Now he only had to make her see the sense of their saying goodbye and everything in his world would be perfect. Girls were running after him in great numbers. He had money, and a social standing he had never dreamed of achieving. Yes, Valentina deserved thanks for that dreadful evening when he had acted like a fool and she had shown him to be one so publicly. In a gush of goodwill towards her, on her birthday in August, the date having been gleaned from Gillian, he sent her flowers and included a card with "I told you I wouldn't forget. Thanks for our May time fling" written on it.

Valentina believed the message was intended to be misconstrued.

"You know nothing happened that night," she said to Gillian, when the flowers arrived.

"You say you didn't encourage him but perhaps he genuinely believed you did," Gillian said warily.

"Come on, Gillian, do you believe I could have led him on? Lead Tony Switch on in the hope of some fun and games in his room that night? Tony Switch?" She gasped in amazement.

"I'm just saying you might have given him the wrong idea. He's used to women falling for him."

"Why are you taking his side in this? You hardly know him. And what you *do* know you don't like."

"You might as well know, I've been out with him a few times and he isn't as bad as you think."

"Oh. I see. And these flowers, are they to show he's forgiven me for something I didn't do? Or are they to remind me he hasn't forgotten his humiliation? Which sentence is the most sincere?"

"He's successful now, so why would he bother to waste time hating you?" Waving her arms, pushing aside Valentina's intended reply, she said, "I don't want to discuss Tony with you. Sorry, Valentina, but it's best we drop this. Now."

"You're probably right. Well, you know what you can do with these!" She dumped the flowers unceremoniously into the rubbish bin and squashed them down firmly with the lid. Brushing her hands against each other as if for a job well done, she went out.

She was upset, mainly because of Gillian's revelation about her friendship with Tony, a man they had both disliked, and partly because the flowers and the message worried her. Remembering Tony's face that evening, she had a revival of her conviction that if an opportunity arose, he would indeed pay her back. Instinctively, she guessed that causing her to lose her job would be what he would aim for, so she had a word with her boss and explained exactly what had happened. Raymond Everett's pale eyes sparkled as he laughed and told her to forget it.

"With a new and successful career, Tony isn't going to risk causing trouble for himself. Besides, I know you and value you for the work you do. I'd be a fool to let you go because of an outburst by a fool like him. There'll be an increase in your money at the end of the month, just to show how valued you are."

"Thank you."

Gillian had left early to go to Leicester where she was meeting Tony after he'd finished an outside broadcast with what she called his "grannies, teenagers and teenyboppers". They were spending a night in a hotel and travelling back separately the following day.

As she travelled home that evening, Valentina felt the excitement of the wage increase and Raymond's kind words slowly fade. She knew the flat would be empty. The let-down was complete once she stepped inside the flat. There was no one to help her celebrate.

There was no point ringing her parents' neighbour, Mrs Frances. Leaving a message wasn't the same as telling someone and her parents wouldn't understand her achievement anyway. Gillian wouldn't be home till late — if at all — and Charlie was working. So she rang Danny Fortune. She didn't explain her reasons for wanting to see him, but arranged a meeting in a cafe they both knew, for seven.

It was almost eight o'clock before he came, rushing through the door with his guitar across his shoulders.

"Sorry, Valentina, I should have let you know I was going to be late but there wasn't time. I had a phone call and I have to do a ten-minute slot in a pub about an hour's drive away. Will you come with me, darlin' girl? The van's busted, and the Jag is faster than a bus," he said with a pleading smile.

She told him her news as they drove, and his response was to say, "Stop the car."

She pulled up at the kerb and as soon as she slipped the gearstick into neutral, he leaned over and kissed her. "That's grand," he said, his Irish accent more than usually noticeable. "Congratulations, me darlin'. What a thrill for you. I bet your mam is excited. They live again through their kids, don't they, mothers?"

"Not mine," she said, slightly embarrassed by his exuberance.

"You've told them?"

She explained about their not having a phone. "Anyway, they wouldn't understand. It's just a job to them. They have no idea what I do."

"Having a daughter leave home, go far away to the big city, stepping outside their world, it probably unnerves them. They can't be a part of it, they can only stand on the sidelines and pretend to understand the rules."

"Mam understands about Michael," she said childishly.

"Ah, but he's the man. Men are allowed to be adventurous. It might be the seventies here in London, surrounded as we are with punks and rockers and Carnaby Street gear and all the bright lights, but where your parents live it's still the fifties. If they're anything like mine, they'll still think the way their parents thought. Would you believe, now, my mother rings me up last month and asked would I not leave off me vest, as the weather in London can be treacherous. And here we are in August. Besides, didn't I give them up when I was ten?"

She smiled then asked, "But she's proud of what you do?"

"So much as she can grasp it, yes. I was born when she was thirty-nine and she's sixty-four now and I sometimes think I've jumped a generation she's so set in her ways. But I love her dearly."

"I'd like to meet her one day."

Danny tapped his watch. "If we don't get on, and I miss this gig, it's me who'll be seeing me mother, homeless and broke and washed up, begging her to let me come home to be comforted and fed!" He kissed her again, then reached out and touched the key. "Will you move a bit faster, me darlin'? I'm running terrible late."

In fact they had to sit for an hour before Danny was called to perform. His ten minutes extended into thirty and even then the packed audience begged for more. Then there were autograph hunters and people who wanted to talk to him to be able to say he had "treated them like a friend". Later, as the pub was closing, he stood and sang once more.

The song was new to her and sweetly sentimental. Valentina watched as couples shared a look and hand reached out for hand. He was sitting astride a chair and for this final number he turned it so he was singing to her. She was pleased, embarrassed, flattered and tense. All in a matter of seconds.

Glancing at the audience who listened in silence, no one in a hurry to leave, she knew Danny was a master, but he still hadn't achieved a strong-selling record. She knew this song wasn't written by Bob Lever; she felt certain this was one of Danny's own.

"That was wonderful," she said as they walked back to the car. "I've heard of having the audience in the palm of your hand but I've never really understood what it meant — until tonight."

"You've never seen me perform before, have you? Apart from singing for you with Bob's musicians and that doesn't count."

"No, but I hope to hear you again." As she drove out of the car park, leaving others chatting and some waving them off, she asked, "Have you heard from

Bob? I wondered if he'd decided to write another song for you."

"He's back from the tour. It went well, I believe. But you'll be hearing this from Gillian."

"Gillian has been going out with Tony Switch and she didn't tell me. I think something went wrong between us the night — well — you know."

"The night he stripped off and did a belly dance on the bed and tried to persuade us it was your idea?" He laughed at the memory. "Gillian felt sympathy for the big fool, I suppose."

"Gillian stayed on and they talked for hours, apparently. And convinced themselves it was all my doing."

"Forget it, Valentina. Tony isn't worth getting into a sweat over. Getting back to Bob, he's written me another song and I'm rehearsing it at the moment, with one of my own for the other side of a single. Want to come and listen? Friday night, Bob and I will be at the rehearsal studios about eight if you can make it."

"I'll try. Are you pleased with it?"

"So-so. He's adding keyboard and drums and maybe another guitar as before. It isn't what I like." He frowned. "They're encumbrances and I'm better without them. I feel closer to my audience when it's just me and my guitar. But I have to listen to what he says. He's a fine musician. I might lose a few fans but if I make a few hundred more I shouldn't complain."

"Bob has given a few performers their first hit. I hope he does it for you, Danny."

"Do you? Do you really?"

"Of course I do."

"That's grand."

She liked the way he said "that's grand". There it was again, that delightful reminder of his Irish roots.

That weekend she made another visit to "her" village, cancelling her plan to see Danny rehearse. His kiss, and his pleasure at her casually spoken wish for his success, bothered her a little, and the way he smiled, and the way he said, "that's grand", and singing to her in that intimate way. She could easily mislead him into thinking she wanted a closer involvement. Best to stay away this weekend. She didn't want complications and misunderstanding to ruin another friendship. She put a note on the calendar stating she would be away till Sunday. She didn't want any more misunderstandings there, either.

The weather was perfect, the evening sky luminescent with the aftermath of a sunny day. The roads were busy when she left London but the traffic eased once she was out of the main getaway routes and heading for the village a few miles west of Cardiff.

She had booked the same room as before and after unpacking the few items she needed, she went down to order a meal. There were about ten people in the bar, some she vaguely recognized from previous visits. She heard one or two London and Home Counties accents; perhaps she wasn't the first to discover the peace and beauty of the area. Her first reaction was disappointment, resenting others threatening its quiet, untouched charm.

She woke early and set off before breakfast to walk around the village. It was then that she saw it. A thatched cottage that looked no larger than two up, two down, with a For Sale notice planted in the front garden. It was hidden from the casual passer-by, being sideways on, down a narrow lane that curved away from sight behind a hedge of overgrown privet.

She stood and looked at it for an age without moving. She wanted it. She had never wanted anything more than that tiny place with the early sun shining on its pink walls. It was called Pink Cottage and at any other time she might have considered that too twee, but even that was perfect.

Before she ate dinner on that Saturday evening, she had examined every room minutely, enchanted with everything she saw. Excitedly, she spoke to John Ellis and Peter Philby, who agreed to travel to South Wales and look at it. They drove down the next day and examined it and, with them negotiating for her, she quickly made an offer to buy it.

Less than a week later, her offer had been accepted and she read the letter, bubbling with excitement. She had decided not to tell anyone about the purchase but John and Peter shared her enthusiasm and warned her they intended to be her first guests.

That lunchtime she ate at Charlie's snack bar and although it would have been tormentingly easy to blurt out her news to Mary and Joe, she somehow resisted. It had to be her secret, somewhere she could be herself, where the villagers and the friends she hoped to make wouldn't know her for what she did but for what she was.

She was aware that buying the property and only being there on occasions would be harmful to the village. If others did — and she already suspected she wasn't the first — then the pretty little village could be dead for months of the year as more and more houses became the Summer Place, where people came and played at being country folk for a while then rushed back to their real lives in faraway towns.

Local amenities like the small shops and the local bus would disappear as fewer inhabitants remained to use them. Property prices would soar, making it impossible for young people to buy, and families who had lived there for generations would be driven away. These sombre thoughts didn't impinge on her conscience for long. She had fallen in love with Pink Cottage and intended to live there permanently one day. At least I'll be using local tradesmen to do what work is necessary, she thought. I'm no use at DIY, which has become such a craze everywhere. And, she decided, I won't fill the car with food but buy everything in the village shop. Conscience appeased, she settled to dream about how she would furnish the tiny place to best advantage.

Despite the buzz of hugging her secret, there was still a feeling of dismay at not having anyone with whom to discuss her plans. For a moment or two she wished Phil were still a friend, or she'd been able to confide in Gillian.

Then she reminded herself that once everyone knew, the place would no longer be her own. Weekends would be catering for friends and never having a moment to savour the joy of owning the place. She needed at least a few months without having to share it. Perhaps when it was furnished she might enjoy visitors, but for now part of its delight was it being hers alone.

She did tell her boss. After all, it was Raymond's confidence in her that had made it possible. Using photographs that, she assured him, didn't show the place in its true beauty, she told him her plans and he listened with amusement.

"Look at you. You're bursting with excitement. If you really believe you'll go another week without telling anyone, I'll put a tenner on you failing! Or perhaps I'll demand a weekend there instead. How's that? A tenner or a weekend in, what's it called, Pink Paradise?"

"You're on," she said. "And you'd better get that tenner ready. I've made up my mind!"

Valentina's parents lived in a council house and their most daring purchase was a bicycle each to take them to work, and here she was holding down a top job in London and being the owner of a cottage in one of the loveliest parts of Wales. It was amazing how far she had come since leaving home, expecting to be a secretary for a couple of years then go back home.

Phil told his friends back in Wales that he still worked for the record industry and helped support his girlfriend, Valentina. It was so easy to convince them; quoting famous names and using the esoteric language of the music world left his friends envious and impressed.

He finally found a position at a record counter in a large store out of central London, but continued to feel strong resentment that Valentina had done so much better than he had. Any mention of her was food for his frustration and whenever the opportunity arose, he hinted that her success was due to her willingness to do anything, to please those who mattered.

He still lived in the flat near Valentina and amused himself keeping an eye on her movements, listing in his mind who she met and where she went. He liked to think that whatever the time, he could guess where she was and what she was doing. Through buying the occasional drink he was able to piece together most of her activities. There were only the odd weekend absences to account for, then he'd be content. He'd heard from Moke that she had arrived at her parents' house at 2p.m. one Saturday, quarrelled and left again a couple of hours later. That was the time she got back late and fell asleep in the car. It should only have taken three or four hours to drive back, so where had she been? And what about last weekend? She hadn't gone home, he'd checked on that, so where had she gone? He had wondered if she had gone away with Charlie Trapp — they had been increasingly friendly of late — but Charlie hadn't left London.

Her weekend disappearances had him itching with curiosity. He asked Gillian but she seemed unaware of her flatmate's movements and what's more, she seemed not to care. Trouble there, he thought with infantile pleasure. Someone else had found Valentina less than perfect. She'd soon learn her lesson and come back to him.

The car he had bought was old but reliable and he determined to keep it topped up with petrol plus keep an extra couple of gallons in the boot. If she set off again on a Friday evening, he'd be ready to follow. Unless he was really unlucky, he should be able to keep her in sight. After all, he was the better driver.

Tony Switch faded out on the romantic song and gave his usual final spiel, this time ridiculing the state of being in love.

"Love," he said authoritatively, "is the most wonderful thing in the world — while it lasts. But the saddest thing is when love fades and dies and the partner refuses to accept it. Torture is what love can turn into," he said grimly, "when someone refuses to let go."

He played a final disc, which was an early romantic song by Danny Fortune, before a sequence that had become a ritual. He asked Marlene for her opinion of it and although, as usual, the listeners heard nothing, he laughed and told her to "Behave, you naugh-ty girl! Blowing raspberries isn't polite." He pretended to listen to her response then said in a shocked voice, "Oh, MarLENE, you shouldn't say such things, even if Danny Fortune is so sweet you feel sick. No, you can't be sick in here! Now don't — oh, MarLENE!" He sighed as the title music swelled, drowning out his pretence of telling her off, and announced the end of the programme.

In her room in the flat, Gillian sat alone listening to him. She turned the radio off and wished she had done the same to Tony. Why had she waited to see him that night and stayed to comfort him? She had been so flattered by his attention at first, but now the snide remarks he made were no longer funny or clever. She knew they were intended for her and they hurt.

She heard Valentina come in, humming one of Tammy Wynette's songs, "Stand By Your Man", and felt a surge of envy. Valentina seemed so happy these days. With an increase in salary, plus, she suspected, a boyfriend hidden away somewhere to whom she scuttled almost every weekend. Once, she would have known all about it. How she wished she could re-live that evening and ignore Tony's need for comfort. But life was not a rehearsal. You only had one crack at everything. If you got it wrong, you had to live with it.

While Valentina was glowing with success, her own life was collapsing into an utter mess. She had ruined any chance she'd had of getting back with Bob. Foolishly, against everyone's judgement, she had taken a gamble with Tony and lost.

Valentina knocked on her door and asked, in a rare conciliatory gesture, if she would like a coffee, but she feigned sleep. She didn't want to see anyone, or talk about what was happening. After a second knock she heard the kettle being filled and coffee being spooned into a cup and wished she had answered.

CHAPTER
SIX

The long day was coming wearily to its end. The trees were spreading the ground beneath them with a carpet of richly coloured leaves and the diminishing cover on the plane trees of London was revealing the bobbles that would remain on the branches through the winter. In the parks, the lack of rain and the long, hot days had taken their toll and in places green grass had been worn down to bare earth by hundreds of feet. Many flowers, their season passed, lay forlorn in dry beds.

The weariness was apparent on the faces of people too, and even Valentina felt a lethargy that was unusual. She had seen Danny at lunchtime and he too was less than his usual cheerful self, as he reported fewer-than-hoped-for sales of his record, "Mostly Magic". Then there was Gillian.

Valentina knew Gillian was unhappy. She put on a show at work and seemed her normal gentle, hard-working self but once outside the office door a gloom settled on her lovely face and she seemed to be deep in depression. Valentina wondered if the romance, if that was what it was, with Tony was going through a difficult time or was indeed over. She didn't feel able to ask; their friendship was no longer that easy.

Gillian's relationship with Tony Switch could never have been that sound, or Gillian would have been open about it instead of hiding it like a dark secret. Now it might be over and still Gillian didn't tell her. What on earth had happened to cause this sad rift? She racked her brain for a reason but found none, unless the affair with Tony was something *he* wanted to keep out of the public eye? She sighed. A few months ago that wouldn't have been sufficient reason for Gillian not to confide in her.

One evening, as they were both in the flat getting ready to go out, she decided to broach the difficult subject. She made coffee for them both and asked, "How is Tony these days? His radio show is popular, I hear."

"Stop trying to pry," Gillian said quietly, her face beginning to show colour.

"I wasn't prying," Valentina replied, equally quietly. "I was trying to make polite conversation between you and me."

"I don't want to discuss Tony with you."

Valentina took her coffee to her room and sat on the bed, wondering if it might be an idea to find somewhere else to live. Working together had once been such fun, but if the atmosphere at home extended to the office, things would swiftly become impossible. Better to accept there wouldn't be a return to the former friendship. She went out to offer the suggestion to Gillian but she had gone, leaving the still-steaming coffee beside her chair.

★ ★ ★

Phil's knowledge of old and new discs and his stories about the makers of them made him popular with customers and sometimes a queue would form at the counter as they waited for him rather than be served by one of the other assistants. He kept well out of the way of the reps that came regularly to sell their company's offerings but news of what he considered his lowly situation had reached Valentina within days.

"I hope he soon gets fed up and goes back home," she said to Gillian when they were told.

"You don't want anyone else to be successful, do you?" Gillian replied.

"That isn't true!" Valentina was hurt by the unkind remark. "I'd be happy for him to be the highest paid man in the industry if he'd go away and leave me alone. You've seen the way he sits at his window and thinks I don't know he's there. Why did he buy a flat with a view of my comings and goings?"

It was becoming more and more difficult working with Gillian since they were no longer friends. It couldn't go on and Valentina decided it was time for a determined effort to clear the air. As she stepped into the flat that evening, she held Gillian's arm and forced her to look at her.

"Gillian. What's wrong? It's more than the hotel disaster with Tony, isn't it? What have I done? If I've hurt you then I promise it was unintentional."

For a few moments Gillian insisted there was nothing wrong, her face blotched with distress, but Valentina insisted. "Is it me? Have I upset you? Or is it someone else? You don't really believe I was the cause of Tony's embarrassment, do you? Can that really be what this is about?" She laughed then, wondering if the affair had ended. Hoping she was right, she tried to jolly her friend out of her unhappy mood. "What a sight, eh? Every time I hear Chuck Berry singing 'My Ding-a-Ling' I'm reminded of it. Pity page three's reserved for girls; he'd have made a fortune!"

She watched Gillian's face to see if her guess had been correct. There was no response. But intuitively she knew she was right. "You and Tony have split up, haven't you?"

"Split up and messed up good and proper," Gillian said at last.

"Come on, you'll get over Tony Switch."

"I *am* over Tony!"

"Don't be sad about it. His is the kind of charm that quickly wears thin. The worst part is getting used to being a single person again. Perhaps that'll be easier you not having been seen together as a couple. Look, what about you and me having a night out? It's time we forgot our differences and remembered how much we share."

"I won't be drinking."

"All right, we'll go for a —" Realization dawned. "You're pregnant!"

"I'm pregnant and d'you know what hurts the most? Not the way he scarpered like a cat with a brick aimed at his ear the moment he knew. It's that Bob and I will never get together again."

"Have you told Bob?"

"I can't tell him. I feel we're still together and I've cheated on him."

"Oh, Gillian." Valentina hugged her, then thought of what her own first option would be if she were carrying a child of Tony Switch. "Abortion?"

"No. And I can't go home either. Not until I've decided what I'm going to do."

"Tell your parents, and tell Bob," Valentina said firmly. "More trouble is caused by concealing disasters than by bringing problems out into the open. Then at least you'll know who's supportive and who will be too wrapped up in their own prejudices. You might be surprised at your mother's reaction. Inside the most moral and upright mother there's a granny just longing to get out!"

With so much to say to each other, so much dead wood to clear from their once open friendship, they didn't go out. Apologies were made and brushed aside and the weeks of animosity forgotten. Much of the evening was spent talking round and round the various options available to Gillian and it was long after midnight before they went to sleep.

Valentina was happy, comforted by Gillian's confidences and a return to a friendship only slightly battered from Gillian's affair with Tony Switch. There was a surge of guilt when she thought of Pink Cottage. Gillian would wonder why she hadn't told her during their long evening of "catch up". The right moment to mention it didn't come in the days that followed and Valentina wondered if she would ever tell.

Perhaps, when they had settled back securely into their normal companionship, she would take Gillian there and surprise her. But, with time passing, leaving behind the renewal of their friendship when they had talked through the weeks they'd been out of touch, it became more and more impossible. Meanwhile, the Saturday arrived when she was actually taking possession. She had saved a week of her holidays and made some vague reference to a motoring tour of Wales to satisfy those who asked.

Staying at the pub for a couple of nights, she attended two auctions, visited a few antique shops and furnished the place cheaply and sparsely, mostly in old pine, including a very old blanket chest. Eponymous pink seemed the obvious choice for carpets and she managed to buy some second-hand curtains that fitted. Everything arrived and was fitted within the week. It meant working long hours but she was proud of her efforts and thrilled with how comfortable it looked.

As she was leaving, she arranged for a man to attend the garden and envisaged a breathtaking display of roses, foxgloves and lupins against the front wall the following summer.

She drove back to London feeling relaxed and fit. She was ready to return to work with renewed energy and enthusiasm and for the first time she felt the benefit of a holiday. Perhaps she would tell Gillian. If she poured it out the moment she went into the flat and told her she had waited, superstitiously, until it was finalised, it would be all right.

Gillian was out when she dragged her luggage in from the car and, thinking about it as she unpacked and sorted out clothes for the following day, she decided to wait a while longer. It was a risk telling one other person, who might inadvertently tell another. Only John Ellis and Peter Philby and her boss knew, and she trusted them completely. But tell just one wrong person and in a matter of days her wonderful hideaway would be public knowledge. No, she would hug it to herself for a while longer.

In September, Danny Fortune's new record was due to be released and at once Valentina had a problem. She knew his previous records hadn't done well. Would she be accused of favouritism if she chose it for hot shotting? On Gillian's advice she went to discuss it with her boss. Raymond Everett was on the phone to his wife and at his signal she sat and waited until he'd finished.

Ray's wife was a mystery. No one had ever seen her and he had explained that she was shy and preferred to be what he called an old-fashioned wife, dealing with all his needs and comforts contentedly at home. He referred to her as Doll, and what her real name was no one had been told. That he loved her was clear to see from the way he looked when they spoke on the phone, but apart from occasional and brief bursts of curiosity, the staff in the office rarely mentioned her.

When Valentina explained her worry, he agreed to sit in on the audition, something he did on occasions anyway.

114

"With the upbeat backing and the easy-on-the-ear voice of Danny, it could do well. You have to decide, Valentina. Lose it, or choose it on merit and not because you once went to one of Danny's gigs, for heaven's sake."

Valentina was aware that he was slightly edgy with her. She knew she had shown a lack of confidence. Phil was getting to her, watching her and asking her friends about her movements. If she weren't careful, he would see her tumble. It frightened her to know that someone disliked her enough to wait for her downfall. But determination was greater than fear and, reminding herself of her good fortune and how much she had to lose, she threw herself into her work with even greater enthusiasm. This was a job she loved and did well. No one was going to take it away from her.

Claire had a new record in the charts that week and it went straight to number nineteen. Her previous offerings had been popular on the radio, with Tony and other disc jockeys giving it plenty of air time, and this, together with a couple of newspaper and magazine fillers, remarking on her reluctance to be photographed or give interviews, had set the record on its way to the top.

Valentina and Gillian wondered about Claire. She was such a private person and at times had an aura of great sadness. They met her from time to time, usually walking alone, wrapped in scarves to disguise herself from curious stares.

"Her black hair isn't natural nor her dark eyebrows, and heavy make-up might be to hide the light tones of her skin," Gillian remarked one day. "Perhaps she's gone prematurely grey?" But Valentina didn't mention Claire's explanation of disguising herself to avoid her family recognizing her.

The secretiveness made Valentina mistrust her. The unexplained statement about avoiding her family hadn't rung true. Although they had spoken several times since, she had learned nothing more to add to the hint of family trouble she had given the night Valentina had almost knocked her down. She gently but firmly refused to give even the smallest detail about her upbringing or her family. So far as anyone knew, for Claire — just Claire — life really began at the age of seventeen. Now, at nineteen, her quiet refusal to tell all hadn't affected her steadily growing success.

Bob Lever had booked a few hours in the recording studio and arranged for Danny and the backing group to be there. Danny was disappointed when Valentina didn't appear. He had invited her again to sit in on the recording, but she had refused. He guessed it was because of the risk of being accused of favouritism.

Some of the group were early and sat around reading magazines, drinking coffee from the machine and chatting. Danny seemed unruffled by the importance of the occasion and played pool with the bass player, hiding Valentina's rejection well.

Only Bob looked anxious. Hiring the studio was expensive and it looked as though Paul, the drummer, was going to be late again. "Why," he asked Danny, "is there always one to make the rest of us wait?"

"Knowing he's good can make the man act casual, I suppose," Danny replied. "Artistic temperament doesn't always go with clock-watching."

Paul eventually turned up and looked surprised at being reminded of how late he was. They went in, the engineer sitting with Bob in the glass partitioned room, looking in on the artists about to record. In front of the engineer was a large control panel, which enabled him to produce what Bob wanted in terms of sound.

They had all rehearsed from the original tape Bob had given them, each adding his own ideas of what the song needed. Then had followed hours of rehearsal, first in Bob's flat, then sessions in the rehearsal room, fining it down, getting it tight.

The drummer put on his cans, waiting for the click-clack to come through and set the tempo Bob wanted. The engineer then added the musicians one by one, a method Bob preferred, and finally, the guitar and voice of Danny.

Each track was played time and again, overlaying each component with another only when the musician felt no improvement could be made and Bob declared himself satisfied. On Bob's instructions the engineer added volume here, widened the sound there. A touch of waa-waa at one point made Danny protest but he was finally persuaded to accept it. He trusted Bob and he wanted this to be a success; partly for himself but also to please Valentina.

At the point when everyone was near exhaustion, it finally came good. Everyone had that sudden flow of adrenalin and after running it several times, listening with a critical ear, Bob threw up his arms and declared Danny Fortune singing Bob Lever's "Darkness My Friend" a sure winner.

One morning, Danny arrived at Valentina's office for a pre-publication discussion with the rep from the record company. Valentina's boss was there as promised and Bob Lever came too. They squeezed into the small room, giving the occasion a party mood.

That the sound was commercial was in no doubt and Danny's voice had been made stronger without making it harsh, by the addition of the extra instruments. There was silence when the last note faded and Danny looked anxiously at Ray and Valentina. In unison, they turned to him and shouted, "Yes!"

Phil heard about it from Bob Lever and wrote a note — unsigned — to Ray Everett, advising him that Valentina was using her position to assist her friends. Ray showed Valentina the note with a crooked smile on his face. "You've certainly rattled someone's cage," he said.

Valentina frowned. "It must be a young hopeful who's resentful about not achieving a place on the wall. It can't be anyone who knows me well; few of my friends would know anyway."

Ray smiled sadly. "In this business there aren't many whom you can call a friend. Most are so anxious to make their mark they're hardly aware of tramping across others to do so."

Valentina shook her head. "This was the action of someone young and impatient. Not even Phil would do this."

"What about Tony Switch? Didn't he threaten vengeance?"

Valentina shook her head stubbornly. "I don't know anyone who'd act so childishly. My closest friends are in the business. I'd trust them with my life," she said.

"Fine," Ray said, "but not with your job!"

Phil was still obsessed with finding out where Valentina went on her occasional weekends. He was in luck the Friday following Danny's record being chosen for hotshotting. Phoning to tell the store manager he was ill, he waited patiently for Valentina to arrive home from work. He had made notes on her movements and a definite pattern had emerged. One weekend away then two staying in London, on one of which she met with John Ellis and Peter Philby and on the other lunch with Charlie. If he'd worked it out correctly, today she would set off for that mysterious rendezvous.

He watched her putting her suitcases in the boot of the car — still on loan from Ray. Then, as she moved off, he followed. The Jaguar could have easily left him behind but he trusted the fact that Valentina never opened her up to enjoy the sensation of power and speed of which the car was capable. The Friday exodus made progress slow and he was anxious about losing sight of her or catching up with her at traffic lights or junctions. Keeping her in sight without being seen was more tricky as the roads became less busy, but by staying well back and allowing other cars to overtake from time to time he thought he was getting away with it.

He had to take a chance occasionally, surging forward to fill a space when more than one car threatened to get between them. He was angry when a driver hooted, afraid she might look back and recognize him, but as the miles flowed under the wheels there was no evidence of her being worried by his presence; she didn't slow down or stop to see if he would overtake her.

He had a map open on the passenger seat and when a chance offered he charted their progress. That her destination was not her South Wales home soon became apparent as she left the motorway and meandered along quiet roads. He wondered who she might be visiting but could think of no one. Where the hell was she heading?

The drive was taking longer than he'd anticipated and his petrol was low when she stopped to fill up, but he didn't dare do the same; he might lose her and after driving for more than a hundred miles he couldn't take that risk. To his relief she did stop a little further on and go into a wayside cafe, which was resplendent with Christmas lights. Through the window he saw her pick up a menu and give an order. He used the opportunity to fill his tank from the spare petrol he'd had the foresight to bring.

As she set off again, he was beginning to think she was on a roundabout route to her home after all, but then she cut off south, down a narrow country road, and pulled up in front of a village shop. Idling the engine, he waited. She came out loaded with groceries, which she put on the back seat, then she drove slowly a short distance, turned into a rutted lane and pulled up outside what he thought was a rather tatty old cottage, for which she had a key. A love nest, was his first thought, but enquiries at the pub satisfied him, and he slept in the car, then drove back to London with a satisfied smile on his face.

The occasional lunch with Charlie had become a regular feature of Valentina's routine as winter crept in with its frosty mornings and cleansing winds. They were approaching the stage where further commitment was a strong possibility. She was tempted, mainly because of Charlie's reliability and because he cared for her in a way that made her feel safe. Meeting his parents was no problem: she had known Mary and Joe before she'd met Charlie. Arranging for Charlie to meet her family was something different and an occasion she dreaded.

"I'm not ashamed of them," she said to Gillian when they discussed it. "It's just that Mam and Dad have lived such different lives from the Trapps and I can't think of a thing Charlie would say that they wouldn't argue with, disapprove of, or not understand."

"You're underestimating Charlie," was Gillian's reply.

That weekend Gillian would be away. She was leaving early on Thursday, coming back on Sunday evening. The pregnancy was confirmed and it wouldn't be long before it would be apparent, so she was going to tell her parents.

"I wish you were coming with me, Valentina. This is the worst. Telling others won't be so bad, I can cope with all that. But telling Mum and Dad, I'll shrink down to a naughty five-year-old again. I'll be that small girl who's broken the rules of behaviour, standing in front of them hoping they won't stop my pocket money!"

"I'd come if I thought you needed me — I could leave straight after work on Friday — but you don't. You and your mother talk like sisters. I don't think she'll berate you for being a fool, she'll just talk it through and remind you of how much she loves you."

"Not telling her who the father is will make it worse, but I don't want anyone to know."

"It's a pity you told Tony."

"Oh, he's probably forgotten by now," Gillian sighed. "What a fool I was."

"You aren't alone in that."

Having the flat to herself for three days was both pleasant and disconcerting. If she invited Charlie for the evening, they would probably spend the night together. She wanted it and knew he felt the same; it was mainly lack of opportunity being the reason they hadn't done so before, that and a certain reticence on her part to making a commitment. She could easily be repeating Gillian's words in the near future, saying, "What a fool I've been."

On the Sundays when they joined John and Peter at The Bull, he had become a part of the group of friends with an ease that had delighted her. She had doubts about him as a lover and perhaps one day a husband, waiting for that special spark, but told herself it was the rarity of their meetings and the slow development of their feelings for each other that gave the relationship its charm.

It was unusual for them to meet in the week because of the restaurant, but he occasionally managed an evening at the theatre or the cinema. If he couldn't get away for the whole evening he sometimes arranged to meet her for a drink. On that Thursday, after Gillian had left, he rang the office and asked her if she was free that evening.

"Don't tell me your parents have nothing better to do than keep an eye on your restaurant," she teased. "Theatre, is it?"

"No," he said, rather abruptly. "There's something I have to discuss with you and I don't think it will wait until a week on Sunday." To her surprise, he sounded angry.

"Come to the flat for a meal," she said.

"I'll be there at seven," he said curtly before putting the phone down.

What on earth could have got into him? He was never sharp with her. Remembering how irritated she sometimes felt after a day filled with frustrations, she

123

made the excuse of problems in the restaurant and began to think about what she would cook.

There wouldn't be much time so she decided on pasta. That was quick and with a few things thrown into a sauce, plus some salad and French bread, it should be all right, specially if she opened a bottle of Charlie's favourite wine.

That he was still in a bad mood was obvious the moment he walked through the door.

"Charlie. Come in. Dinner will be about ten minutes."

"Don't bother. I don't think I'll be staying."

She stared at him in disbelief. "What is it? What's happened?"

"I don't know what happened. I thought we were building a trusting, loving friendship. I'd hoped it would grow into something stronger. I really believed we were getting close. I thought you could wait for sex until we were both sure, but I was wrong, wasn't I? You've been amusing yourself with me, perhaps laughing at me. Slow, boring old Charlie, someone to spend a little time with to fill the odd empty hour. Why, Valentina? Why did you do this to me?"

"Do what? What have I done?" She flopped back into a chair and stared at him, hardly recognizing his face, it was so distorted with anger.

"Where do you go on the Sundays we don't meet? Why could you only spare me one out of three? I thought you'd been going home but you haven't been near your parents for weeks, have you?"

She lowered her head. Her secret would have to be told; she couldn't have him think so badly of her. "I've bought a cottage. I know I should have told you, but first of all it was for me and I didn't want anyone else to know and once I'd kept the secret I found it harder to tell anyone. Not even Gillian knows."

"Oh, and I should be pleased that you didn't tell Gillian either? This is me, Charlie. We've been seeing each other as often as we can manage for months. If you'd been free we'd have spent every Sunday together."

"I should have told you. I'm sorry, but at the time I needed a bolt-hole. Being watched by Phil, a responsible job, Gillian and I not speaking, it was easy not to tell her, and —"

"Stop this pretence! You're wasting your time with these inventions! I can see by your face that you're making it up as you speak! Forget your lies, I know the truth. You're living with someone in some village in Wales, using a run-down thatched cottage that should be condemned."

"Run down?"

"And using me to prevent you becoming bored between the times when you can meet."

"Run down? Charlie, you haven't listened to a word I've said."

"I'd hoped you'd at least honour me with the truth once you knew I'd found out."

"That is the truth. It's simply that —" She stared at him and suddenly she no longer wanted to explain, to make him understand. If he could think her capable of such a thing he wasn't worth the effort. "You'd made up your mind not to believe me before you came, hadn't you? Now please go."

"Gladly!"

There was such disgust in his voice and so much outrage on his usually calm, gently smiling face, she couldn't bear to look at him anymore. If he really thought her capable of using him, deceiving him in that way, she didn't want to see him ever again.

After the flat door closed and she heard the sound of his footsteps running down the stairs, she wished she'd asked how he'd found out about Pink Cottage. Apart from Ray, who had lost his £10 bet, and John and Peter, no one had been told. She rang and spoke to Peter, who assured her they had spoken to no one. Yet someone had found out. The letter to her boss, and now this.

She shivered. It had to be someone who was watching her every move. Phil. It had to be Phil. She looked across to where the window of his flat glinted in the last of the day's light. He could have written to Ray, exaggerating her slight involvement with Danny, but the cottage? How could he know about that? And who would describe her lovely cottage as a run-down ruin that should be condemned, she wondered with a mixture of anger and disappointment.

Gillian returned from her weekend to find the flat had been thoroughly cleaned and the fridge re-stocked. Covers had been washed and replaced, old cushions and tatty lampshades thrown away and new ones bought. Windows shone so they were invisible, the sky a clear blue beyond them.

"Good heavens, Valentina! What got into you? You've made it into a palace!"

"Yes, and I wish I were Rapunzel, locked in my lonely tower and with my hair cut so there was no escape!" She looked at Gillian's smiling face and said at once, "Forget my weekend. How was yours? You told your mother?"

"You were right. She's already knitting tiny bootees."

The baby was due in April and they discussed the need for a child-minder and the possibilities of surviving in their small flat with a baby. At first, Gillian insisted she would find somewhere else but Valentina convinced her it wasn't necessary. "Whatever we decide, we're together in this." Valentina saw the reddening of her friend's cheeks as she thanked her. "Now, Gillian, don't get all sentimental on me. It's selfish really. I don't want to lose you and I rather relish the idea of being an auntie. We have lots of those in Wales. All the neighbours and friends are aunties to the children."

"Thanks," Gillian whispered, tears falling. "You don't know what it means to have your support, especially when I was so stupid about —"

"Old 'Thing'? Forget him. We'll be better off staying together. There isn't a spare room here and I don't think we can put a baby in the cupboard Moke tried to sleep in, but your room is big enough to accommodate a small child, for a while at least."

"Not if you believe my mother." Gillian sighed. "She has visions of going out and buying everything from cot and pram to dishes and dolls, right down to her first bike."

"We won't have room for everything but I'm sure we'll fit in the essentials. Don't worry, leave it to Auntie Valentina. It'll work out."

It was as they were getting ready for bed that Gillian asked about Valentina's three days alone. "Or were you alone?" she asked, tilting her head questioningly.

"Oh, Charlie did call but he didn't stay long." This was the moment to tell her about Pink Cottage; there would never be a better time. "Gillian, I haven't been completely open with you. No, he didn't stay the night and now he never will. He found out that my trips to Wales have been to visit a cottage I've bought." She looked at her friend, expecting to see a frown of disapproval. "I didn't tell anyone. I know it sounds stupid but I wanted it for myself, at least for a while. It's such an exciting thing, to own a house."

"I can understand that. Where is it? Tell me about it. You lucky thing."

"Charlie was told about it. He called it a ruin that ought to be condemned. He was also told that I go there to meet my lover. Can you believe he thinks me capable of such deceit?"

She told Gillian what had been said and her worries about how he found out when no one was supposed to know. "Anyway, he believes what he was told and wouldn't even listen to my explanation."

"Ditch him!"

"Consider him ditched!"

128

Now Gillian had told her parents about the baby, she prepared herself for telling Bob. No longer together — in fact already part of the way along the unpleasant route to divorce — she nevertheless dreaded telling him.

"You were right about my not needing you when I told my parents," she said a few evenings later. "But telling Bob is different. Will you be there?"

"Of course. As Little Lever's deputy auntie I have a great interest in everything about him." Then she stared at her. "Gillian? Come on! You don't believe Bob will hit you, do you?"

"No, I really believe that was a one-off and I should have understood. But he's sure to be angry and I don't want to upset Little Lever."

Little Lever became their name for the baby.

They met several friends, including Bob, at The Bull the following Sunday. Gillian didn't wait until the last minute; as soon as they had ordered their meals she asked Bob to go outside with her and there, beside the cold river, she came straight out with it.

Bob looked shocked. His lips were stiff as he said, "I didn't know you had someone serious, Gilly. I'm — I'm pleased for you." His next question was forestalled.

"Don't ask me who the father is. I won't tell you and no we aren't serious and no we won't be getting married. It was a mistake." She looked at him, her cheeks pink, her eyes bright with unshed tears. "There, now you have it. What have you to say to me now, Bob?"

White faced, he stared at her then said gruffly, "I've lost my appetite but I'll stay and watch you digest lunch while I digest your bombshell."

"I thought you'd go screaming mad," she said, watching his face, like her own, filled with pain.

"I haven't exactly been living like a monk. I was more careful or perhaps luckier than you, that's all. Come on, love, the others will be looking for us."

She sat across the table from him, between John and Valentina. Every time she glanced at Bob he was watching her, but he looked serious rather than angry. He smiled once or twice and even winked on one occasion. She had expected anger but all she could see was sympathy and understanding.

"Tell me who it is then we'll talk it through," Bob said as they left to go to their respective vehicles.

"Sorry, Bob, but I don't want anyone to know. Not even you. These things have a nasty habit of seeping out and I want Little Lever to be mine and no one else's."

"Little Lever?" he queried.

"That's what Valentina has nicknamed him."

"What will his real name be, Gilly?"

"Little Lever will do for now."

He walked her to the car then walked back to the pub garden and punched the wall with an explosion of fury. Guitar playing would be difficult for a week or so, but it was worth it.

130

CHAPTER
SEVEN

Since the quarrel with Charlie, Valentina had refused to go to the cafe for lunch. She and Gillian had been using a small takeaway on the corner of the lane, which had a counter and a few stools for those with time to sit.

"Such a pity. Charlie's is so convenient." Gillian sighed. "And I've got a bit of a thing about cheese and onion rolls dripping with coleslaw. No one makes them like Mary."

"I'd rather eat stale bread and green margarine than have to look at him again."

They called at the takeaway one day and found the place closed. With an even deeper sigh, they settled for another, further away. They ate there for a week but on Friday, as they were leaving the office at lunchtime, they were hailed by Joe Trapp, who called his wife, both of them leaving their cafe to catch them up.

"Valentina! Gillian! Where have you been? We thought you must be on holiday," Mary said reproachfully.

"You haven't stayed away from us because we have a stupid son, have you? Please come and eat at Charlie's, we miss you," Joe added.

"It isn't because of the baby, is it?" Mary asked. "You don't have to worry. If you want kippers with marmalade and coleslaw, you can have it."

Valentina raised a quizzical eyebrow at Gillian and in accord they followed the couple back to the cafe. "Why not?" Valentina said with a smile. "Because Charlie behaved stupidly, it needn't deprive us of a good lunch."

"Today it's on us," Joe said.

"Bob was in earlier, with someone called Claire," Mary told them as she handed them their food. "Quiet girl. Sad, but very beautiful," she added with a glance at Gillian to see her reaction. She saw Gillian's skin begin to colour. "Sorry, perhaps I shouldn't have mentioned him." She leaned closer to Valentina and added, "They're here often but never at this time of day."

"D'you think there's anything between them?" Gillian asked when they were back in the office. "She is beautiful and very talented. I couldn't compete now, looking like this and about to blow up like Michelin Man."

"Pregnancy gives you a glow and your shape won't be like that for more than a few months. From his reaction, I think Bob still cares."

"He's disgusted with me," Gillian said, as she sorted out the sales sheet for the week.

"He hasn't said so, you haven't seen him, so what makes you say that?"

"Because he would have been in touch if he wasn't disgusted. I've pushed him into someone else's arms. How could I have got myself in this mess?"

"You aren't the first."

"How trite!"

"Sorry, but I can't think of anything I haven't already said, except go and see him again. You can't sort it unless you talk."

"I don't want an argument. Not in front of Little Lever," Gillian added with a grin.

"Will that be his name? Does Bob know? Gillian, you have to talk to him."

Bob Lever was having a run of success. Claire's new record was high in the charts and Mobile Nubile, for whom he had also written, were rising too. With Danny's "Darkness My Friend" being hyped and predicted to reach the top ten, he was much in demand. But he was far from happy.

Keeping himself busy all day and for much of the night didn't guarantee him a good night's sleep. As soon as he switched off the light and allowed his body to sink into the mattress, his thoughts flew inevitably to Gill. What a fool he'd been to hit out that day. Never before or since had he felt that impulse. Why hadn't she believed him when he promised it would never happen again?

He wondered about the baby, tormenting himself with thoughts of her with another man. Which man? Was it someone he knew? Someone he met on occasions and perhaps shared a joke with? A cavalcade of possibilities passed across his mind's eye as he tried to guess which of their acquaintances had been her lover. Even when he was doing something that took most of his concentration, the wondering went on. Her lover was a shadowy figure, sometimes young, sometimes old, haggard or ridiculously adolescent. He woke several times each night with a frown on his face, trying even in his unconscious to see the features, recognize the man and solve the unsolvable. Pain twisted him and drove sleep far away, time after time.

On Saturday he was free until the afternoon, when he'd arranged to meet Danny to go over some songs for a proposed LP they were planning. He was wide awake at 6a.m. and decided to go to the flat and talk to Gillian, make her tell him who the child's father was. Once he had a picture of him he might get some rest. He soaked in a bath, seeing in the steam the faces of their mutual friends, accusing then dismissing them in a parade of unanswered questions. Frustration urging him on, he was knocking on the door of the flat before seven, demanding to be let in.

Valentina was up, still in her dressing gown, making tea for them both. She opened the door and with hardly any reaction at the early call, asked, "Tea or coffee, Bob?"

"Where's Gilly?"

"Wait there," she said firmly, seeing the anger in his eyes. "I'll go and see if she's awake."

He stood exactly where he was and waited, his tapping foot the only evidence of his agitation.

Valentina came back and said, "She's getting dressed. Now, tea or coffee? Or aren't you planning to stay that long?"

"What d'you mean?"

"You look as if you've come for a shouting match and a stormy exit."

He walked to a chair and sank into it like an old man and she at once felt sorry for him.

"It's all right, Bob, I'm not accusing you of wanting a fight. I know this must be difficult."

"Who is he?" he asked in a low voice, as though talking only to himself. "Who is this lover of hers? I have to know, it's driving me mad."

"I'll leave that for you and Gillian to discuss. I'll go out for an hour to give you privacy to talk."

"No need for that," Gillian said, coming into the room wearing a smart two-piece with a full skirt and bunched-up top.

"God 'elp," Valentina whispered. "You look ready to pop instead of only a few months gone!"

"Who is he, this boyfriend of yours?" Bob demanded.

"I don't have a boyfriend. This —" She patted her belly "— this was a terrible mistake."

Valentina put coffee beside them both and went into her room, closing the door firmly. She stood behind it, listening anxiously for raised voices but the low murmur that reached her was reassuring. However he was going to cope with it, Bob was showing no sign of violence. Distress was his strongest emotion, she guessed, and she wondered if, even with this added difficulty, there was still a chance of them getting back together. That they still loved each other was in no doubt, but was it powerful enough for Bob to cope with bringing up another man's child?

She realized there was no sound coming from the living room and the low conversation had died. After a minute or two she opened the door and looked in. Gillian was alone; Bob had gone.

In Charlie's restaurant, Carl Stevens was having lunch with Tony Switch. They were waiting to give their order when Phil walked in with Bob Lever. The latter two had arrived separately but at once Bob saw Carl and Tony and went to greet them. Phil, aware of the animosity between himself and Carl — whose job he had tried to steal — turned away and sat at a table on his own. Carl called him over.

"Might as well sit with us, Phil, I won't slap you," he said. "Although it's a pity someone doesn't," he added in a low voice.

Somewhat uneasily, with Carl and Phil eyeing each other antagonistically, the four men settled to peruse and discuss the menu. Tony did most of the talking at first, telling them about his new life as a disc jockey and about the girls who threw themselves at him. "Everyone wants me now I'm a household name," he boasted. "Specially pluggers, eh, Carl?"

Phil gradually opened up, amusing them with stories about his customers, imitating the voices of some, jeering at the hopes of others, who were desperately wanting a career in show business. Buying records, taking them home to sing or play along with, convinced they only needed that little bit of luck and everything in their lives would be perfect.

136

"For most, the nearest they'll get to a career in music is talking to people like me." He laughed. "There they are, wasting the here and now, dreaming of that distant day when everything will be wonderful. They wouldn't know how to handle success anyway. They're a lot of nobodies who think one day they'll be somebody, passing their time in dreams. It would be funny if it weren't so sad. They gather anecdotes and cherish them, perhaps telling them to others as though they are the heroes of encounters with the famous." He fell silent, knowing he was talking about himself. The others too were quiet, remembering their own dreams.

As they finished their meal, Phil sang a snatch of a song:

> "Pity the lonely dreamers,
> Empty hands that want to hold the world."

Aware of the others listening, he went on,

> "Pity the lonely dreamers, who believe,
> One day they'll have it all, so they believe,
> All will turn to gold
> From shabby, dismal grey
> Shabby, dismal grey.
>
> Pity the lonely dreamers, who believe,
> That special day is coming, they believe
> Lady Luck will hand,
> To them her jewelled crown,
> Them her jewelled crown

Pity the lonely dreamers,
Empty hands, oh empty, empty hands,
Empty hands that want to hold the world."

Phil looked up, saw Bob watching him and immediately stopped singing. Embarrassed then, at his lapse into sentimentality, he said, "Poor silly sods, the lot of them."

"Is there any more?" Bob asked.

"To the song, you mean? Well, there's a bit more about how life is frittered away, while they wait for the special day. You know, Bob. The usual rubbish."

"Bloody awful tune," Bob said.

"Yeah," Tony said. "Don't ask me to give that one air time!"

Charlie came with their coffee then and with a few pleasantries, including asking about Valentina and Gillian, returned to his post at the kitchen door.

"How is your wife, Bob?" Tony asked casually.

"Pregnant," Bob replied.

"Oh, um, congratulations? Or commiserations?" Tony asked, quirking an eyebrow.

"So you're together again?" Phil asked in surprise. "I thought I'd seen you going into the flat a few times."

"No, it's nothing to do with me."

"Me neither." Carl laughed. "I'm too old for lovely young girls like Gillian and, besides, my wife would kill me!"

The others repeated their denials.

"She's serious with someone then?" Phil asked.

"Mind your own business, Phil! And stop using your flat as a lookout tower or I'll close both your eyes for you!" Bob stood and waved at Charlie for the bill.

"Temper, boy, temper," Phil murmured. "That was how you lost her in the first place, wasn't it?"

"Shut up!"

Sensing trouble, Charlie came across and offered them a second coffee.

When they eventually parted, with ruffled feathers back in place, Bob found himself repeating the words of Phil's song. He couldn't put it aside; the words sang in his head and a variety of different treatments until he got hold of something that had him running up the stairs to his flat and into his studio with a look on his face that Gillian would have recognized and described as "full tilt into a new song".

He used the eight-track in his soundproofed room. It was enough for him to play around with until he had something approaching a completed song. At four in the morning, he was sitting and wondering to which of the people he wrote for he should offer it. He slept for a few hours and woke up thinking of Danny Fortune. It was different from Danny's usual choices but he might give it a try. He woke Danny out of a deep sleep at 7a.m. to play him the tape and ask him if he liked it.

"No, Bob! No way!" Phil's reaction to Bob's suggestion that Danny should sing his song was anger and hurt. Danny, of all people, someone Valentina supported. Without the thought being more than a split-second old, he said, "I want to sing it. Me! Right?"

139

Surprised and more than a little disappointed, Bob's first reaction was to pick up the song, tear it into pieces and leave but, what the heck, he didn't have much to lose by listening to him. He reached for one of the guitars Phil had on a stand in the corner and began to tune the strings.

He sang the song through twice himself, then nodded towards Phil. Disappointment began to fade and he asked him to sing it again. Phil's voice started weak but confidence grew and he produced a powerful baritone that filled the room. Bob tried a few different chords and said, "One more time, Phil."

"I can't. I'll be late for work."

"Sorry," Bob said, looking at his watch. "I'm inclined to forget time when I'm working on a new piece, you ask Gilly — ask anybody."

"I could meet you this evening?"

"Not tonight. I'll see you a week from tonight in my flat. I'll call a couple of mates and we'll see. I can't say more than that, mind," he warned.

Charlie called at the girls' flat one evening and he remained silent while Valentina fussed with coffee, each waiting for the other to speak. He was hurt by her secrecy over the cottage, which he now believed had explained her absences and Valentina was still simmering with anger at the ease with which he had believed that she had a secret lover.

He apologized repeatedly after she made coffee and a lemon drink for Gillian but she brushed them aside. "I

140

would never have believed a similar story about you, Charlie," she said. "Who told you this anyway?"

"I — I just heard it somewhere," he said evasively.

"Phil. It must have been Phil. But how did he find out about my cottage?"

"I don't want to discuss how I heard. It was wrong and I was an idiot."

"It *was* Phil!" Watching his face, she knew her guess was correct. It was so like Phil to behave in such a spiteful way.

Slowly the threads of their anger began to break down. Once they began to talk, they quickly made up their quarrel, Charlie insisting that it was the newness of their relationship, the lack of commitment, that had caused the lack of trust. But Valentina wondered if they would ever return to their once relaxed and easy closeness.

She didn't blame him for half believing the story but if he respected her he would have withheld judgement until he had heard her explanation. She didn't want to commit herself to a man who needed reassurance on her loyalty, or who would accuse her on the word of someone like Phil.

Christmas passed with Gillian going home and Valentina spending a few days at Pink Cottage. When it was over, she and Charlie returned to their occasional Sunday lunches, but never at some out-of-the-way place on the Thames as so often in the past, but always at The Bull, with John and Peter.

"Safety in numbers?" Gillian queried. "That's hardly necessary with Charlie."

"Not exactly. More a cooling-off period. This way he isn't my date, he's just one of our friends."

"I might not come this Sunday," Gillian said one day.

"Going home?"

"No, I'm just avoiding going to The Bull."

"Why?"

"I just don't like being there on my own. I hate not being one of a couple.

"Neither of us has let that bother us before."

"I wasn't pregnant before."

Phil was nervous when he went to Bob's flat. The appointment had been delayed several times; Bob was busy and Christmas intervened. He had never given up hope of making a record. Although he had auditioned for several bands, he had either been turned down or had been unhappy about the kind of music they played.

He should have come to London and forgotten Valentina. She had made him lose his way. Instead of searching for a compatible band, he'd been forced to search for a job. He'd forced his way, lying and cheating, into that job as a plugger and he'd lacked the necessary skill to keep it and it was Valentina's fault. All of it.

He was a performer and the reason he hadn't made it until now was her. She had ruined everything for him then left him. Bob liking his words and maybe letting him sing them was unexpected and definitely a final chance to make a record.

One of the groups applying to audition for hotshotting that week was Square Clock. Valentina turned them down without seeing them. A few days later, she and Gillian were at a reception where a recording company was introducing new recordings and, as part of the entertainment, Square Clock were playing.

"I think I'll slip out," Valentina whispered when they were told. "I don't think I can face my brother at this moment."

Tony Switch was there and he came over, smiling as if he and Gillian were brief acquaintances. "Valentina, Gillian. Great to see you. I hear congratulations are in order, Gilly."

"Gillian. I prefer Gillian." Only Bob calls me Gilly, she thought with sadness. "And yes, I'm expecting a baby." Then she added loudly, "I'm on my own with this. The father wasn't man enough to cope with a child."

She glared at him, wanting to shout and let everyone know that the news was hardly a surprise to Tony. He had been the first to be told and he'd made it clear that he would never accept it, warning her not to accuse him unless she wanted to be laughed at. No one had seen them together, he'd made sure of that. At the time she'd believed it had been to protect her from the media. How stupid she had been.

Valentina took her friend's arm and led her away. There was a dais on which members of the group were gathered. Too late to disappear. She couldn't leave Gillian on her own now; her face was blotchy and her eyes over-bright. She guided her to a seat at the back of the room to listen to Square Clock. To her surprise, Moke wasn't playing.

Mildly curious, thinking he had been unavailable for this one night, she asked someone sitting near her and was told that Moke had been sacked. "Apparently", her informant said, "he wasn't that reliable. He wouldn't attend rehearsals, said he didn't need them and often, being out most nights and wandering the streets during the day, he was incapable of playing when he did show up. When he twice failed to show for an actual performance, he was given the big heave-ho."

Valentina decided to ask Phil how her brother was managing. Refusing to use her position to help was one thing; seeing him without any money, perhaps without a place to sleep, was something else. Phil couldn't help.

"Why don't you ring your parents?" Gillian suggested. "He might have gone home."

"D'you really think my brother has that much sense?"

"Well, no, I suppose not."

The following evening, Valentina went to his last known address only to be told that Moke had left owing rent and no one knew where he'd gone. Not wanting to worry her parents, she rang their neighbour and asked if they would phone her back with Moke's address, saying she'd lost it.

A few minutes later a breathless Gwennie Francis rang. "Your mam is very worried. She thought Michael was with you and Gillian. She wants you to tell him there's money here for him and would he please to get in touch."

"Money is the sure way of persuading him to contact Mam," Valentina said to Gillian. "Her door and her

144

pocket are always open to him. He won't need telling, he'll smell it!"

But she was wrong. Days passed without a word. She tried Phil again and contacted members of Square Clock but no one knew where to find him.

"He could be in trouble," Gillian mused, "but it's more likely he simply doesn't want to be found by his doting mother. Remember how she took over in that house he shared? What an embarrassment that would be, having Mummy come to make sure he ate up all his greens! I bet he'd even miss a payout to avoid something like that happening."

Valentina wasn't so sure.

CHAPTER
EIGHT

Phil saw the young woman enter the shop where he worked on the music counter and stopped what he was doing to stare. Glamorously tall and slim, beautifully dressed, she had the legs mini skirts were made for, he mused. She hesitated then came across to his counter. He pushed aside the young girl who went forward to serve and smiled his best smile.

"Phil Blackwood at your service. How can I help you?"

She offered an elegant hand. "Penelope Masters. I've just arrived here from the States and feel lonely for the sounds of home. Do you have any records by KC and the Sunshine Band?"

"I can get them by tomorrow and any others you want." His mind went frantically into overdrive as he tried to think of ways to persuade her to stay longer than it took to fill out the order. She explained that she was to take up a new position with the BBC and at once they had something in common. Phil offered to lend her some of his record collection. "Including," he added with an air of self-conscious pride, "a few tapes of my own. And I'm making a record. My lyrics and the music is by a top songwriter. It's predicted to go right to the top."

"You make records? Wow!"

"I had a band but gave it up to concentrate on my own songs," he said. "I've always been interested in music and I have a huge collection including some of the best American sounds. Come to the flat and have a look. Come this evening if you like and help yourself to any you want."

"I couldn't do that," she said with a wry grin. "You're going a mite too fast for me."

"Tell you what, meet me tonight and I'll introduce you to some of the sights and sounds of London instead." She still looked doubtful as she thanked him and prepared to leave. "Come on, Penelope, you'll be safe with me. Don't you Americans boast about your friendliness? Well, let me tell you that we Welsh are the same."

"Welsh, are you? My folks came from a place called Maesteg."

"There you are then, we're practically related." He went on talking about Wales and about the music scene, trying to persuade her. "So, we'll take a look around London, is it?"

She smiled that special American smile and his heart began to pound. "All right, Phil Blackwood. Tomorrow, but only if my friend can come too."

"That's fine by me. I'm going to rehearse my new recording tomorrow afternoon but I'll be through by seven."

★　★　★

147

The week that followed was one Phil would never forget. It was March and if the weather was bleak he was completely unaware of it. The friend was soon dropped and he and Penelope walked the streets of London together. They saw several plays and shows for which he willingly paid top prices. They went to the best restaurants for late-night suppers before taking a taxi back to her hotel and sharing increasingly passionate kisses when they parted.

His overdraft was alarming but he optimistically told the bank manager he was expecting huge sums once his record was released. For the first time he realized what money could bring and he loved it. He forgot Valentina and her mysterious visits to the cottage. Penelope was so much more his style.

Then, one terrible day, Penelope told him that she wouldn't be seeing him any more as her job was about to begin and she wouldn't have time for much else.

"I'm starting as a research assistant for Radio Three," she told him.

"Radio Three? I thought your music tastes were more in line with mine, popular rather than the classics?"

"I like both, but my training is with the classics and it's there I want to develop my career."

"Meet me after your first day. I want to know how you get on. Don't lose touch, Penelope."

He met her after the first day and saw at once things had changed. She walked out of the building with a group of people dressed in trendy clothes; she was carrying piles of books and sheet music. Standing there in his usual clothes of denim and leather, he felt self-consciousness flood over him like a wild wave. She waved an arm in casual salute but didn't approach him. He watched with growing pain as she stepped into a car and was driven away.

Even from a distance her eyes looked glazed as she looked past him and beyond. He had been a fill-in who was no longer needed. Going to a phone box, he dialled Valentina's number and with his lips pinched together he left an aggressive message about her lack of loyalty and the way she used people.

He tried over the following weeks to speak to Penelope, phoning her hotel and her office, but there was no response. She was no longer interested and it hurt. He had to make a success of this record. He'd be somebody then. That would change her mind — and a few others would take more notice of him then too.

Winter was releasing its grip and Phil returned to watching the girls' flat for hours. It was now an obsession, needing to know where Valentina was at any given time. Tonight, though, he had missed her leaving with Gillian, off to spend the weekend with Gillian's parents.

Valentina had driven them in the Jaguar, with Gillian's new suitcase in the back filled with everything she might need for a hospital visit. It was a joke, packing for herself and Little Lever, but even though the baby wasn't due until April, she had been advised against travelling too far from home unprepared.

They reached her parents' home without incident, laughing at the way they had outwitted Phil, imagining him looking out from his window and wondering where they were. "Or," Valentina said grimly, "wasting his time driving to Pink Cottage presuming we're there."

There was a meal waiting for them, her room welcoming with flowers and chocolates, and Valentina reflected sadly on the difference in welcome between Gillian's family and her own. The baby would be welcomed too and cocooned in love and tenderness. For a moment, tears touched her eyes, but whether for the joy of the soon-to-arrive baby or self-pity for herself, she didn't dare consider.

It was made clear during the evening that Gillian was restless and at bedtime she was unable to sleep. At 4 a.m., Valentina was woken by her moans and within moments the household was awake.

"I said you should have come home before this," her father grumbled, walking up and down, searching for something with which to excuse his agitation. His wife smiled and asked him to start the car. Glad to be given orders and something positive to do, he ran to the garage and drove the car out onto the drive.

Outwardly calm but filled with apprehension, Valentina collected what Gillian would need and went with her to where her father was gunning the engine and waking half the neighbourhood. She watched them drive away and, filled with excitement, picked up the paper on which Gillian had written the number of the hospital, wondering how long she should wait before phoning.

150

On her third enquiry, she was patiently told things were going well and to ring again in an hour. She sat in the quiet house and stared at the phone. At eight she rang again, trying to guess more from the voice on the phone than from the actual words, excitement giving way to fear that something was wrong.

Little Lever was born at midday on Saturday and immediately named Dylan Robert. Gillian had deliberately added Bob's name, a part of her still hoping, as she stared down at her small son, that they might still be a family one day.

On a visit home the next weekend, where he hoped to have his ego soothed, Phil drove by way of Valentina's cottage. He guessed she would be there and saw from the parked car that he was right. He prepared a smile and knocked on the door.

"Oh, it's you." Disappointment showed on her face.

"Hello, and pleased to see you too," he replied, pushing past her into the small living room.

"It *was* you who told Charlie, wasn't it? Relishing the trouble you were causing me. How did you find out?"

"Easy. Everyone knew. You can't keep secrets like this for long."

"How?" she insisted.

"Gillian, I think. Come on, aren't you going to offer me coffee or something?"

"Gillian didn't know."

"Says you!" he said, but his determination to bluff it out faded when he saw the anger glittering in her eyes.

"All right, I followed you. In my clapped-out car, I followed you in your fancy machine with ease."

Valentina was relieved. She hadn't wanted to think it had been Peter or John who had spread the news after giving their word. "Why?" she asked then. "What made you go to so much trouble just to split up Charlie and me? Well, it didn't work and I'm grateful to you for testing our friendship."

"Haven't seen as much of him since though." He glanced at her quizzically.

"Will you please go, Phil. I want to do a bit of decorating and time is precious."

"Give a hand if you like?"

"Goodbye."

"At least a bite to eat before I go. What about the local pub? I had quite a decent meal there last time I came."

"Please, go. I only want people here who have been invited and so far that's only Gillian."

"So it isn't for you and Charlie to get away from Mary and Joe?"

This time she didn't answer at all, just opened the door and held it until he walked out without another word. She closed the door firmly and leaned against it with a worried frown on her face. Phil knew when she would be here. From his sky-line view opposite her flat, he could watch her movements. Next time, she decided, she would make sure to pack the car when he was out of his flat. And she'd alter her routine, perhaps come again next week and this time invite Gillian and Little Lever.

The following week, Gillian returned to the flat with all the paraphernalia needed to support herself and the baby. And a week later, making sure she was seen, she got into a taxi with all her cases and headed for the underground station. What Phil didn't see was her being picked up a few minutes later by Valentina as she set off for Pink Cottage.

In the several times she had stayed at the cottage, Valentina had hardly spoken to her neighbours. She smiled at people and made herself known to the shopkeepers, but she hadn't connected houses with the people in them. So on this visit she was surprised to find out that people in the shop, both assistants and customers, seemed to know a lot about her.

"Got a very important job, I hear," was the first surprise, as she had determinedly refused to talk about work. "Music records, isn't it? Pop and all that?"

"How did you know that?" she asked in alarm.

"Your boyfriend told us."

"I don't have a boyfriend." Knowing glances were exchanged. "No boyfriend," she repeated firmly, "and, if it was the man who came last weekend, it's just wishful thinking on his part! Right?"

With great determination, ignoring hints, she managed to keep clear of people who seemed keen to be invited in to see what had been done since the cottage had changed hands. With the baby in his buggy, they took short walks and enjoyed eating in the garden, still overgrown but peaceful. Valentina enjoyed sharing

153

Gillian's excitement as she saw everything for the first time.

"I'll be glad when you're back at work and I'm helping to look after Little Lever." Valentina sighed. "I'll miss you both after this weekend."

"Why don't you get your brother to stay for a while?"

"No thanks! Besides, I don't even know where he is. I don't think Mam does either. The last time I asked she went into a rage, blaming me for whatever he's up to. What is it about me that makes my mother hate me and Phil become so obsessed with hurting me?"

"Jealousy. It'll fade in time."

"And Tony Switch? He threatened revenge on me, although he was the one who was stupid."

"Don't mention him," Gillian said seriously. "You'll upset Little Lever."

Tony was feeling on top of the world. His programme was a success, talked about on the way to work each morning by a growing band of fans. There were personal appearances on television and now the promise of a book telling the life story of Marlene, his "naugh-ty" invisible friend. On top of all that, there was a succession of beautiful women, who were attracted by his fame.

They were all fleeting romances without a thought of anything more. No one moved him and made him want to give up all the rest. Life was good and he was going to enjoy it. One day perhaps he'd meet that special woman, but until then he was having fun. He looked back on the foolishness of his record-making years and sighed. The brief fame had gone to his head in a big way and he'd behaved like an idiot. Thank goodness he'd had the strength to ride the ridicule and not hide from it. To have come so far in a new career was hard to believe. Coffee spilt on his hand and he felt the pain and smiled. No, he wasn't dreaming.

The rehearsals for Phil's new song, "Pity The Lonely Dreamers", were not going as he'd hoped. He knew this was a wonderful chance and almost certainly his last. Fortune didn't smile too often in a lifetime and the opportunity to record his own song, with music written by Bob Lever, was the widest smile he could ever hope for. But Bob was insisting on using another guitarist.

"You aren't good enough, Phil," he'd insisted when he had been forced to listen once again to Phil's clumsy attempts.

"If I record the guitar separately, so I could concentrate, I'd be —"

"You'd be rubbish and you know it!" Bob finished. He stood up and glared at Phil, then snatched the instrument out of his hand and flung it on the couch. "Forget it. I'm wasting no more time." He switched off the power and unplugged the amp and the tape deck.

"All right, have it your way," Phil said. He placed his guitar in its case. "You're right, I need an expert musician."

"Last chance, Phil," Bob snapped. He dialled a couple of numbers and arranged for a meeting at his flat for the following night. "Eight o'clock, Phil. Be here!"

Phil trembled with relief. He'd almost blown it.

Before he settled to sleep that night he suddenly remembered that he hadn't checked on Valentina. The conversation with Bob had made him forget. The car wasn't there. She given him the slip and gone off for the weekend with Gillian. Next day a call to the inn confirmed they were at the cottage. They must be stupid if they thought they could outwit him.

Late on Sunday, the car was still not in its place. He looked at the clock: past eleven. Getting up and adding a dressing gown to his pyjama trousers, he made a hot drink and sat by the window to wait. He dozed and woke stiff and cold at 3a.m. and stared in disbelief at the empty parking place. He knew she had appointments on Monday; Bob Lever had mentioned a sales meeting.

At four, he pulled on trousers and a sweater and went to see if the car was parked somewhere out of sight, but there was no sign of it. He was angry and frustrated; her absence was like another rejection. Picking up a convenient piece of shattered kerbstone, he attempted to heave it towards the window of her flat but the weight was too great and instead he smashed it against the entrance door.

He ran off, away from his own place, to return a few minutes later, strolling back innocently, convinced he had deceived anyone looking out. He glanced with satisfaction at the stone leaning against the door, surrounded by chipped paint and shattered glass, then went back to continue his vigil. She didn't appear.

He was late for work and went straight to a phone to discover Valentina was in her office. They'd tricked him again. Anger flared his nostrils and his customers were treated with irritable speed and without his usual jocular friendliness.

One evening Valentina answered a knock to find the singer Claire standing outside. Puzzled, she invited her in, made coffee and waited between brief attempts at conversation to be told the reason for the visit.

"Do you think we should worry whether our family approves of us or not?" was Claire's surprising opening.

"We do, but whether we should or not is something for psychiatrists to delve into," Valentina replied. "Approval is something we all need, I suppose. I know I'd be happier if my mother was proud of what I've achieved, if she boasted a little to her friends. But perhaps it's weakness in me to expect it."

"My mother has sworn never to speak to me ever again."

"Why?" Valentina asked, then, seeing the closed expression on Claire's face, apologized. "Sorry, I don't want to pry. I mean, you must ask yourself why and decide if her attitude is deserved. If it isn't, you have to accept that it's something she can't cope with. Don't let the guilt of her unreasonable rejection ruin your life, accept it if it's undeserved. That's what I try to do. Am I making sense?"

"I do feel guilty. What I did couldn't be helped, but it hurt my mother dreadfully."

"If it's right for you, then you have to live with it, but guilt is a self-inflicted agony that most of us shouldn't feel."

"You said you and your mother can't be friends?"

"I can't live my life the way she thinks I should. She's proud of my brother, whatever he does, so I don't think she's cold or unfeeling. Somehow I've let her down."

"So you live with the guilt?"

"Let's make a pact. We'll both try to accept ourselves for the way we are and not blame ourselves for the failings of others. Right?"

Claire left after an hour and Valentina lay awake for a long time, wondering about the girl's sad secret and whether she had helped in a small way to alleviate her misery. Perhaps Claire's ability to sing a song to touch people's hearts was partly because of the unhappiness she carried with her.

Over recent weeks, every time she updated the wall, Claire's name was there. Her records were hitting the charts and each stayed for a while in the top ten. But obviously her success was being spoilt by her mother's rejection. As sleep slowly claimed her, Valentina thought of Moke and wondered idly where he was. She should have made an effort to find him. Perhaps if she did her mother would be pleased.

Pleasing her mother, she thought sleepily, was something that had tainted her childhood and was still affecting her now. The need to please and be admired: surely that was something she, like Claire, should have outgrown?

CHAPTER
NINE

Valentina woke the morning after her strange talk with Claire with the need to find her brother still on her mind. When the weekend came she would go to the addresses at which he had lived and hope to pick up some clue to his present whereabouts. All the addresses were multi-occupation and talking to a different person might illicit a different answer.

Before she set off on the Saturday morning, when she hoped to catch many of the tenants still at home, she telephoned her parents' neighbour, Mrs Francis, and asked if she had seen Moke. No, she was told, and her mother was beginning to worry.

Three places resulted in blank looks and disinterested responses. The houses were all in poor areas. The population of the rooms changed frequently and no one knew the names of people who had lived there before them and certainly had no interest in someone who had lived there weeks before. Of Moke, there was no memory at all.

On Sunday she went to The Bull for lunch, wishing she had invited Charlie to join her. John and Peter were there, and she explained her predicament to them. "I have no idea where my brother is and it's impossible to tell my parents."

"You must tell them," John urged. "Nothing ever gets sorted out while it's hidden." John spoke seriously but he was looking at Peter. "You have to expose things to the light and only then can things start to find solutions."

Taking a chance of offending, Valentina asked, "You haven't told your parents about you and John yet, Peter?" It was the first time she had referred to their relationship and, to her alarm, Peter walked away.

"John, I'm sorry. I shouldn't have said that."

"Why not? I've been saying it for months. People who care accept us for what we are; it's only Peter's family who haven't been told. Or guessed," he added with a sad smile.

"Like me, they might not need to be told." She smiled. "They must be aware of the facts and can surely see you are happy." They both watched anxiously as Peter returned.

"We're going down to see them together, tomorrow afternoon, and they'll be told," Peter said. John continued to look doubtful. "Really," Peter assured him. "I've just phoned to tell them we have some good news. It's all fixed."

Valentina left them discussing this new stage in their relationship and sat near the small window looking out at the Thames making its placid way down to the sea. It had seen everything and was surprised at nothing, she mused. In the length of time it had been flowing along

160

more or less the same route, petty worries or fierce wars were brief and of little importance, soon forgotten.

When the two young men re-joined her, they both looked relaxed. It was a while before they talked of other things, but when they did, they planted an idea in Valentina's mind that wouldn't go away. There was a property to rent in the row of assorted shops called Cranbury Parade, only a short distance from the flat. Without explaining further, she asked them to hold it until she could look at it.

Reading her mind, John said, "It's a good area, attracting large numbers of shoppers. Passing trade too, with even some parking, would you believe. There isn't a record shop anywhere near it."

"You, John," Valentina scolded, "are too sharp for your own good!"

"It will be a while before it's actually for rent," Peter told her. "The owner has some legal things to sort out and he plans to do a few repairs first."

"It will give you time to do some thinking," John added.

Driving back, putting aside the dream, she forced her mind back to the problem of Moke. She admitted to herself that she had to do what she should have done first: ask Phil to help. She hated having to ask him. She wanted him out of her life and the tenuous thread of their close roots was something she wanted to sever. But if she were to find Moke, Phil was the one to ask. When she knocked on his door, to her surprise it was opened by Bob Lever. Invited in, she found three other musicians drinking beer and sitting amid the remnants of a meal.

Phil looked up and a smile opened out on his face, his dark eyes glowing with undisguised delight. "Valentina!"

"How is Gilly?" Bob asked at once.

"Well, and enjoying being a mother to Little Le — to baby Dylan Robert," she corrected.

"It's all right, Valentina. I know you nicknamed him Little Lever."

"You haven't seen him?"

"No, I don't think it's anything to do with me anymore."

"By it do you mean Gillian or the baby?"

"Leave it," Bob said sharply, glancing around the room at the wide, interested eyes of the group.

"She'd love to see you — why don't you phone her?" Valentina whispered under the noise of feet shuffling as a place was found for her to sit. She stood at the window for a moment and, glancing down, saw with an uneasy feeling just how clear a view Phil had of their flat.

"Why did you come?" Phil asked. "Are you going to give us an unofficial audition?"

He hadn't stopped staring at her since she arrived. The smile was still fresh on his face and it made her uncomfortable. He mustn't take this visit to be a change of heart.

"I'm asking everyone I can think of if they know where my brother Moke is," she said, looking at all the faces except Phil's. No one had heard anything of him and Valentina prepared to leave. "Thanks, anyway. Sorry to disturb you."

"Aren't you going to hear my song?" Phil asked. Bob glanced at her and shrugged.

"My music, Phil's words," Bob explained. Surprised, Valentina sat again to listen.

She soon wished she hadn't. Phil sang the song to her and there was pleading in the song, wanting her to love him and make his dream come true. She looked down as if concentrating and only looked up when the last chord faded.

"I wish it luck and hope it does well." She struggled to her feet again and said quickly, "Now I really must go." With instruments abandoned on the floor and plates and glasses spread untidily around, she lost her balance and grabbed the windowsill to steady herself. The curtains shifted and revealed a small telescope hidden behind it.

Phil saw her to the door and tried to kiss her. She pushed him away, fear as well as exasperation showing in the strength of it.

"It's all right, you don't have to worry," Phil hissed. "I didn't write it for you. There are plenty of other women to enjoy!"

She pushed her way through the door and took deep breaths of the cold air. Why was he watching her? What did he intend to do? That telescope wasn't there to watch the London sparrows, that was for sure. She hurried back to the flat and pulled the curtains across the windows facing Phil's eyrie. He was as tightly coiled as a spring in her grandmother's bed, she thought with a shiver.

When she was beginning to think Moke wouldn't be found until he wanted to be found, she had news of him. Unfortunately, it came from Phil. He came into the office on a Monday morning and asked to see her.

"What d'you want?" she asked ungraciously. "I have a very full morning."

"I wish I hadn't bothered. I thought you'd like to know where your brother is, that's all." He turned to go.

"Sorry, Phil."

"He's in prison."

"I don't believe it!" She said it in a voice that implied she believed it utterly. "What an idiot. Where is he? What happened?"

"He tried to steal a bus." She stared at him, waiting to be told that he was joking. "No joke. He did it for a dare."

"This is terrible."

"A spell in prison might do him good!" He handed her a piece of paper with an address and phone number. "His social worker. Posh, eh? Having your own social worker?"

Valentina had a second shock that day. She was so frightened by what Phil had told her and what a telephone call to the social worker had confirmed that she ran into her boss's office with hardly a knock. Claire was with him and Valentina was just in time to see them separate from an embrace. A look at their

164

faces told her they had been kissing, the creases and the lack of lipstick on Claire's face revealing the passionate nature of it.

"Oh, I — sorry — I'm so sorry — I'll come back later."

"Get out!" Ray said, his voice guttural with rage. "Get out!"

Valentina swivelled around the door into the outer office, shut it behind her and leaned on it, her eyes wide with shock. Ray was having an affair with Claire. Was this what had separated Claire from her family? An affair with a married man? The door opened and she fell back, knocked by Ray as he prepared to step out.

"You'd better come back in," he said peremptorily. "Close the door."

"Look, this is nothing to do with me," she began shakily. "Can't we forget it happened?"

"Can we trust you to do that?"

"Of course. It isn't my business."

"Thank you," Claire whispered.

"What did you want?" Ray asked, and she couldn't think for a moment. She looked at Ray and shivered. His eyes were cold and anger tightened his mouth. This would come out all wrong, she knew that. "It's about my brother, Moke."

"I know, he played with Square Clock. What about him?"

"He's in prison."

"And that brought you bursting in like that? Hardly urgent. He isn't going anywhere, is he?"

"I wondered if I could have some time off to visit him."

"Arrange it with your assistant."

"Thank you."

"And not a word about what you might have seen."

"I didn't see a thing." By this time she was in tears.

That evening she went to see Danny, who seemed so pleased to see her she felt like crying again. She had left Ray's office believing she hadn't a friend in the world apart from Gillian. "It's Moke," she explained. "He's in prison." She told him as much as she knew.

Danny's arms were around her, soothing her distress. "What did your parents say?"

"I haven't told them."

"Afraid they'll blame you? No doubt about it, they will. Instinctive to twist the facts and find someone to heap the blame on. It's a great pity, me darlin', but it's sure to be you." He held her gently, touching her hair with his lips. "You mustn't believe them, that's the thing."

"But I do," she wailed.

"Typical of you to take responsibility when there's no need. A grown man, he is, and able to make his own decisions. He didn't ask your advice before doing that stupid thing? No, he did not. And would he have listened to you if he had? No, he would not. Isn't he his own man entirely?"

He held her closer and kissed her wet cheek; brushing her hair back with his chin he kissed her again, closer and closer to her lips. It would have been so easy to succumb to the comfort he offered, but she

166

turned her head and lightly kissed his cheek and moved away.

Danny looked at her and sighed sadly. "Wasn't that grand? Will we do it again?"

She smiled at him, shaking away her misery. "Let's go and eat, shall we? I'm starving."

Taking up her jocular attitude, he said, "All right, if it's the best you can offer. If you're turning down a night of unbridled passion, we'll eat."

They went to Charlie's and Charlie joined them when they were at the coffee stage, pausing first, in his polite way, for their permission.

"Have you had any luck in your search for your brother?" Charlie had been the first to whom she had mentioned her concerns about Moke.

"I don't know about luck," she said sadly. "He's in prison." A smile began to light up her eyes. "He was — trying to steal a bus!" The stupidity of it struck them all and they laughed until they were helpless. Even the serious-minded Charlie succumbed.

"Can I do anything?" Charlie asked eventually

"There isn't anything anyone can do," Danny said. "I've been trying to convince Valentina of that. Moke has to pull up his own socks."

"I'm going to see him as soon as I can, offer to put him up for a few days while I try to persuade him to get a job and a proper place to live."

"Doesn't she make it all sound simple," Danny teased. "Will all this be achieved in the first hour or will it take two?"

"He'll have to sort himself out before Gillian and the baby come back. There won't be an inch of room to spare then."

"Would he consider a job in the kitchens?" Charlie asked. "He'd have to stay clean and tidy, and respectful of the others. I am very particular about my staff, you know that."

"Thank you, Charlie," Valentina said, although she had no intention of risking the embarrassment of her brother being sacked from the kitchen of Charlie's restaurant.

Visiting Moke was an experience she didn't want to repeat. The bare room and the melancholy atmosphere depressed her spirits even before Moke appeared. He was prickling with defiance and apart from asking her not to let their parents know where he was, said very little. "I'll be out of here in a week and they need never know," he said, and she agreed.

"I'll let you stay at the flat, but only for a night or two. Gillian and the baby are coming back soon and if you're sensible and find work I'll do what I can to get you started with a small place of your own."

"How noble of you," he sneered, "but no thanks. I'm not friendless, you know. You've never helped me in the past so why should I indulge your need to be noble now?" He walked off before the end of the allotted time.

Gillian was staying the night and the next day was Saturday, with its promise of an extra hour in bed. On the way back to the flat after an evening of new recordings and live performers, they decided to stop for a coffee and to unwind from the events of the evening. Before getting out of the car, still upset by seeing Claire and Ray together, Valentina told her friend what had happened. As with most promises not to tell, there was just one exception.

"Charlie would give us coffee," Gillian suggested, when they had discussed it for a while.

"No, not Charlie's, let's go somewhere we aren't known."

They stopped at a small cafe and ordered coffee and toast. They sat there mulling over the music offerings of the evening, and Valentina went through notes she had made of the records they had heard.

They were getting out of the car at 11.30 when they saw Claire.

"I don't believe this," Valentina muttered. "What is it about this area that attracts her? Claire!" she called. "Fancy a coffee?" It was late and she and Gillian were ready for their beds but she was curious.

Claire stepped towards them, paused in the light of the street lamp, glanced at her watch and shook her head. "Thank you, but I have to go."

"A lift, then?"

"No thanks, Valentina. It isn't far."

"What can she be doing out so late?" Valentina wondered.

"Perhaps she isn't Ray's mistress," Gillian suggested. "Out so late and obviously with an appointment, has it occurred to you she might be a prostitute?"

"She's too successful to have to do that," Valentina protested. "Why would she?"

"Big debts? Family in need? Forced to continue with something she started before she was successful? These things happen, don't they?"

"But surely Ray wouldn't — would he?"

"We've never met his wife — he never brings her to any social gatherings. Perhaps she's an invalid, or suffering with some illness he can't cope with?"

"I doubt if we'll ever know, not now."

"What d'you mean, not now?"

"Gillian, I don't know how to tell you this, but I'm considering leaving my job."

"But why? You've been so successful."

"Ray isn't the same with me now. I blew it, walking in on him and Claire like I did. Besides, I feel it's time for a change."

"What will you do?" Gillian asked as they got out of the car.

"I'm sorry, but I can't tell you at present, but when — and if — I can sort it out, you'll be the first to know."

Later that day Gillian went back to her parents' and Valentina drove to South Wales to visit hers.

They were both late leaving, having overslept, but even so, Valentina decided that if, when she reached her parents' home, she was unwelcome, she wouldn't stay. She would drive back to Pink Cottage to sleep.

"What have you got involved in now?" were her mother's first words.

170

Valentina stared at her mother. Hatred was bursting from her like evil gases. "Dad?" She looked to her father for support but he was watching his wife, trying to soothe her.

"Ashamed, I am," Valerie went on. "You and that Gillian with a baby and no husband. What's been going on up there in London? Ashamed of you, we are."

Something snapped inside Valentina. "Me? You're ashamed of me? It's your precious son you should be saying that to, not me!"

"Never helped him. Your own brother and you've never helped him. Where is he now? I've lost touch with my son and it's your fault."

Her decision not to worry her parents with news of their precious son was forgotten. "Michael is in prison!" she shouted. "Drunk and incapable probably! How can you blame me for that?" At once she was ashamed of her outburst. Valerie turned to Dewi, who held her and then led her towards the bedroom with only a brief, angry glance towards his daughter.

Valentina flopped into a chair and stared at the pattern on the carpet, foolishly counting flowers, petals, leaves and swirls.

Her father came back down and stood looking at her. "She's been frantic with worry. She's even been to London looking for him. She hasn't slept properly for ages. She wants him back home. The doctor has given her something to help her sleep but I regulate the doses, she's in such a state, see."

Cynically she said, "Sorry, Dad. I was selfish, expecting you to welcome me with a hug!" Her

171

shoulders drooped. "I want so much for her to be proud of me." He said nothing and she sighed and went on, "I shouldn't have come. Affection is too much for *me* to hope for in this house."

"You shouldn't have told her about Michael like that. Best we know, but you should have told me first."

"If you had a phone I might have but I could hardly have left a message with Mrs Francis," she replied in frustration. "Whatever I do it's wrong."

She handed him the details of Michael's situation and he telephoned the social worker from a phone box to arrange a visit.

"I can give you a lift back tomorrow if you like?" she offered.

"No, best you go. We'll go up on the train on Monday. Our appointment isn't till four."

"I was intending to stay until Sunday."

"Best not. You're like a red rag to a bull with Mam at present, see. She's in a state, see, and best you go, love."

She stepped back as if from a blow. Best she didn't stay? Why did she keep hoping her mother might need her? Want her?

"Is my collection of teddies still in my room?" she asked, choking back tears. "I thought I'd take them for Gillian's baby."

"Go quiet, then. Don't disturb your mam."

The furniture had been rearranged and Valentina remembered how often that had happened when they were children. Restless and bored, Valerie would exhaust herself struggling with the heavy furniture, getting brief satisfaction from the new look she had achieved. Now, her dressing table was in Moke's old room and it was in there she found the teddies, packed away in a cardboard box with her other favourite pieces, no longer on display. Her mother was gradually squeezing her out of her life, Valentina surmised, sadly.

She searched for a few ornaments and books she had treasured, nothing of value, just childish things she had once enjoyed. They were all missing. She emptied the box and began packing it with a few things she didn't want to lose. There were still a few of her school books, and the copy of *A Tale of Two Cities,* won as a prize for recitation. They were thrown together in a box with old papers and oddments, together with an envelope containing old photographs.

She went through them, taking one or two, replacing the others in the drawer. One showed a man she didn't recognize and, turning it over, she read the name: Ernesto. Italian, she wondered? He was dark and rather small, standing against the doorway of a house: this house, she realized with curiosity.

"That," her mother's voice said from the doorway, "is someone I knew a long, long time ago."

Something in her mother's voice made her stare. Was he important, this friend from long ago? Was the man in the photograph a clue to the way her mother rejected her? She glanced again at the image of the man and knew her questions were not likely to be answered; her mother had silently returned to her room.

CHAPTER
TEN

After staring at the photograph for several moments, Valentina followed her mother into the bedroom and asked her to explain, but Valerie refused.

"It's something long forgotten," was all she said.

"He's been here, in this house, so he must have been a friend. So why haven't you mentioned him? Is it something to do with me?"

"The world doesn't revolve around you," Valerie snapped.

Ignoring the remark, she asked again, "Who is he?" Her mother's obdurate expression made her give up and leave the room. She wasn't going to get any further, that much was plain to see. She went down but her father had gone out. No help there either.

She immediately began inventing reasons for her mother having kept the photograph, which grew wilder and more terrifying as the moments passed. By the time her parents returned, solemn and uncommunicative, and coffee had been poured, she had reached the worst explanation of all. Had her mother been the victim of rape?

Had she been conceived as a result of a sordid and terrifying attack? Was that why she was so hated? Rape.

The ugly word filled her mind and she stared at her mother, willing her to sense her distress. Unable to ask, she silently pleaded with her mother to tell her that wasn't true, that she was born of love, and not hate and fear. But her mother stared into her lap and refused to utter another word.

She stood up. She couldn't stay in this unhappy house where her thoughts were so distressing. It was late, but she preferred a long drive to spending the night here, where, for whatever reason, she was not wanted.

"I won't stay," she said when they had finished their coffee.

"Just as well," her mother said, stacking the dishes on the work surface. "I need to finish clearing that room."

"I'll take the toys for Little Lever and you can throw out the rest."

Valentina gathered the few treasures she decided to keep, half of her mind wondering how she would find room for them, the other half desolate with the feeling that she was being dismissed from her home, an item surplus to requirements. She was carrying boxes to the car when she saw Phil.

"What are you doing?" he called. "You can't be leaving home — you did that a long time ago."

"That's exactly what I'm doing," she said, her eyes suspiciously bright. "Leaving in disgrace, but I don't know why."

He took the boxes from her and put them near the car and held her in his arms. It was her undoing. She began to cry and, still holding her, he took the key from her hand and, opening the car door, guided her inside. He threw the boxes in the back and sat in the driving seat and took her once again into his arms.

"I'd better drive you where you want to go, love. You aren't in a state to be on your own."

"I'm all right. I'm always all right. I just need a minute."

"No, give me a moment to explain to my landlady and I'll go back with you." Clutching the key, he ran off, to return quickly with a bag across his shoulder, which he threw in the back. "Now, back to London, is it?"

She nodded, uncaring where she went. What did it matter?"

Phil didn't ask questions but sang quietly, allowing her time to relax and recover. She would talk when she was ready and he wasn't going to spoil his chances by rushing things. He planned to make the drive last as long as he could; having her captive wasn't an opportunity to waste.

At a junction where they could continue to London or stop at the cottage, he slowed down. "Do you want to go straight back or stop at the cottage and go on in the morning?"

"Phil, I don't want you to expect anything. You're just driving me home. Right?"

"No strings," he promised. "I just thought you might like to spend the night at the one place you can call your own. I won't stay with you. I'll get a room at the inn. I haven't known a comfortable couch yet and yours looks worse than most."

"Thanks. I don't think I can face the flat tonight. It'll be different when Gillian comes back with Little Lever and we have him to look after."

"She's bringing the baby back to London, is she?"

"We've arranged a childminder, and her job is still open. We'll manage."

"What about Bob?"

"He isn't involved," she replied quickly, even in her distressed state making sure she didn't allow any wrong information to escape, but then Phil made a wild guess based on a few unsubstantiated rumours he'd heard.

"He's not the father, no, everyone knows that. But Bob still cares for Gillian. I've spent a lot of time with him with my record underway and it's clear to see, and they're still married after all. This baby, though, it's down to Tony Switch and I don't think Bob can cope with that."

"What did you say?"

"You heard."

"This has nothing to do with that creep! Whatever gave you such a ridiculous idea? We both think the man's a fool."

"They were meeting on the quiet, mind, but things get out." He patted her thigh. "Don't worry, love, I won't say a word."

Pushing his hand away, she glared at him, his face dark and smiling in the reflection of the facia lights. "Tony Switch is not and never has been involved with Gillian, get that?" She forced a laugh. "What a joke. If you only knew what laughs we've had at the man's vanity and lack of talent."

"Who then?" He grinned, unrepentant. "You must know."

"I don't. Someone from her neighbourhood, I believe." She settled herself more comfortably in her seat and closed her eyes. She hoped her lies had convinced him. The last thing she wanted was for stories about Tony being the father to percolate through to Gillian, or to Bob.

Phil drove steadily on, pleased with the success of his wild guess. He always knew when Valentina was lying.

When they reached the cottage, Phil disappeared, ostensibly to arrange for a room, but he returned with bread, milk, coffee and half a dozen eggs. "Breakfast," he announced. "And we have a table booked for an hour's time for supper."

"And your room?" she asked suspiciously

"Come on, Valentina, don't you trust yourself?"

They ate a meal of steak and kidney pie with fluffy mashed potatoes and vegetables and, without waiting for coffee, Phil walked her back to the cottage.

"Coffee?" he suggested and Valentina nodded agreement.

Phil busied himself in the kitchen while Valentina sat near the electric fire, still wearing her coat. The distraction of eating had worked only briefly and the moment she sat down, her thoughts returned to her distressing departure from her home. Closing her eyes, she saw her mother's face, dislike emanating from the eyes. And behind her, her father, staring in a helpless way at Valerie; a weak man, prepared to give up his daughter rather than upset his deeply unhappy wife.

178

"What are you thinking about, love?" Phil asked, placing a steaming cup beside her. "Did your mother tell you things that upset you?"

She turned her head and looked at him curiously. "What d'you mean?"

The question wasn't angry, more conversational, and he sat down beside her and said, "Tell me what's bothering you and I'll fill in where I can."

"My mother wishes I'd never been born," she said in the same conversational way. "My brother Michael is the one she loves. I don't think she ever wanted a daughter."

"That's not so, love. I've just learned from my landlady that there was a man your mam wanted to marry. He was a lovely man apparently, an Italian, and —"

"Ernesto?"

"That's right. He worked on a farm as a prisoner of war and when the war ended he stayed and they fell in love. They would have married if her parents hadn't sent him away and denied her any further contact."

"I don't understand. How does that make her hate me?" One of her imagined explanations came to mind and breathlessly she asked, "Is Ernesto my true father?"

"No, love. Dewi is your father, no doubt about that." He cautiously slid an arm around her. "He came back, see, this Italian. Gran told me all about it ages ago. Talk of the village it was at the time. He came back, and wanted her to go back to Italy with him. He had never married but by then you were born and her parents had insisted she married your father." He pulled her into his arms. "They saw a lot of each other while he stayed and, well, your Michael was born the same year."

"He's Michael's father?"

"That's the story, love."

"If I hadn't been born she and this Italian would have married?"

"If you hadn't made your untimely entrance, or she'd given the child up for adoption, she would have found him. She knew where he lived. A letter was all he needed. They'd promised to wait for each other until she was twenty-one, you see. But she was young and still unable to defy her parents and the opinion of others. As time passed, she turned it round until she could blame you."

Coming out of the shock of what she had learned, she pushed him away and ran to her room, locking the door. She didn't try to sleep.

Phil was there when she went down very early the next morning. Ignoring him, she began to pack the car, ready to leave.

"What's the hurry? We could stay here for lunch and still be back by early evening."

"I have to go."

"All right, we'll go. We'll be back at the weekend anyway. You have to give me a lift home to collect my car."

Valentina drove them back to the flat, driving like a maniac and cutting up people angrily. At a roundabout she prepared to overtake a small van which moved into the outside lane without warning. To swerve to the right would have placed her perilously close to the barrier and a pile-up might have ensued. She gripped the wheel tightly and through an agony of seconds that seemed like hours, prayed that the van driver would see her and pull left, which he did.

Phil let out a slow breath and asked, "Want me to drive?"

"No, I don't!"

When they stopped outside the flat, her arms ached with tension and she wanted to get inside and unwind, alone. With as much politeness as she could manage in her state of mind, she dismissed him. "Would you mind if I don't ask you in? I'm very tired and I've got a lot of stuff to check ready for tomorrow's appointments."

"When will I see you?" he asked, putting the last of her boxes on the floor.

"Phil, I'm very busy for the next week. In fact, would you mind if I gave you the train fare instead of driving you back to pick up your car next weekend?" She didn't look at him as she spoke and was startled when he grabbed her and swung her round to face him.

"What? How d'you expect me to get to work this week? I need a lift, Valentina, every day. I abandoned my weekend, left my car behind and came with you when you needed someone. You have to at least get me to work and take me back to collect the car. What d'you think I am, some doting idiot who'll take what crumbs you throw?"

"Phil, please, can we talk later?"

"All right, love." His voice had softened as he stepped forward to kiss her but she picked up a box and held it in front of her like a shield.

"Later," she said firmly.

"How much later?" The anger was back in his voice, his lips a tight line. "This year, next year, sometime never?"

She drooped with unhappiness and fatigue. "I'm sorry."

"You will be, I promise you that." He spoke slowly and with a smile on his lips that didn't reach his eyes.

His gran had taught him the way to make people behave. Later, his dark face, darker with the need of a shave, stared back at him from the bathroom mirror and his eyes lit up as a plan began to grow in his bruised mind.

Gillian and Little Lever moved back to the flat and life was frantically busy for both Gillian and Valentina. Their day began early and ended late; Little Lever went to a childminder at eight every morning and the two girls went to the office feeling more like going back to bed.

On Sunday, a week after Gillian's return, Valentina met Charlie for lunch. She admitted that she wasn't very hungry, only tired.

"It isn't that he's a difficult baby," she told Charlie. "He's happy and absolutely gorgeous and I love him. It's getting up at night that's so draining. We're supposed to take it in turns to see to him but each time he wakes we both get up. We don't want to miss a moment of him while he's so small and neither do we want him to wake up alone and think no one cares."

"Thank goodness you have the weekend to recover. Gillian plans to go to her parents' Friday till Sunday, doesn't she?"

"Unless there's a function we have to attend. It's practically impossible for us to manage in the limited space, but somehow we do."

"I thought you were looking for a larger flat?"

Valentina looked at him, wondering whether or not to confide in him. Speaking of her plans before they reach fruition seemed to be a risk. But that was only foolish superstition, she admitted, nothing more.

"Charlie," she said hesitantly, "I'm going to rent a shop."

"Where is it? What will you sell?"

"Records, of course," she said with a smile, answering the last question first. "It's in a parade of shops and in a good position. There's a flat above too and although it isn't much larger than our present abode, we'll have to move into it because I wouldn't be able to pay rent on both, not for a long time anyway."

"You've known about this for some time?" he asked.

"A while, yes. If it all goes well I hope to open it in August."

"Would you like me to look at it before you make up your mind?" As always he didn't force her to involve him but he was more than a little disappointed that he hadn't been privy to her intentions.

"Thank you, yes, I would."

"You only had to ask and I would have helped you look for a property," he said and Valentina looked at his calm, smiling face and sensed his feeling of rejection.

183

"It didn't happen like that, Charlie, or I would have discussed it with you. It was Peter and John's idea. I was a bit disgruntled with my job. I still enjoy it enormously but there's a slight problem with my boss that has made me less content. They mentioned the shop, pointing out the perfect position, and the idea came. I started making enquiries and once I'd spoken to a few people, record companies as well as the bank, and John and Peter had spoken to the owner, well, the thing took off."

"Then it's all settled?"

"Not quite, but things have moved a long way in the past couple of weeks. I should be able to start work on it at the end of May and the record companies are vying for my permission to help me with the shop fitting. It's very exciting. A bit scary too. Ray knows, of course, and he supports my move."

She looked at him and felt guilty at excluding him. "Sorry, Charlie, but I didn't think it would work out. It seemed too wonderful to happen to someone like me. I was afraid that if I spoke too soon, everything would fall apart and I'd have no shop and no job."

"You don't have to explain."

"Please come and look at it. I'd appreciate your advice. There's so much to do and it needs serious planning before it becomes a place where people would enter voluntarily, and with limited money I can't afford mistakes."

"I don't think you need my advice, Valentina. You'll manage perfectly well on your own. Worse luck!" he added with a smile. "But I would like to see it. Ring

184

Peter and make an appointment. If you're free Monday lunchtime, we'll look at it then."

"What did you mean, 'worse luck'?" she asked.

"I want to marry you, and if you needed someone strong to lean on I think I'd stand a better chance."

"Marry you? But —"

"Will you marry me? Soon? I wouldn't change anything, except perhaps not share our home with Gillian and Little Lever, but we'd make sure they are safe and secure. And we'd see them often. I'd quite like to be a surrogate uncle."

"Charlie, I don't know," she said hesitantly.

"You'll think about it?"

"I'll think about it," she promised.

"Surely it can't be right if I have to think it over?" she asked her friend that evening.

"There are no rules. I always wanted to marry Bob."

"I always thought I'd marry Phil. The frightening thing is, I would have if I hadn't come to London. What a mistake that would have been."

Gillian had returned from the weekend with her parents and she looked more relaxed than the previous week.

"You and Little Lever had a good weekend?" Valentina asked as she took the baby from his mother's arms.

"Bob was there. He wanted to see the baby."

Valentina stared at her friend and there was brightness in the blue eyes, and the mottled look on her rosy cheeks was increasing; she knew she was going to cry.

"What happened?" Valentina wondered if Bob had asked for a divorce to marry someone else. She couldn't think of anything more devastating for her friend. "Is everything all right?"

"I refused to see him. I made Mum say I was out."

"Why?"

"If he has ideas of trying again, he'd ask me to give up Little Lever and I couldn't."

"Are you sure he'd want you to?"

"Of course he would."

"For goodness' sake, Gillian. Ask him! Talk to him." She took the baby into Gillian's bedroom and removed his outdoor clothes and undid his napkin for him to have a good stretch and kick after being in his cot for the journey.

"You do see it would be a mistake, don't you?" Gillian asked from the doorway.

"Bob loves you and he'll love Little Lever too. He's half you, isn't he? How can it be a mistake? You and Bob were meant for each other." She looked away from Gillian's unhappy face and added, "My mother married a man she didn't love because I was on the way. I ruined her life and that caused disaster for us all." She explained the reason for her mother's resentment and her intense love for Michael.

It was as they were settling down to eat supper that Valentina told her friend her other news. "It seems the shop opening might really happen. So, do you mind if we move into the flat above? We can decorate it as you like but it will be a while before it looks like home. Can you face the upheaval?"

"We'll have a look and decide on the cheapest way of doing it. Next weekend?"

"Can you manage tomorrow lunchtime? Charlie is coming to see it and I'd rather you were with me."

"You're going to turn him down, aren't you?"

"I rather think I am."

Moke had been out of prison for some time before Phil came across him. He had been reduced to begging on the street and sleeping where he could. Phil found him a room, in the area where he and Valentina lived.

"What *do* you really want to do, Moke?"

"Play guitar and sing."

"Pity the lonely dreamers," Phil sang softly. Moke told him to shut up.

Tony Switch thought life couldn't be more perfect. His unexpected career had risen unbelievably fast and he was feted and admired wherever he went. Autograph hunters came in droves to add his scrawl to their collections and admiring girls offered untold delights. Then there was Penelope Masters, an unbelievably lovely American girl whom he hoped would share his life forever. They had met at the BBC and at once she had become his girl. It was his arm she held as if it were a lifeline every time they went out. She was like a uniform which showed him to be a member of the "success club", being seen in all the best places, and with his own stunningly beautiful woman.

He had proudly introduced her to people who might further her own career, taking her gratitude in through his skin like sunshine, warming him and increasing his feeling of wellbeing. He looked down at the woman lying beside him in his king-sized bed, in his fashionable bedroom in his smart flat, and sighed contentedly. Everything clean and new, his woman-who-does coming every day to change sheets and make sure the whole place was spotless, replacing anything that showed even the slightest sign of wear.

And nothing could go wrong. He was into advertising now and was making money even as he slept. Television was already taking an interest, with a game show at the signing stage. Things were getting better, every day a new target conquered. Admiration glowed in Penelope's eyes and made him feel invincible.

Oh, Marlene, he silently told his imaginary friend, thank goodness I had the sense to ditch Gillian. Imagine me, Tony Switch, stuck with someone like that. He looked at the woman sleeping beside him and sighed happily once again.

It was in the same buoyant mood that he set off to record a new show later that day. It was one in which he was to star. He had studied his script and added a few jokes of his own that he would make sound like ad libs and he fervently hoped that the members of the public would remember their lines and say them as intended. Not like the last time, when a nervous woman had changed the words slightly and made a nonsense of his rehearsed reply.

Penelope looked dazzling in white fashion boots with gold laces, a white leather waistcoat with western-style fringes and gold trim, and a short, tight-fitting body-hugging gold top which hid very little.

To Tony's irritation there were people in the audience that he knew. That stupid no-hoper Phil Blackwood with the equally stupid Moke and, nearer the front, Valentina. Worst of all, Gillian Lever was with her. What did it matter? He shrugged. He'd be able to stay clear of them without any trouble. As the star he was protected from the riffraff. He guided Penelope over to where the producer and his team were standing and introduced her to those she hadn't already met.

Valentina turned to Gillian when she saw Tony. She knew that the embarrassment of seeing the father of Little Lever hadn't eased for her.

"Phil is over near the doorway and he looks angry. And, don't worry, but you-know-who has just arrived. Don't let him upset you. We're here as guests to please some of the recording companies; it's just part of the job."

"It isn't as though I didn't know he'd be here. The 'star' can't not turn up, can he? But he still makes me nervous. Who's that with him? The new girlfriend?"

"That's Penelope. Quite a dish isn't she? Phil had been dating her for a while, and had boasted about 'his' girl. She must have broken it off. She looks very expensive to me, more than Phil could afford."

Valentina looked between the heads of the crowd as people were being shepherded into their seats and was shocked at the pain and envy showing on Phil's face.

His expression was raw with unhappiness, alone in a business of which he so desperately longed to be a part, and she felt the need to comfort him. There were still a few minutes before the recording and she took Gillian's arm and guided her through the lighthearted audience to where Phil stood, staring at Tony's girl.

"Hello, Phil, what a specimen Tony's found for himself. Too brittle to be pretty, don't you think?"

"She's lovely," Phil snarled. "And she deserves better than that creep."

"If she's got brains, she'll soon discover what an idiot the man is. We saw that straightaway, eh, Gillian?"

Taking the cue, Gillian said, "Remember when he stripped off, convinced Valentina was out of her mind with desire for him and wanted nothing more than a romp on his bed? What a sight, eh?"

Shouting above the continuing noise behind them as people were told where to sit, they were unaware of a man standing near them. As they walked away to find their own places, the man turned and spoke to Phil.

The news was hardly new but it was worth re-hashing and when the reporter spoke to Tony and was treated to his fury, the item made greater prominence than it otherwise would. It would probably have ended up in the bin, discarded as being yesterday's news, not worth a mention, but a photograph of the reporter with a black eye and a swollen nose gave it the necessary spice.

Overnight, Tony was faced once again with trying to live down embarrassing publicity. Penelope refused to talk to him and was soon regularly seen with a television producer who was, he assured her, looking for an assistant to take part in a "Guess The Object" show.

CHAPTER
ELEVEN

Claire called to see Valentina just as she and Gillian were about to eat. For a fleeting second, Valentina was afraid she had come to complain about her bursting in on her and Ray kissing, even though so much time had passed, because she looked so tense. But then she smiled and with relief Valentina invited her in.

"Come in," she invited, "but please don't raise your voice, the baby is sleeping."

"Can I see him?" Claire asked and with a questioning shrug towards Gillian, Valentina opened the door of Gillian's bedroom and led their visitor to the cot.

The baby was sleeping on his side, rosy and so beautiful that Gillian and Valentina weren't surprised to see tears in Claire's eyes. He stretched, his mouth pouting, his arms tensing and his hands making tiny fists. Claire bent down and touched the soft hair on the baby's temple then, reaching into her bag, gave Gillian a small parcel.

"For Dylan Robert," she whispered. "I hope he will like it."

"Thank you, what a surprise," Gillian said as they went out of the room and softly closed the door. She opened the beautifully wrapped parcel and gasped with delight at the content. It was a silver christening cup, chaste with a design of angels and flowers and obviously old. "Claire! This is beautiful, but it must have cost a fortune. Thank you." Tears filled her eyes and, laughing, sharing her friend's delight, Valentina handed her a handkerchief.

"I haven't any other children to buy for," Claire replied.

She accepted their invitation to stay for a meal, a curry, which was easily divided between three with extra poppadoms and chunks of bread to fill it out.

She didn't stay long after they had eaten and when she left, Valentina again had the feeling that the rather mysterious young woman had wanted to talk to her. Perhaps if they were alone she might be persuaded to trust me, she thought, and as Claire went to the taxi she had ordered, she called after her, "Are you free tomorrow evening? Will you come for a meal with me? Just me. Gillian will be out."

Claire nodded. "We could eat out. I'll call for you at nine."

"It's a bit late for me. I don't think I could last until nine o'clock for a meal," Valentina said as she and Gillian cleared the dishes. "But I know she wants to talk to me. She's unhappy and probably needs a friend."

"If it's family problems then you're the one!" Gillian said with a laugh. "With your parents and your brother you could write a book!"

"Mam and Dad had no reason to marry, apart from me. They have very little in common except disappointment, yet here they are, more than twenty years on, still together, still unhappy. It isn't a marriage, it's a life sentence."

On Monday lunchtime Valentina drove with Gillian to the shop where Charlie was waiting, looking, Valentina remarked, "Not like a lover, more like someone's uncle." He carried a huge umbrella.

"But he looks so —" Gillian searched for the word "— so dependable. You could do a lot worse than marrying him. See how his face lights up when he sees you."

Sure enough, Charlie's face broke into a huge smile of welcome and he hurried across to greet them. "I reckon he loves you enough for both of you," Gillian whispered.

"Not the best reason for a marriage."

"Liking and respect? Believe me, there are worse. There are your parents for a start," she reminded her. Then Charlie was there and he kissed Valentina on the cheek and Gillian winked and tilted her head questioningly, making Valentina laugh as she stepped out of the car and under the umbrella.

It was raining steadily, the skies dark and threatening an even greater downpour. The shop door was locked, barred and padlocked and Valentina led them to another door at the side. She took them first up brown-painted stairs to the rooms above the shop. She was apprehensive, wanting to be reassured that she had made the right decision. The need for Charlie to be impressed was making her heart race. On such a gloomy day it wasn't going to look its best and even its best wasn't much. Prepared for his disappointment, she was on the defensive, waiting, expecting criticisms and doubts.

"There's a lot to be done . . ." Charlie began and before he could say any more she snapped a reply.

"Don't state the obvious, Charlie. I know it isn't a palace; we're looking at potential not perfection."

"The position is excellent, the rooms are pleasantly proportioned," he said with a touch of a smile. "The bay window is an attractive feature, the curving staircase is elegant."

"Now you sound like an estate agent!"

He laughed aloud then and hugged her. "Valentina, it's a mess but I would willingly bet that within a month you'll have it looking superb. D'you agree, Gillian?"

"She'll be sloshing paint around like a maniac as soon as she gets the key and I suspect most of her friends will be involved too. Specially me!" Gillian pulled a mock-serious face.

Charlie walked around, touching walls and testing the floorboards, and finally said, "Staining floorboards and 'sloshing' some paint on the walls wouldn't cost much, and with a few rugs and things you could be very comfortable here for a while."

"Only for a while?" Valentina demanded. "You don't think I'll make this work?"

"On the contrary, my dear. I'm sure you will. You'll be living somewhere more comfortable once you've got the business running successfully." He was hoping that her next move would be to share with him, as his wife, but he didn't divulge this. The next time he proposed it had to be the right time and place, and a dark gloomy day in a dark gloomy property was neither.

Danny Fortune called that evening, as Valentina was waiting for Claire.

"I have a thirty-minute slot at the pub we went to before," he told her. "Will you come?"

"Sorry, Danny, I'd love to but I've arranged to go out."

"With Charlie?"

"No, with Claire. You know her, don't you?"

"The maiden of mystery. Who she is, where she lives and where she goes are intriguing speculations to while away the time when we're hanging about in rehearsal rooms and the like. Some think she's a prostitute, did you know that?"

"That isn't true, and you can squash that speculation right away."

"Friend, is she, now?"

"Hardly that, but she calls to see us occasionally."

"Honoured you are, me darlin'. She doesn't talk to many."

"Sorry about tonight. I hope it goes well, although why you do small bookings like this I don't know. You don't need them now, do you?"

"Ah, but I do. Friends, they are, and I don't intend to forget them and pretend the people I've met since are more important."

"Sorry. I was being stupid."

Claire came earlier than arranged but with apologies. "Sorry, Valentina, but I have to cancel our dinner. Something came up."

"Oh, what a pity, and here's me starving."

"Another time? What about next weekend?" Claire suggested and on impulse Valentina invited her to the cottage. The invitation was a surprise and one which Claire accepted with alacrity.

"That would be wonderful. I need to get away for a while."

"And that leaves you with no excuse for tonight, me darlin'," Danny said. "If I promise to feed you, will you come?"

"If someone doesn't feed me soon I'll start on Little Lever's baby food."

Danny had a small car, not new, although with the success of his new record Valentina knew he could have afforded better. Everything about Danny was unpretentious. He wore comfortable clothes, ignoring the fashion for glitter and the outrageous. Tonight he was wearing jeans and a carelessly ironed shirt and he carried a clean but far from new sweater. On his feet he had good quality slip-on shoes that shone with regular polishing. Shoes, she thought with a smile, were Danny's extravagance.

"Are you still living in the same house in Islington?" she asked as they set off to find a restaurant.

"Sharing with the same three lads, yes. There seems no reason to change. I could move to somewhere bigger or with a more impressive address and be miserable."

They pulled into the car park of a pub advertising bar food and, with a sigh, Valentina accepted that tonight's meal wasn't going to be a memorable feast.

"You don't enjoy the trappings of success, do you?" she remarked when they had ordered pizza and salad.

"To be honest, I don't enjoy anything about it. I'm happier with what I'm doing tonight: a performance for the people who supported me when I was unknown and who still treat me as a friend. And," he added, "taking my girl to a pub for a bite to eat and a chat."

"Your girl? Since when?"

"Since the first moment I saw those merry eyes."

The words were spoken lightly but she was surprised at how much they pleased her.

The atmosphere at the small venue was more like a gathering of friends than an evening where Danny was booked as an entertainer. The audience gathered around him and called out requests and added stories and even sang a few songs of their own. The hours flew past and Valentina was surprised when they all began to leave.

"That was wonderful, Danny, you were wonderful," she told him as he drove her back home.

"Wasn't it perfect because you were there."

On Friday, Claire arrived at the flat at six, ready to set off for South Wales. She said very little on the journey and Valentina was beginning to think the weekend would be long and boring. There was no phone at the cottage or she might have been tempted to ring Gillian and ask her to ring back with an excuse to go back to London.

Once there, the cottage seemed to break Claire out of her shell. She ran, as far as possible in the tiny rooms, in and out of doors, up and down the stairs and out into the untidy garden, obviously loving every inch of the place.

"It's perfect," she said at last. "This is a place to be happy, I can feel it. Oh, Valentina, I can understand why you had to have it."

They ate at the inn and walked around the fields, Claire surprising her with her knowledge of wild flowers, and of the birds that filled the air. A robin followed them as they walked along a hedgerow.

"A sentinel making sure we, the intruders, leave without causing trouble," Claire mused. "They're so brave, flaunting their red breast like a naval flag, warning us, 'I am not to be trifled with'."

When Claire showered and came down ready for bed, Valentina stared in surprise. She was pale without her make-up, more vulnerable, almost afraid. Gone were the dark eyes. Now pale blue eyes stared at her, waiting for her reaction.

"Cocoa?" Valentina gulped, unable to comment for fear of frightening the young woman away for good.

"The disguise is good, isn't it?" Claire said softly. "I pad my cheeks a little when I think I might be photographed. It's so my family won't recognize me."

Valentina waited, so afraid of saying the wrong thing. She knew without doubt that explanations were the reason Claire came this weekend and didn't want to ruin everything. The expression in Claire's eyes was tragically unhappy. She needed to talk, and soon, or she would break down completely.

When the silence went on too long, Valentina said softly, "I've always known my mother doesn't love me. I've only recently learned the reason why. I was the result of a brief affair with my father which prevented her marrying the man she really loved."

"My mother divorced when I was three. I hardly remember my father; he hasn't even written since he left. Then my mother married again, a younger man —" Claire broke down and it was a long time before she could go on.

Valentina thought Claire's confession was going to be abuse by her stepfather but when it came it was a new slant on an old problem.

"My stepfather and I fell in love. He left my mother and we met whenever we could. Success is a two-edged sword, Valentina. It brings happiness and in my case, danger. I was underage you see. We waited until I was sixteen then I moved out. We never did anything wrong, neither of us did anything wrong. We just fell in love."

"But I saw you and —" Realization came. "Ray Everett!"

"Ray and I live together as man and wife, but no one knows. I'm trusting you with a secret that could lead to suicide if it got out."

"Suicide?" The calm way the words had been spoken chilled her.

"I'd kill myself if I had to give him up."

Valentina shivered again at the calm, utterly believable words. "No one will learn of it from me." This was a promise she would never break.

"It was music that brought us together. He encouraged me to do something with my voice and came with me to singing lessons, helped me to rehearse." She smiled at Valentina, her face, free of make-up, looking young and bearing the beautiful innocence of a child. "He makes me utterly happy and if only we could be open about our love, life would be perfect. But we can't." She looked at Valentina again, wondering if she had been wrong to tell.

"Your secret is safe with me," she assured her again, and she hugged her.

The weekend was one Valentina enjoyed. Besides admiring the greenness of the area with distant hills adding a backdrop that was breathtaking in its splendour, Claire opened her eyes to the delights of the immediate countryside. She taught her where to look for bird nests, and found the routes taken by foxes and badgers and other creatures that lived secret lives.

They stayed Sunday night, both having arranged an extra day, and planned to leave at midday on Monday. That last night was magical. They found a gap in a hedge where the sharp-eyed Claire had spotted badger hair caught on a twist of barbed wire and they stood patiently waiting, downwind, at dusk. Claire touched Valentina's arm before she heard a thing, and pointed along the narrow, well-used path. A family of badgers, including three young ones, were off on their search for food.

Besides scratching in the soil for earthworms just below the surface and finding lip-smacking pleasure from the slugs and other creatures they found, they played. They chased each other, pausing occasionally to scratch and groom themselves, completely oblivious of their enthralled audience.

They set off for London before midday, intending to find somewhere to eat on the way. Claire was wearing the contact lenses that hid her blue eyes and heavy make-up was in place. The relaxed girl was gone and Claire, just Claire, was ready to face the world. The joy of the previous night still filled their minds and Valentina didn't drive fast. They weren't in a hurry for their brief holiday to end.

At first Valentina didn't take any notice of the car behind. She glanced in her rear-view mirror occasion-ally and they had been on the road for an hour when she realized that although many cars had passed her, the same green car was there for much of the time, disappearing then returning but never out of sight for long.

She still didn't find it odd. After all, they couldn't expect to be the only ones to enjoy a relaxed drive through pretty countryside, travelling slowly to admire the burgeoning hedges with the blossoms of hawthorn still displaying its annual extravaganza. There were few cars using the roads Valentina had chosen and as she watched the car more closely, she began to wish she had taken the regular route and avoided the quiet lanes.

The car suddenly speeded up alarmingly. The driver seen in her mirror was only a blur. Very little face was showing, mostly concealed by what appeared to be a black balaclava, and sunglasses hid the rest.

"Claire, the fool's going to ram us!" she shouted. "Look out, he's trying to run us off the road!"

Frantically she straightened the car and began to increase speed. She had to outrun him. But her reactions were slowed by fear and the car was on them again. The Jaguar jerked as the green car hit them. Backing off, the driver gave them a chance to recover then rammed them again, metal screeching a complaint as the back bumper broke away. Valentina tried to escape but they were hit again, this time at an angle, making the car veer towards the edge of the road where there was a grass verge and a ditch.

There was a second or two of quiet as he backed off once more, playing with them, tormenting them. Then his engine roared and he came at them and this time the two vehicles joined together. The Jaguar didn't react to her pulling on the steering wheel as she tried in vain to straighten up. Inexorably, slowly, almost dreamily, yet amid nightmarish noise, as metal scraped and was crushed, they rose up onto the grass and down into the ditch. The green car pulled away with more scraping and screaming of tearing metal and their attacker drove away. The ensuing silence was broken only by the ticking of the engine as it cooled.

"Are you all right?" Claire asked.

"I think so. Are you?"

"My chest hurts where the safety belt gripped but I can move my arms and legs and my neck feels all right."

Slowly, as if all their joints had seized, they got out of the car to stand looking down at it in bewilderment.

"Who was he?"

"Why were we attacked in that way?"

"He must have mistaken us for someone else."

Outwardly calm, but with voices that trembled, they relived the outrage, asking questions to which neither could give an answer. They were dazed by the unbelievable event and before they recovered sufficiently to go and summon help, a car pulled up. They held each other, convinced the driver of the green car had returned. But the driver was a woman and she offered to go to a phone box and seek help. Both girls continued to stand beside the upended car, shock making their limbs dance a jig.

The police took their statements but nothing they told them was any use in finding the driver. No, they couldn't describe him, no, they weren't even sure if it was a man, except he was big. No, they didn't take the number of the car and no, they weren't sure of the make.

"All I can remember was the way the car windscreen filled the mirror and seemed to be riding on my shoulders," Valentina said. "I was never so frightened in my life."

They returned to London by train and taxi, after arranging for the car to be collected by a local garage for assessment and repair, arriving very late in the evening. Claire insisted on Valentina being dropped off first then took the taxi on to where she lived. Valentina was still shaking as she told Gillian what had happened.

"Who could it have been? Was he after me, or Claire?" The questions went on and they decided that the man was deranged, and had chosen them at random, looking for some fun. The news later, that the car had been found abandoned and had turned out to have been stolen, seemed to confirm this.

As they were getting ready to go to bed, Bob phoned.

"Either of you know where Phil is?" he asked. "We'd arranged a meet today but he wasn't at work. A neighbour told me he'd been away all weekend."

Valentina and Gillian stared at each other, joined by the same thought.

The result of the police questioning revealed that Phil had been at a hotel all weekend, with a woman. Valentina studied the map and wondered if he could be at both places but it seemed unlikely. Back to the idea that someone had been out for a bit of fun. Although, an alibi can be arranged.

Charlie's reaction to the news of the girls' ordeal was shock. He took Valentina to lunch at a small Greek restaurant and over a meal of dolmades with some fine Greek wine, he listened without interruption to her story. When she finished, with her suspicions about Phil's absence, he reached over and took her hand.

"It has unnerved me, I admit it," she told him. "'Specially now, when I have to face living in the new flat. Not knowing its sounds and its shadows, I'll start imagining someone creeping in, watching me. The man in the car hasn't finished with me yet, I know it. I'll be all right when Gillian is there, but going out in the evening and walking back into the strange new place, alone. Oh, I'm a wimp. Sorry, Charlie, you've caught me at a vulnerable moment. Gillian was right. He was a nutcase and it happened a long way from London."

"We'll go to the shop and make a list of everything we need to make it safe from burglars and nutcases," he promised.

"Thank you, Charlie."

"But that's short term. Marry me, Valentina. I promise I won't change anything you don't want changed. I'll just care for you. I know how badly you want to make a success of this new venture and I'll give you help if you need it and stand back when you don't. Please, say yes. I love you so much and I want to keep you safe."

"Charlie, I can't agree to marry you because I'm afraid of living alone."

"I'll settle for that."

"Oh, Charlie, I don't deserve you."

"Marry me. Let's announce our engagement. We'll have a party for all our friends. Make it a Sunday and we can use the restaurant. Please, Valentina. I'll do everything in my power to make sure you won't regret it."

He had chosen the place and moment well. Valentina leaned across the narrow table and kissed him. He turned to the waiter and said, "We're getting married!"

"Congratulations, sir. You have a beautiful bride. I wish you much happiness and many babies."

Telling Gillian was a thrill, and they discussed the few plans she had considered. But then she began to

206

realize how little she and Charlie knew about each other.

"Where will he want us to live? Will he really accept my working at the shop? And there's that waiter, wishing us many babies. I don't know whether Charlie wants any. I don't know if I do!" she wailed.

Tony Switch's "Tony and Marlene" show introduced a new item in June. On each programme he had a "Guess Spot".

"How many more times? It's not a misprint, Marlene," he scolded. "It's a surprise guest and the listeners have to *guess* who he is." He was silent for a moment as if listening to the imaginary Marlene. Then, "What d'you mean, 'Why bother if I'm going to tell them anyway?' It's fun, that's all." Another pause. "Yes, it's a he, and no, you naugh-ty girl, you can't peep into the dressing room while he's getting ready."

The guest that night was Danny Fortune. Neither man liked the other and Danny was dreading the whole thing. Tony's sense of humour was increasingly outrageous and some of his guests had been humiliated to the point where they lost their temper; many others refused to take part. Newspapers and magazine columnists were running lists of people who had survived intact, and Danny knew he was unlikely to be one of them

"Come with me," he pleaded to Valentina as the day drew near but she refused. She didn't want to be involved. Tony was capable of announcing they were a couple and spreading rumours that would upset Charlie.

Danny was dejected when he sat in the small outer room waiting to be called into the recording studio to face Tony's questioning. But the interview wasn't the cause of his dismay. He had just been invited to an engagement party. Valentina was going to marry Charlie Trapp.

During his spot he was so downbeat, so willing to agree with every wittily unkind remark Tony made about the poor quality of his voice and the boring songs he wrote that the interview failed to create the usual fireworks and Danny was pronounced a winner against the dreaded Tony.

Danny was puzzled. No one believed a word he had said. He *was* a failure, his songs *were* boring and he *was* untalented. Without Valentina he was nothing and now it was too late. He had lost her.

The advertising team for Danny's recording company turned the interview round and decided the publicity was too good to waste. Danny Fortune, singing the latest Bob Lever song, called "Phoenix From The Ashes (Of Our Love)", was chosen to be hyped. Interviews in newspapers and magazines emphasized Danny's sincerity and humility and he began to feel a fraud.

"All this makes me want to go into hiding," he'd complain to anyone who would listen. Even that sounded — and was interpreted by some — like false modesty. But orders for the record came in faster with

208

each hour that passed. Danny Fortune was a name on everyone's lips.

When "Phoenix" hit the number one spot, Valentina waited for him to call, but he didn't contact her and when she had a moment free she rang to congratulate him. A recorded voice asked her to leave a message on tape and she felt dejected, cut off from him at the moment she wanted to share his success. She remembered the times he had asked her to go with him and she had refused, treating his friendship so casually it must have hurt. Her vanity told her she had been letting him down lightly, aware of his growing affection for her, but she should have been there when he did the Tony Switch interview. He had needed a friend that day.

"Am I turning into a career woman with no thought for anyone else?" she asked Gillian.

"Don't be an idiot."

"I'm serious. I'm so wrapped up in my own life, I can be oblivious to the troubles of friends."

"Danny, you mean?"

"I'm fond of him and I've treated him unkindly. I . . . This might sound vain but I thought he was more than a little in love with me. So I've been careful not to do anything to encourage those feelings; that's why I've turned down some of his invitations. But I allowed him to hear of my engagement to Charlie from someone else. I could have at least told him myself."

"Go and talk to him."

"I've tried ringing but he's never there."

"Hardly surprising. His social life must have trebled with all the publicity. Don't worry about him. Here." She handed Dylan Robert to her friend. "Forget about some of the other loves in your life and burp your favourite young man!"

Valentina smiled as she took the sleepy baby, but the smile faded as she admitted to herself that deep down she wished she were a part of Danny's hectic social whirl. But that was stupid. Her job kept her occupied more evenings than she wanted, the shop was a prospect she looked forward to with joy and she had Charlie to fill her future. Her life was altogether too exciting to suffer what seemed like jealousy at the thought of someone else being a part of Danny's life, sharing his success. How could she be jealous over someone she didn't love?

Late on Friday of the following week, Valentina was in her office dealing with the last of the day's mail. Gillian was putting letters into envelopes and checking that everything important had been answered. Both were hurrying, anxious to get away.

As they worked, they were discussing Gillian's search for a flat suitable for herself and her young son. Despite the offer of the flat above the shop, she had decided the time was right to find a place of her own.

"I'll stay at the new place for the first week whether I find a place or not," Gillian assured Valentina. "Longer if necessary. Just until you feel the place is really yours."

"Thank you." Valentina smiled, touched by her friend's thoughtfulness. "As long as Phil stays away I'll be fine."

"You don't really believe it was Phil who forced you off the road, do you?"

"No. Phil is an idiot but I don't think he would do anything so terrible. He wouldn't physically hurt me, he just wants me to fail and go back to him."

"Any chance?"

"No!"

Thoughts of Danny and Phil and Moke kept her awake for much of the night. Of Charlie, she thought not at all.

CHAPTER
TWELVE

The police called on Valentina twice, once to tell her they had no information and to clarify a few details of her statement, then to tell her that investigations were continuing but they had little hope of finding the driver of the stolen car.

"It had been stolen from a house in Barry," the constable explained, "and after the attack on you, it was abandoned in a quarry."

"You're sure it was the one that rammed me?"

"The damage on both cars matched. Paint was exchanged from both vehicles," he explained. "If you think of anyone who might have a grudge against you or your friend, please let us know at once." He saw her slowly shake her head and frown as possibilities passed through her mind. "Even if it's only a faint possibility," he encouraged.

It wasn't Phil. She wouldn't believe him responsible of an attempt that might have caused her serious injury or even death.

With the embarrassment of the damage to Ray's car, Valentina didn't ask anyone for help. She used trains and buses until Danny arrived on her door one evening and offered his services as chauffeur. With a thought of how she used people, she declined, assuring him they could manage, but he cheerfully insisted and drove them to work, promising to be there to take them to collect Little Lever and then back to their flat.

"Why didn't you ask me?" Charlie asked when he was told of the arrangement. "I'm a part of your life now, aren't I? We're a couple and you have to learn to involve me in any problems you have, darling."

"It takes a bit of getting used to," she apologized, but she and Gillian still continued to accept Danny's help.

"Come out for lunch," Danny said on the third day. And, true to form, he took her not to a smart restaurant but a small pub, where a menu was ignored and his offering was a ploughman's of cheese, bread, an apple and some pickle.

They talked shop for a while, Danny explaining that he and Claire were rehearsing a duet, written by Bob, which they hoped would be their next record.

"You're really successful now and I'm so pleased," she said with difficulty, struggling with a tough crust.

"Is it all right?" he asked anxiously as she pushed aside the inedible piece.

"Danny, it's fine. I was starving."

"You always are," he teased. "Not what Charlie would have given you though."

"Sophisticat you are not, but great company. I can relax with you."

"And not with Charlie, that man you've promised to marry?" he asked softly.

"Charlie too," she said firmly but without convincing him.

"Claire has asked me to sing with her at your engagement party, but I don't think I can do that," he said, after collecting two coffees and some apple pie.

"You'll come though?"

"I don't think I can." The gentle green eyes were shadowed with pain as he stared at her, as if trying to look into her heart and find hope. "How can I celebrate when I know Charlie isn't the one for you?"

"Please, Danny."

"All right, if it's really what you want of me, then I'm your man."

Valentina had been trying for days to talk to her parents about her engagement. She had left messages with the neighbours and had written three letters, each one less effusive than the last. The fourth said simply: "I am going to marry Charlie. Will you come on 30 June to meet your future son-in-law?"

This one resulted in a phone call.

"Thanks for phoning, Mam," she began after her mother had announced herself. "You and Dad will be here for the party, won't you? I'll book you into a hotel as the flat is so crowded. I didn't dream how much room one small baby can need."

"I didn't phone about that!" her mother replied sharply. "It's Moke. We haven't heard from him and your father and I are worried."

"I might have known," Valentina said softly, disappointment like a stone in her heart. "Sorry, Mam, but apart from staying with Phil for a few days when he came out of prison, his whereabouts have been a mystery. I don't know what I can do. He knows where

214

you are and where I am. If he wants to find us he can easily do so." After listening to her mother for a while, and saying little more than "Yes, Mam" and "All right, Mam", she sadly replaced the receiver. Her engagement was of little importance and was turning into a non-event in her own mind as excitement had never developed in the way she had once imagined it would at such a life-changing affair.

Guilt, brought on by her mother's phone call, resulted in her going to see Phil. She didn't want to, but he was still the most likely person to have seen Moke. She was edgy and a little afraid, wondering if he knew something about the attack on her and Claire. If he had become so lacking in control, wasn't visiting him risky?

"I'll go with you," Gillian offered. "We'll take Little Lever and he wouldn't dare start anything with him to protect us!" She smiled encouragingly. "Honestly, Valentina, I was convinced it was Phil simply because there was no one else who was more angry but I've had time to think and if Phil wanted to hurt you he'd have done so in a simpler way than following you from the cottage. How did he know what time you'd be leaving? What did he do, hide in a hedge until he saw you passing? No, this is down to a local nutcase, believe me."

Valentina wished she could.

It was Danny who went with her in the end. "I want to see Phil about this record of his, 'Pity The Lonely Dreamers'. I like it and as soon as I can I'd like to add it to the songs I sing at my gigs. Isn't it due out about now?"

"I haven't heard a date yet, but Phil is sure to know."

Phil smiled when he saw her but was soon scowling when he saw she had Danny with her and explained she was seeking news about her brother.

"What, again?" he complained. He stepped back and with a jerk of his head gestured for them to enter.

His hair was greasy and longer than ever and pulled back carelessly behind his ears. His feet were bare and he wore a shirt from which the sleeves had been carelessly cut. The flat was as untidy as its tenant, with clothes draped over chairs and shoes, with socks attached, dropped near the chair where he had obviously taken them off. His leather stage clothes hung outside a cupboard and wrapped around a hook was a black woollen scarf. Three guitars were standing in a corner, one bearing the legend Square Clock. Knowing it might belong to Moke, Valentina stared at it then at Phil. "He's here?" she asked.

Phil shook his head and explained that Moke had left it with him before he was arrested.

"Do you know where he is?" Valentina asked.

"I'm only across the road but you only see me when you want something," he grumbled. "But still, that's your way, isn't it? Using people. Danny's your chauffeur, I'm your private eye. What's Charlie? A chance to acquire prestige and money?"

They didn't stay long and Valentina was upset when they returned to the flat.

"Will I come in for a moment?" Danny asked and without waiting for a reply, went to the kitchen and busied himself making tea.

"Why does he live in such a mess?" Valentina wondered.

"Why does he still believe you belong to him?"

"There's such clutter in that miserable room. He hasn't tidied it for weeks. I doubt whether he's used his stage clothes recently yet he hasn't bothered to put them away, and there are oddments of clothes that must have been left by friends, which he hasn't bothered to return. Like that black scarf of all things. That must belong to someone else. He's too macho to wear one of those."

"Now that's a funny thing," Danny said thoughtfully. "I didn't have a proper look but I thought it was one of those balaclava things. Didn't you say the driver who pushed you off the road was wearing something like that?"

"No, Danny. Not Phil! It was a black scarf, that's all. An ordinary scarf. Perhaps he does wear it. Phil always wears a lot of black."

"You know him best, but promise me you won't go over there on your own."

Valentina hadn't wanted the engagement party to be formal, and had refused to agree to a sit-down meal. Nor had she sent invitations. "Word of mouth will do, surely? Tell someone and ask them to tell others. I bet the grapevine is more efficient than Her Majesty's mail," she had assured Charlie.

217

"I want our engagement to be special, and catering is my profession. Please, let me do something superb for you, my darling."

"It's a celebration, Charlie. I don't want my friends to come bearing gifts then stand around wondering what to do. I want a huge buffet with lots of food, drink and laughter. And I want music. The liveliest I can find. Music is my profession, remember."

Unhappy but determined to please her, Charlie had agreed but now he was very anxious. It would soon be time for the guests to arrive and she wasn't there. The food was set out, the tables and chairs arranged casually as she had requested, and the room was beautifully decorated with flowers. As he stood anxiously waiting for her, he began to wonder if the low-key attitude had made her forget the occasion herself. "It will be a disaster," he told his parents. "No one important will come."

Valentina spent a little time in the flat above the shop, where she had left her gift for Charlie. She looked around the new flat that would one day soon be her home. It looked a mess but she began to imagine how it would look when she and Gillian had made it liveable. Glancing at her watch, she was alarmed at how much time she had spent daydreaming. It was time to leave.

She went into the bathroom and in haste slammed the door harder than intended. The lock made a loud click and curiously she tried to reopen it. It wouldn't move. Somehow the door had slammed and locked itself. She didn't worry. She checked her hair and make-up in the spotty old mirror they would have to replace and daydreamed a while longer. She tried the door again. It was firmly locked and she began to panic.

Valentina's parents were the first to arrive at the party, hoping to see their son, and as others drifted in Valerie began telling anyone who would listen that Moke was the talented one, Valentina had just been lucky. Members of Music Round staff entered noisily, including the girls from accounts and stock control. Several reps and one or two from the BBC arrived, all excited and intent on enjoying the party. Danny came with Claire and they sat together discussing the song they were to sing. Danny had altered the words to make it relevant to the occasion and they sang quietly as they rehearsed.

Valerie cried with relief when Moke arrived, having heard of the party through friends. His clothes startled the conservative Charlie. Moke was dressed in a long robe over which he had a shawl decorated with sprigs of flowers and bows of brightly coloured ribbons. A band made of braid surrounded his head and it too bore a cheerful display of flowers. The front of his robe was covered in badges and buttons and on his back was the symbol of nuclear disarmament.

"Hi there, brothers, I'm Moke. Call me brother." He stood and blew kisses all around until Charlie grabbed him and dragged him aside.

"A throwback to the hippies," someone muttered.

"Come and sit in a corner and talk to your parents. They'd like that, wouldn't they?" an embarrassed

Charlie pleaded. Flustered and increasingly angry, he took time away from his vigil watching the door, to assure his family that it was all a bit of fun and Valentina would soon be there. To his surprise, Mary and Joe seemed to be enjoying it. Perhaps the worst was over and once Valentina finally deigned to appear, everything would settle down. But there were greater worries to come.

Carl Stevens arrived with his wife at the same time as Gillian, who had come straight from her parents' home, having left the baby with them for an extra day. She accepted Charlie's kiss and looked around, searching for Bob. Valentina would surely have invited him. She had thought of nothing else all weekend. Her pale hair was carefully styled and she wore a new figure-hugging dress, revealing how well her body had recovered after the birth of Little Lever. The room was crowded but if Bob were here, she would find him and maybe they would talk.

She wandered through the mass of lively people, most of whom she knew, and she stopped several times to join a conversation but all the time her eyes searched for Bob Lever. When her watch showed her it was after nine o'clock, she began to think he wasn't coming. Tears threatened and reddened the rims of her blue eyes. More and more guests continued to arrive and, like Charlie, her eyes watched the door.

The variety of dress made Charlie despair. Where were the suits? Apart from his father and himself, he hadn't seen one. He didn't consider himself out of date but thought the general untidiness showed lack of respect for the occasion. Every aspect of fashion was displayed, from girls in smart hotpants to the scruffiest denim. There were plenty of jeans. Full length, torn at the knees, patched and cut down to become very revealing shorts, on both men and women. He could see people in black coats that reached the ground standing beside the briefest and garish of mini skirts, all adding to the colourful and dazzling display of modern youth, but to Charlie it was a nightmare. When he thought he could see nothing worse, punk arrived. Five members of a popular band came in carrying instruments, posed in the doorway and sang a little of their latest hit. This was followed by applause and a rowdy cheer of welcome from the guests.

Charlie couldn't look at them. They wore earrings and nose rings. He shook their tattooed hands without raising his head and immediately wanted to wash. He was relieved when Gillian came and took them away to introduce them to people she knew. Gillian was seriously worried about her friend's non-appearance but Charlie insisted there was nothing wrong and Valentina would be there any moment, that she was probably planning a surprise. She shared her concern with Danny, who went to stand where he too could watch the door.

The pile of gifts grew on side tables, the crowd and the noise level increased, and still Charlie stood at the door waiting for his future bride to appear. Phil walked in at the same time as Peter and John and he laughed when Charlie told them Valentina had yet to arrive.

"Aren't you worried?" John asked.

"Angry, that she can keep everyone waiting like this!" Charlie's voice was sharp.

"Angry?" Danny said. "I'm worried! She hasn't phoned to explain the delay? You told us she was held up after visiting friends and wouldn't be very long. It's after ten o'clock! I'm going to the flat to see if she's there." Danny excused himself from Claire. "I'll find her and be back to sing our duet," he promised. "But I have to make sure she's all right. She might have fallen, hurt herself, anything."

"I doubt that," Charlie retorted. "She's waiting to make an entrance. She likes to feel important — her parents told me she's always been like that. It's very thoughtless of her."

"We think you should start the buffet before everyone gets fed up and leaves," Joe said, and Mary nodded agreement.

"I can't. Not before Valentina comes."

"If you don't there'll be no party when she does come."

Charlie waved to stop Danny leaving. "Don't go, Danny. Wait a little while longer, please."

Phil laughed and said, "Or Claire will go looking for you and we'll have to send someone to look for Claire and there'll soon be no one left!" He was looking to others to share the joke but no one smiled.

Valentina was shivering with cold. The premises hadn't been lived in for a long time and the bathroom had no heating. She called from time to time although she knew it was impossible for anyone to hear her. She looked at her watch repeatedly and wondered how long it would be before Charlie came to look for her. She wondered sadly if he would. She could imagine his embarrassment, her failure to arrive being his strongest emotion. But then she dismissed that idea. Of course he would be worried. He loved her and would be here soon. She concentrated on listening for the sound of the door opening.

Danny went to the flat the girls still shared but it was empty. He went back to the party, hoping she would have arrived in his absence. She hadn't appeared but someone else had.

Heralded by a couple of young girls and pausing to make an entrance, Tony Switch walked in. He wore white slacks and white socks with brown highly polished shoes, and one of the girls who trailed behind him carried his brown leather jacket. Gillian left her punk friends and slipped quietly into a seat beside Mary and Joe. This was becoming a disaster. And where was Valentina?

Striding across to Charlie, aware of every eye on him, Tony said, "You're lucky I could fit this in, Charlie. I've got another appointment in an hour." He handed Charlie a piece of paper. "Here's my account."

"What? But this is a —"

"I know," Tony said airily, "a record you want me to give air time to. Really, Charlie, you're becoming quite the impresario. Danny and Claire, isn't it? Come on then, tell them to get on with it. I can't stay long."

"Just a minute. I didn't invite you to listen to anyone. This is my engagement party, mine and Valentina's. You've been misinformed. In fact, I don't remember your name mentioned at all." He stuffed the account in the breast pocket of Tony's shirt.

"What? Don't tell me this is another of Valentina's tricks! She seems to spend her time making me look foolish!" Tony's eyes flashed angrily.

"Have a drink," Joe offered.

"And do stay for some food," Mary added.

Gillian looked at him and said nothing.

Tony went straight into his act.

"Hey, get off Marlene's lap," he said to Carl Stevens in mock alarm. "She was there first!" Carl good-naturedly jumped out of the seat and began apologizing to the invisible Marlene and at once the guests looked to Tony for laughter and fun. He didn't let them down. He joked and teased and made outrageous remarks about many of them and they laughed and begged for more.

Charlie reluctantly agreed to his parents' growing insistence that they start the buffet. Tony stayed on the dais and continued to amuse everyone with his witty stories between music both recorded and live. Gillian stood with Danny and Claire, unable to relax, certain something was wrong. Valentina wouldn't have forgotten her own engagement party. She tried to imagine her visiting a friend and forgetting. There was no way that would happen, so where was she?

"It isn't long since someone pushed her car off the road," Gillian reminded them and, overhearing the

224

conversation, John and Peter admitted sharing their concern.

Ignoring Mary's request for them to sing their duet as arranged, Danny left again, with John and Peter.

"They won't be long," Charlie assured everyone, but in fact he was so unsure of Valentina's love he was convinced they would find her in the flat watching television and eating some of the chocolates he had given her the evening before.

While the buffet and Tony's entertainment kept everyone occupied, John, Peter and Danny slipped away and Gillian went with them, forgetting her handbag in the anxious moments and also regretting leaving while there was still a chance of Bob turning up.

"I have a feeling she's at the shop," Danny said. "She's excited at owning it and she pops over there now and then to look and plan and dream."

"She wouldn't go there and make herself late for her engagement party."

"She wouldn't have intended staying this long. She'd need hours to get herself ready if I'm any judge," Peter said.

"I still want to check."

"I think we should too," Gillian agreed. "She might easily have fallen, with builders' rubbish all over the place."

John and Peter looked at each other. "There isn't anywhere else to try, is there?" John said with a shrug.

The parade looked deserted. Most of the shops used their upper storeys for storage, not accommodation. There were few people about. Parking John's car in front of the shop, they checked the door which was used for access to the upstairs flat but it was locked. They shouted and banged on the door but the building remained dark and silent.

"Well, she obviously isn't in there, so where do we look next?" John asked.

As the two men walked back to the car, Danny stared up at the premises. Gillian paused to wait for him.

"What is it, Danny?"

"I have a feeling she's there. Valentina?" he called repeatedly.

"You think she's in there?" she asked. "But there isn't a light showing and she didn't answer when we banged on the door."

He didn't reply and she turned to get into the car. With her hand on the door, a shout from Danny startled her and with John and Peter following she ran to where Danny was pointing up at a small window.

"Have you seen something?" Peter asked.

"She *is* there. I knew it, look!"

A hand appeared, the ends of fingers waving from the tiny window of the bathroom, which opened only a couple of inches against security wire. John gathered some old pieces of wood and boxes abandoned by builders and using them he climbed up until he could reach the drainpipes. His long, gangly frame looked precariously balanced as he slowly pulled himself up to a point just below the window.

Peter hid his eyes, afraid to watch. "Be careful, please," he murmured.

226

Reaching the window, John tapped and called her name and a tearful Valentina answered. "I'm locked in," she sobbed. "The door's stuck."

"Are you hurt?"

"No, just cold and frightened."

Danny immediately called the police.

"The gap isn't wide enough to push a coat through," John called to her. "But put your hand through the window, my darling, brave girl." When he saw the small white fingers he gripped them, foolishly trying to warm them with his affection for her. Then he kissed them and promised she would be out in no time at all.

The police came quickly and assessed the situation. They ordered John and Peter and Danny to stay where they were while they went in, but Danny pushed them aside and ran up the stairs two at a time and was at the bathroom door before they reached the landing.

"Valentina, me darlin' girl, I'm here!" The stiff lock turned and he was hugging her, wrapping her in his coat and soon guiding her out to John's car.

Wearing Danny's coat over her flimsy dress, Valentina insisted on going to see Charlie. Surprisingly, it was not yet midnight.

"Shouldn't you be home and in bed with a duvet and someone like me?" Danny joked. She had hardly let go of his hand since the bathroom door had been opened.

"He'll be so relieved to know I'm safe," she said, ignoring his words.

"To be sure he will, to be sure," Danny replied, trying unsuccessfully to hide his doubts.

"We can go and tell him," Gillian admonished. "You should be going home."

"He'll worry if he doesn't see me," Valentina insisted, snuggling into Danny's coat to quell her shivering.

When they walked into the restaurant, Tony was dancing with Mary, his tall figure making the diminutive Mary look like a doll. Joe was talking to Charlie in a corner near the kitchen door, where a team of waiters were arranging the remaining food onto fresh plates for those who were still hungry.

To give Valentina a chance to talk to Charlie, Gillian left them and went to find Claire. Danny signalled to Claire that it was time for their song. It would take attention off Valentina's arrival for a moment if they were quick. But first, Danny went to collect a plate of food and a hot drink.

"Don't I just know the girl will be starving," he said.

After hurried explanations, Claire and Danny were ready and Tony made the announcement.

No one had noticed Valentina's entrance. Charlie didn't come to meet her but stood where he had been for most of the evening, against the kitchen door. She went towards him, her face pale and her body feeling as though it had been encased in ice. She still wore Danny's coat around her shoulders.

"Where have you been?" Charlie demanded.

She was disappointed but not surprised at his first words. He had so much wanted this evening to be a success, his mind had refused to take in the fact she had been in trouble.

"Aren't you glad I'm safe?" she asked softly.

"Safe? Well, yes, of course. But I want an explanation."

"Didn't Peter ring to tell you? I was locked in the bathroom and —"

"Come on, Valentina. You can do better than that!"

She stared at him and realized very clearly that Charlie was not the man to think of spending the rest of her life with. "No," she replied. "I can't do better than that. You think I did it on purpose? Some sort of joke, perhaps? You'll believe the police when they come to interview you tomorrow. They'll want to know who was here and who wasn't, so look around you and make sure you have the answers."

"Police? But what happened? You mean you were really locked in? Why didn't one of the other tenants hear and let you out? Why did you have to be so dramatic and call the police?"

Sadness, not anger, was her strongest emotion as she explained. "I was locked in the bathroom above the shop, Charlie. Stop being pompous for a moment and listen. I went there to pick up the present I'd bought for you. I went into the bathroom, slammed the door and couldn't get out."

"I'm sorry. This party had filled my mind so much, all I could think of was that you were ruining it, letting me down. I'm so ashamed I didn't believe you. Are you hurt?"

"Now if that had been your first question, there might have been a future for us."

"Don't say that. We can work it out. I was in the wrong. I must have been mad not to realize you were in trouble."

"Danny knew. Gillian knew. And John and Peter. All you could think of was your embarrassment. Perhaps that tells me something. I'm so very lucky with my friends. So many people in my life who really care."

Phil listened with interest to her story about being locked in. Then she had come out and cancelled her engagement! His gran was right. Locking someone in was the best way of making them see sense. He looked at Valentina, so lovely and so vulnerable, huddled up in Danny's coat. No, if being locked in a clean bathroom upset her so badly, he could never lock anyone in a cellar or a coal hole with beetles and spiders and mice, no matter how much they deserved it.

Danny and Claire finished their duet and although the call for an encore was tempting, Danny, who had hardly taken his eyes off the doorway where Valentina and Charlie, just within sight, were talking, he shook his head. He beckoned to Phil and asked him to sing, offering the use of his guitar. He escorted Claire back to her seat beside Gillian, then nodded to Tony to take over once again.

Valentina was white. By contrast, Charlie's face seemed about to explode. Hurriedly, Danny went across. He said nothing but just looked at Valentina.

"Please, Danny, take me home," she said.

CHAPTER
THIRTEEN

Tony Switch decided to make the most of his most recent mistake. He telephoned the evening papers and a couple of days later a lighthearted leg-pull appeared in several. "Tony gets it wrong again," announced one. "Switch gets his wires crossed," said another. They explained how Tony gatecrashed a private party and expected a fee. Each described how he turned up at the party having been misinformed about his role. Photographs of a smiling Tony showed him to have taken it all as a huge joke. "Valentina and I are friends," he was reported as saying. "She knows I'm always good for a laugh."

The day after the disastrous party, Valentina didn't want to go to work, and it was tempting to stay in bed when she woke to find her limbs and neck stiff and painful. Lying in that bathroom, tensed against the cold and increasingly sure of being left there all night, she hadn't realized how tightly she had clenched her muscles. If it hadn't been a day on which Ray was going to be absent, she would have stayed home, but with Ray out of the office for the whole day, and with auditions arranged, plus preliminary interviews for her own replacement, she had no choice.

The first thing she did on reaching the office was to ring Charlie, but there was no reply. Flowers arrived at ten o'clock and, thinking they were from him, Valentina indifferently handed them to Gillian to put in water, not even bothering to read the card.

"It was nice of John and Peter to send flowers, wasn't it?" Gillian said as they sipped coffee in a break between appointments.

"John and Peter? I thought they were from Charlie." She wasn't disappointed, just angry with herself for the assumption. "What vanity," she said. "Me thinking he would go to that trouble. I doubt he's given me a thought."

"He'll come soon. Perhaps he's on the way here this very minute."

"Charlie will still be smarting over his embarrassment. What was I thinking of, getting myself locked in a bathroom and ruining his engagement party! If he thinks of me at all, it'll be much later, when his ruffled feathers have relaxed."

"Don't be too hard on him. You must admit it was a lot to cope with. An engagement party for all those people, including both families, plus the rich, the famous and the Gawd-'elp-us. He wanted to impress them all and show you how well he would fit into your world and, lo and behold, his fiancée doesn't show!"

Gillian began to smile and soon the two of them were giggling helplessly at the absurdity of it.

"I'd have loved to have seen his face when the punk rock band walked in," Valentina said with more laughter.

232

Charlie's mother phoned to ask if she had recovered. "I'm so relieved to know you're all right. We all are."

"Except my loving fiancé," Valentina muttered as she replaced the phone.

More flowers arrived, this time from Tony Switch. The card simply said, "Sorry you missed your party."

"File them under Bin," Valentina said, throwing them in Gillian's direction.

To Valentina's delight, her brother Moke called into the office to tell her he was going back home.

"I'm sorry you didn't make your mark, Michael, but at least you tried and that's more than most people do. Hundreds of young people must be sitting safely at home, dreaming wonderful dreams. Wanting to take a chance but lacking the nerve. I'm proud of you, really I am. But I do think it's the right thing for you. Music will always make you popular and it's a wonderful hobby. Best you forget your ambition for something more and try something new."

"Have you finished?" Moke said, his voice filled with anger. "I *haven't* forgotten my ambition. I'm just going home for a while to think about what I'll do next. I'll be back. And I'll be there for the opening of your precious shop, too!"

Valentina had hoped to discourage him; he was lacking in common sense and she was afraid that rather than admit failure he might become involved in something worse. But all she said was, "I see. Well, take your time, be sure it's what you really want. And be very careful not to fall into traps promising an easy way out. London can be a lonely place."

233

"So can home," he muttered.

Danny called in soon after Moke had gone, to check that Valentina was fully recovered. Several friends telephoned to be reassured by Gillian. Many remarked on the newspaper articles that revealed Valentina and Tony to be friends. Valentina shared their joking remarks but felt nervous, wondering who had invited him, and how he really felt about being made to look a fool again.

John and Peter rang several times, and to her surprise she had a call from Tony's secretary, expressing his wish for her speedy recovery from her ordeal. The message sounded genuine, implying his real concern, but she still felt doubtful.

Danny called towards the end of the morning to see if she was free for lunch but she declined, explaining there was too much to do, mainly auditions, and telling him they would manage with a sandwich in the office.

Valentina tried again to ring Charlie but again there was no reply. He was out and hadn't bothered to see if she was recovered after her frightening experience. Seething with hurt and irritation, she nevertheless became aware of relief that the engagement was over before it had begun. Charlie was not the love of her life. She had been feeling very much alone and she'd had an aching need to have someone special in her life, someone who loved and cared for her. Charlie was kind, gentle and so easy to be with, she had mistaken her need for love.

There were three applicants for her job to be interviewed that day and each was more useless than the last. With a sigh, she checked the list of people they had decided were worth seeing and as there were so few, she asked Gillian to re-advertise in several trade magazines and phone around the agencies once again.

Claire came into the office as Gillian was leaving. She asked Valentina if she and Charlie were meeting that evening.

"I haven't heard from him," Valentina replied briskly. "Not since the party disaster. I've tried to ring him but there is no reply."

"The flowers?" Claire nodded to the huge bouquet, stooping to smell their fragrance.

"From Peter and John."

"Oh, I see. Then if you're on your own, d'you fancy going to the cinema? My treat, a belated thank you for our weekend?"

"With Gillian leaving early, I don't think I can," Valentina told her. "I'll be lucky to get away before seven."

They met instead for a snack meal. Valentina didn't want to — she was exhausted — but again sensed in the strange girl that lingering need to talk. Claire talked a little about her mother, whose name Valentina didn't learn. Claire was so used to keeping her life a secret it was unlikely that she would ever trust anyone enough to give names and details, Valentina thought sadly.

Claire showed her a few photographs of herself, though, taken with her father when she was very much younger. "My father died when I was three and Mum and I were very close, then when I was fourteen she married again."

"How long since you spoke to your mother? Is it worth trying again?"

"I frequently try to talk to her but she refuses. She slams down the phone as soon as she hears my voice."

"You must know where she lives? Can't you go and see her?"

"No, never!" Claire was adamant. "She mustn't know who I am or what I do."

Valentina wondered why talking to her was important yet seeing her was out of the question. Risking Claire withdrawing her confidence, she asked her.

"I don't want her in my life before we can talk and be friends. She's so angry, she'd ruin everything for us. My career, Ray's happiness, everything. How would we cope with the publicity?"

The evening was very warm, the London pavements sending out the day's stored heat, the fumes of cars and buses choking in the still air. Valentina was achingly tired. It had been a long and busy day and she was still weary after the trauma of the previous evening, so she excused herself from Claire and treated herself to a taxi home. The flat would be empty as Gillian had gone to her parents' and was going straight to the office the following morning. Tonight, though, she would have preferred company. Not to talk, she was too weary for that, but just to have someone there.

Her heart fell like a broken lift when she saw her parents standing outside her door. All she wanted was to flop into bed. Now she would have to listen to their version of events.

236

She made coffee and tried to concentrate on what was being said. Something about Moke, predictably.

"He's coming home to settle down," her mother said. "So don't start putting ideas in his head about music and London, right?"

"I don't think he plans to stay, Mam. He wants to have a break then he'll come back and try again."

Valerie looked knowingly at Dewi. "Didn't I tell you what she's like? There you go, Valentina, encouraging him. Leave him alone. I don't want him unsettled all over again."

"I don't have any influence on Michael, Mam. He never listens to me or he wouldn't have come to London in the first place. I certainly don't encourage him to stay," she insisted wearily.

"Nonsense. It was you with your bragging about your wonderful job and the famous people you meet that made him leave home," Valerie insisted.

"I told you about my job because I thought you'd be p —" She was about to say proud of me, but even with her mind dulled by tiredness she knew that was as unlikely as snow storms before morning.

"When do you open the shop?" Dewi asked but without giving her daughter a chance to reply, Valerie interrupted.

"What a crazy idea. Someone like you running a business? You've got to be educated for that sort of thing."

"I know the business, Mam, and —"

"It's sure to fail, isn't it, Dewi? And who will help you out of the mess, then, eh?"

Valentina sat while her mother went on about her plans to find a good job for Moke, only half hearing what was said. Her mind was tumbling with thoughts of a driver who was nothing more than a dark, threatening silhouette, and the dark passages of the new flat, empty and redolent with danger and fear. Sleep overtook her temporarily and she jerked back to hear her father insisting they left.

"Come on, love, we'll leave Valentina to sleep. From the look of her she's exhausted."

"Thanks, Dad." She sighed with relief. "I admit I'm not feeling at my best."

"All right, I've done my best to make her see sense but I doubt it's done any good."

Dewi kissed her and wished her luck in a self-conscious whisper. Her mother's parting shot was, "At least you've had the sense not to marry Charlie. He's too old and set in his ways."

Valentina thought that for once her mother had got it right.

She undressed quickly and prepared for bed. Ten minutes after her parents had gone, as her head was about to hit the pillow, there was a knock at the door. With a groan she got up to open it. Charlie was standing there with a bottle of wine in his hand. Beside him, reaching higher than his waist, was a huge basket filled with roses.

"I guessed you'd need a day to recover and I didn't want to talk to you while you were at work," he explained. "It was difficult but I made myself wait until this evening."

She said nothing, just stared at him.

"I've been standing across the road in a porch for two hours waiting for your parents to leave," he went on. Then he took her in his arms and said softly, "Forgive me, my darling. I must have been insane not to worry when you didn't turn up. I was like a manic conductor, keeping the orchestra in order when the house was falling down, doing the job he'd been programmed to do and ignoring the chaos around him."

She still didn't speak, just stood there, making no effort to hide a yawn.

"I went out early. I walked by the river where we first had lunch together, to think about us and how I'd let you down so badly. I'm so very ashamed, my darling."

He came inside and closed the door behind him then followed her into the living room. He gave her a chaste kiss and looked into her eyes; he saw tiredness and pushed her gently into the bedroom and onto the bed. "I won't stay now. You need sleep. We'll just have a drink together and I'll leave. We'll do the serious talking later, when you're fully recovered." He went to find glasses and a corkscrew, chatting intermittently as he opened and closed drawers in the search. "Tony rang, to see how you are. Wasn't that kind? And Phil, and several other friends. You have a lot of loving friends, Valentina." When he came back with two brimming glasses of wine, Valentina was asleep.

He sat looking at her for a while, regretting his stupidity in believing she had put something before him and their engagement party. How had he been so easily convinced? Phil's words came back to him about how she had done something similar to him when they had first come to London, walking away when everyone believed they would marry. He had believed Phil, convinced she was one of those women who lose their nerve when it comes to a commitment. Leaving a note for her to find when she woke, he let himself out of the flat and returned to his place in the restaurant.

The wall was updated but Valentina had hardly glanced at it and unusually none of the new listings penetrated her tired brain. It wasn't until much later that Valentina really studied it and memorized the names and sequence. She sat with Gillian and they both cheered when Danny's name took its place more than halfway up the list. Claire's name was there too and, reminding her friend that both were written by Bob, Valentina suggested she rang him and congratulated him.

"I can't. Much as I wish it wasn't so, it's over and was from the moment I knew I was expecting Little Lever."

"Talk to him," Valentina insisted, but Gillian shook her head, her eyes beginning to redden.

"He was at the party but he didn't speak to me. I might be wrong but he seemed to go out of his way not to stand near me."

"He must feel as awkward as you do. Someone needs to bang your heads together."

The morning was so hectic they needed to get out for a while and they went to Mary and Joe's for a sandwich, having allowed themselves twenty minutes.

240

Mary came across and kissed Valentina and made the usual enquiries.

"My Charlie is very rigid sometimes. You'll be so good for him, Valentina," she said.

Valentina hugged her and, knowing this couldn't be left until a better time, said, "It's over between us, Mary. I'm so sorry. I couldn't imagine a better mother-in-law than you but I don't have what Charlie needs. It's best, to be honest."

"What did Charlie say?"

"I haven't told him. I fell asleep when he came last night. He left a note to say we'll talk about it when I've recovered. But it's over. I'm so sorry, Mary. Please don't discuss it until I've made it clear to Charlie, will you?"

"Perhaps he'll persuade you to give it another try?"

Valentina shook her head.

That evening, Charlie came again and Valentina, still not ready for the unpleasant discussion that would end their relationship, asked her flatmate to tell him she wasn't available. Gillian answered the door and explained that Valentina was still suffering from her ordeal, but he insisted on coming in.

Once Gillian had left them to put Little Lever to bed, Valentina took a deep breath and said, "It's no good, Charlie. I love you, but in the way I love Danny, and Gillian, John and Peter, no more than that. Not enough to marry you. I'm sorry, you're a lovely man, and I really thought it would work, but Sunday evening showed me clearly that you and I have too many differences."

He argued and pleaded but she wouldn't be swayed. She was lonely for affection and love and Charlie was so big and strong and reliable — but she knew that if she married him it would never be enough, for either of them. With the new flat to get used to and the new business looming up with all its incipient worries, she felt more vulnerable than ever before. It was a lot to tackle alone. To relax and sink into his arms would be so easy but she knew it would be so wrong. Charlie didn't deserve that.

Over the next few days, flowers and gifts arrived from him. He also wrote several notes and made phone calls — most of which were intercepted by Gillian.

"Once he accepts I made a terrible mistake, I hope we'll be friends," Valentina sighed. "But it's going to take some time."

With Gillian's help, Valentina wrote letters to party guests and explained why she was returning their gifts. The engagement, she wrote, was off and would never again be on.

She felt very guilty for the emotional see-saw she had made Charlie ride, but gradually her mind was filled with other things. Her mother rang, very irate, telling her Moke had been home but had left again. That her mother blamed her, Valentina didn't need telling. Then her father rang to tell her Moke had stolen money from the house.

"I'm not his keeper!" she told them both angrily, and immediately felt the rush of returning guilt.

"I'm beginning to wish this new shop was somewhere miles away and with no telephone," she told Gillian.

The shop Valentina was renting was small and, having been boarded up for a long time, dirty and shabby. Hardly a place to encourage people to come and relax and choose music. With Gillian helping when she could, she gradually cleared it of abandoned rubbish and carpeting and tattered curtains. She always went back to the flat to bath — nothing would persuade her to use the one above the shop even though the bathroom had been thoroughly cleaned and fitted with a brand new door.

Moving old carpet revealed worn and weak floorboards and touching wallpaper loosened plaster that showered down, often onto a floor she had just scrubbed. It seemed hopeless at times and she was tempted to tell Charlie she needed him, to share the problems; to have someone always there to boost her morale would have been a luxury. There were other times when she was so excited at the prospect of bringing order from the chaos, dealing with it all on her own, and these times became more and more the norm.

Builders came and went, dealing with the more serious damage. Gradually the neglected property became a place where she could take off a coat and put it down without finding it covered with dust and plaster and rubble when she picked it up again. One day soon, this would be her home.

At the start, every time they went there, the place looked worse than on a previous visit. Now, every evening, when she and Gillian called to look at the progress, things were better. Walls were painted over fresh new wallpaper and carpets covered the uneven floors. Curtains hung at sparkling windows. The flat was a hasty job, as it was necessary only to make it fit to live in, but without involving a lot of time or expense. It was the shop that was most important and its design was the first consideration. There was so little room she dare not waste an inch by including anything she didn't really need.

Once news of her acquisition had spread, she had received offers from the record companies willing to design it for her. She had already been told they would arrange for the window to be topically dressed every week. Popular music was a transient business. With new lists out every Tuesday, it was not a good idea to have a display based on the previous week's top ten with a centrepiece of last week's number one. They would re-dress it every week when the new lists were announced.

One company sent a representative of the shopfitters to see her and he told her that, small as it was, she would need to partition off a section of the shop to hold her stock. This area would be fitted with slim sections to hold her supplies, he explained.

Danny happened to be there when the man came to check on a few measurements and he at once took an interest. After that, he came often and asked how he could help. Valentina explained the system and talked of her plans. It was a relief to discuss her fears as well as her hopes. Danny was a good listener, hearing her out when she was convinced she would fail, then shooting her nebulous arguments down in flames with a few words and a lot of laughter.

During those weeks, with Danny a regular companion, she had mood swings with every success and setback. Full of hope one minute, the next flooded with despair. She would be calmly discussing something and Danny would misunderstand or something would make her lose her temper. Danny took it without showing offence or disappointment, saying constantly with his lovely, soothing Irish voice, "It'll be grand."

The selling display in the main area of the shop consisted of sloping display units, each containing record sleeves. These were separated under several headings and, not wanting to sell only top singles, were varied in appeal. Each record sleeve was placed in a plastic "master bag". This transparent bag bore the label containing details of the artist, band or group, plus the date purchased and all the other information Valentina would need to re-order. A customer would make his choice and take the empty sleeve to the counter, where Valentina would pick up the record from the stock area to sell. The empty sleeve would then be returned to the display. When the last one was sold, the master bag would be put on a table, a reminder to re-order.

Danny understood immediately and wrote clear, easy-to-read signs for the slots holding the stock, in alphabetic order, one section for each of the recording companies.

A record player was built in to play both background music and to allow customers to hear a single or a track before buying. To help acoustics in the high-ceilinged room, the shopfitters hung circles of polystyrene, which improved the sound and gave the place a modernistic appearance. To Valentina it was magic and she grew impatient to start her new business. Then her mother's words would come back to her and she would see the shop falling back into its previous abandoned chaos, leaving her financially ruined.

Until the premises had reached the stage when it looked like it might one day be a record shop, Valentina still worked with Gillian and Ray Everett. Inevitably, a few weeks before she was to leave, Gillian, with the rest of the staff, decided to arrange an office party to send her off and wish her luck.

"I'll be embarrassed, having you all seeing me off as if I were a long-standing, valued old dear about to retire," Valentina told Gillian with a laugh, but she was pleased to know they thought well enough of her to arrange it. "What shall I do, ask Mary and Joe to book a table?"

"You are to do nothing!" Gillian said in mock alarm. "You don't get involved at all. Just come at the time and the place we tell you. Right?"

"As long as it isn't at Charlie's Restaurant. I don't want to be reminded of that occasion." She shivered as she remembered. It was a Saturday evening in September, a few weeks before she was actually going

246

to leave, and the venue was a room in a pub not far from the river. A taxi was ordered for eight and Gillian had made arrangements to leave the baby with the woman who looked after him during the week. Having been told it was a pub, Valentina wasn't too anxious. There wouldn't be many there, just the staff, plus a few of her friends.

"A long cotton skirt and a cheesecloth top will suffice, won't it?" she asked. "It's so hot."

Gillian disagreed. "Oh no you don't! I want you looking the part of a successful businesswoman. Wear something bold and dramatic."

More people turned up than she had expected. Instead of just the staff, others had heard of the party and had either wangled an invitation or gatecrashed. Danny was there, standing at the door waiting for her, and inside she saw her boss Ray talking to Charlie. Amid the sea of faces she was startled to see Tony Switch shouldering others out of his way to kiss her cheek and wish her well, the flash of a camera ensuring the gesture was recorded.

She reached for Danny's hand as she went forward to the bar, where drinks were available with money handed in beforehand. She was hardly surprised to see Phil. He always knew what was going on in her life. Standing behind him was her brother, Moke. He was dressed in a long robe with lots of braid, and wearing flowers and row upon row of beads.

"Moke!" She smiled. "I'm so pleased to see you! Have you —"

"No, I haven't rung Mam," he interrupted warningly. "And if you mention Mam or Dad just once, I'll strip off my clothes and do a streak! And it wouldn't be the first time," he added with a grin.

Claire arrived at ten o'clock and sang a song with Danny. There were dozens of good luck cards displayed around the bar and Bob Lever called briefly and gave Danny a card to pass to Valentina later.

As Bob was leaving, the babysitter arrived with Gillian's baby and he stopped in the doorway and stared down at the sleeping child with a frown. Seeing him there, Gillian's heart gave a lurch and she pushed her way through to collect the baby and talk to him, but before she reached the doorway Bob had gone.

CHAPTER
FOURTEEN

The search for a person to take over her job was a little embarrassing for Valentina. She had turned down so many applicants perhaps Ray thought she was trying to make it appear she was impossible to replace. Most of the letters she received were clearly by people who understood the music scene but not in the wider sense that was necessary for the complicated job. Few women had thought it worth applying for such a high-profile position. Her trail-blazing effort of opening up the possibility of a woman in this top job was going to fizzle out.

She remembered how hard she had worked to convince Ray his decision had been the right one, and there had been plenty of people who had wanted her to fail. Including Phil, of course. But she had been successful and she held the receding hope that another woman would come along and fill her shoes. It didn't seem very likely, though, she thought, looking at the new batch of applicants.

Some were from people selling records at small outlets, others were musicians themselves and thought this would be sufficient qualification, unaware of the organizational skills required to run the busy office, and the important decisions that had to be made.

One letter sounded particularly promising and to her delight it was from a woman. The writer, a Myfanwy Mayhew, had been involved with a record and music shop of her own, and she had a collection of records and sheet music dating back to the thirties. Popular music was her hobby as well as her career and she lectured occasionally on the influence of music on the young and how music style charted the changes in fashion and dance and general attitudes.

Following the spate of ads placed by Gillian, Valentina chose three for interview, including Myfanwy Mayhew, and arranged them for the following day.

The first two were faint possibilities but when she met Myfanwy Mayhew she knew she had found the perfect person for the job. The woman was a musician, playing piano and guitar, and a singer in a choir and also a solo performer. She had never made a record; had never wanted to.

"I've been content," she told Valentina and Gillian, "to run the business and enjoy making music as a pleasurable hobby. Now, with my son ready to take over, I want to do something more demanding."

"Your husband?" Valentina coaxed. "Does he take an interest in your talents?"

"I'm divorced," was the reply. "I only have my son, Jeremy."

"Is he musical?"

"None of my abilities have been passed on." The woman spoke harshly and Valentina wondered if there was some disappointment over her son's inability to follow his mother.

"Before we go, I'd like to arrange for you to meet my boss. Can you manage sometime today? Say four o'clock?"

"Of course, and thank you." Myfanwy smiled as she left.

Valentina gave a huge sigh of relief. She looked at Gillian. "She's the one. I think we've made a real find there." Gillian agreed. They talked about the woman for a while and looked at her letters of recommendation and her references. She certainly sounded exactly what was needed. Now she had to convince Ray. The woman had to be someone he could work with.

Claire made one of her occasional visits that morning and invited Valentina to go to a function where new recordings would be heard. One of the reasons for the evening was to introduce a singer with a style similar to her own.

"It's a bit of a publicity thing," Claire explained. "The usual crowd will be there, including Tony Switch and several other radio names. Television too. Tony gave me tickets and suggested I invite you. It won't do any harm for you to be seen there, Valentina. More customers for the shop, eh?"

During lunch Valentina and Gillian talked again about Myfanwy Mayhew and the end of their search.

"Won't it be marvellous if Ray decided to appoint another woman? I'll be so relieved if this works out. I didn't want to leave before Ray was satisfied with a replacement and I knew you wouldn't want the responsibility, even for a short time. Little Lever is enough for you at the moment, isn't he?"

"Perhaps, if I hadn't decided to keep him, I might have applied for the job."

Valentina looked alarmed. "But I didn't think you were even slightly interested?"

"Oh, don't worry, I would never want something so difficult. I like being a support," Gillian assured her friend. "I could never cope with being on the front line."

"If I'd thought you had even the slightest idea of going for the job, I'd have helped you every way I could. You must know that."

"I wouldn't have been suitable, we *both* know that. I lack the confidence and that's what you need plenty of to do what you do," she said with an affectionate smile.

"And this Myfanwy Mayhew? D'you think she's got it?"

"I have no doubts about her."

"You do have plenty of confidence, Gillian. And you're brave and that's even better. You faced up to being a mother and you're doing a marvellous job caring for Little Lever. I'm truly impressed. If only you could be brave when it comes to Bob."

Myfanwy Mayhew came at four, and Valentina opened the door to Ray's room and closed it behind her. She gestured "fingers crossed" to Gillian and waited.

They didn't have to wait long. There was a scream of anger and a torrent of words in a high-pitched tone, before the door opened and was flung back on its hinges. The woman burst through, still shouting abuse at a white-faced Ray, who followed her to the door.

In the main office doorway she bumped into Claire, who was waiting for Valentina, and the girl covered her face and gave a low, ululating moan. The two women then stared at each other.

"I — I knew it was you," Myfanwy said in a guttural tone, close to Claire's face. She strode past Claire then, hitting out at her to move out of her way.

Claire was holding onto the door she had clung to, to save herself from falling from the blow. At the outer door, Myfanwy turned and screamed a stream of abuse at her before hurrying out. The door slammed behind her and Ray came forward and slapped Valentina's face.

The ensuing silence was electrifying. Valentina stared in disbelief then jumped up from her chair and backed away from Ray's malevolent stare, her eyes fixed on him in horror. In support but understanding nothing, Gillian ran to stand beside her. Claire remained at the door, still holding on, needing its support. Valentina was unaware of them; she was mesmerized by the hate on Ray Everett's face.

The tableau seemed frozen for ever, but Valentina finally asked fearfully, "What have I done?"

"Are you pretending not to know?" Ray spat out. "You brought her here and you pretend you didn't know what you were doing?"

"I swear I didn't. I received a letter, I interviewed her and that's all I know."

"She's my mother," a tearful voice whispered and Valentina turned her head to see the anguish on the girl's face.

"Oh my God!" It was Valentina's turn to cover her face. "Claire, I promise you, I didn't know!" she wailed. She didn't know what else to say. She wanted to go to Claire and hold her, comfort her, but she was unable to move, locked in the tableau, staring from Claire to Ray and back. Neither looked at the other; the pain was too great for both of them.

"I'd better go," Valentina said at last. Fumbling, hardly able to see for the tears that filled her eyes, she found the letter with its Herefordshire address. "This is all I know." She handed him the letter with arms that were stiff with shock. Her whole body was rigid and she wondered how she'd be able to get to the underground and home.

Beckoning Gillian to follow, she went through the door, passing the unmoving Claire. She turned as she reached the outer door and spoke to Claire in a shaky voice. "I'll be home all evening if you want to talk. I promise you, I didn't know who she was, and I also swear I've told no one about this. No one."

Valentina sat up long after midnight, but Claire didn't come.

Working in the office was unbelievably difficult. Ray didn't speak a word to her and it was he who arranged the remaining interviews, ignoring her offer to continue to sieve out unsuitable applicants to save him time. Every evening, she fled the building like a prisoner escaping an evil master. It was Gillian who told her the appointment had been made and she wasn't surprised to learn that it was a man, and one she had discarded as unsuitable.

On the day she finally left, she did something she had wanted to do ever since that unfortunate appointment. She telephoned Myfanwy Mayhew. She was shaking when the woman answered and it was tempting to replace the phone, but she managed to say, "Mrs Mayhew. It's Valentina Robbins. Please, don't hang up. I want to tell you how sorry I am about what happened."

To her relief the woman replied calmly.

"It wasn't your fault, Miss Robbins. That much was clear from the expression on your face. You know how news gets around when people who are in the same business get together. You probably won't know him, but it was someone called Phil Blackwood. He indirectly told me about the vacancy when we met at a charity function. I'd never have heard about it otherwise and I certainly hadn't thought of moving to London."

"Yes," Valentina said thickly. "I know Phil Blackwood."

After a few pleasantries in an effort to hide her alarm, Valentina rang off, convinced that somehow Phil had discovered Claire's secret and had arranged the unpleasant meeting, making sure she was involved. She met Bob Lever as she was heading for the underground and told him what had happened. The secret was out now; there was no longer any need to hold her promise to Claire.

"He really must hate me," she said, on the edge of tears. "What shall I do?"

"The least you say the better. It could be nothing more sinister than a coincidence."

"No. It was Phil."

"You've moved away from there anyway."

"Not far, though. I'd hoped to buy my stock from Music Round. In fact, my business depends on it."

Moving out of the flat they had shared and into the rooms above the shop was not easy for Valentina. The excitement of opening her own business was intoxicating but it was not enough to make her forget her confrontation with Claire and Ray. Day by day, as the actual hour drew near, the girls carried boxes of bedding and china and small items of furniture they had gathered during their tenancy. No longer having the use of Ray's car, John, Peter, Danny and others helped.

"The more people in and out the better it will be for her," Gillian told Danny and he made sure he was there whenever they needed transport.

Larger items of furniture had been bought, mostly second hand. Armchairs and a couch were covered with cheerful Mexican-style blankets to hide their worn appearance. Chests of drawers and cupboards had been cheerfully painted. Long before they moved in, it was looking like a home. But still the shadows troubled Valentina. She imagined movements where there were none and an unexpected sound would startle her. She tried to hide her nervousness from Gillian but Gillian had foreseen her anxiety and together with Danny had done everything possible to ease the transfer from the old and familiar to the new and strange.

When she walked through the door on the day she would move in permanently, Valentina tensed herself for what she called the heeby-jeebies. But the air was filled with music, and the sound of voices and laughter flowed down the stairs to greet her. Flowers had been arranged in vases both in the entrance hall and at intervals up the stairs. People — at that time she had no idea who — had heard her arrive and faces peered over the banister with welcoming smiles, and hands holding drinks aloft waved greetings.

The first people she recognized were casual acquaintances who had so recently attended the party intended for the engagement that never happened. Superstitiously she began to think of ill omens. Then, as she reached the top of the stairs, all fears faded as familiar and loved faces swam into view. Danny stepped forward and hugged her, and wished her well. To her delight, her mother appeared, although, as usual, she was unable to hide the fact that she was looking for Moke!

Charlie called but couldn't stay, and Gillian's parents were there, holding Little Lever. Danny had composed a song for the occasion and her eyes sparkled with pleasure as John and Peter somewhat shyly sang it with him. Moke appeared with a bag over his shoulders, obviously hoping to stay.

Gillian saw him and said, "Hello, Moke, your mother's over there. She'll be so pleased to see you."

She turned to look for Valerie and when she looked back, intending to tell Moke where Valerie was sitting, she saw him running down the stairs, stumbling in his haste not to be seen, and out of the flat. There didn't seem much point in telling anyone he'd been there as, by the time she had gone down and opened the door, he were nowhere to be seen.

"We aren't stopping, love," John called, as Peter handed her a glass of wine.

"And we don't intend getting you drunk," Peter added with a smile as Danny came with another. "Pleasant as that might be."

There were about twenty people crowded into the small room and it was a smiling Valentina who stood beside Gillian and waved them off about an hour later.

"Howzat for a welcome to our new home, then?" Gillian said proudly.

"Perfect. Thanks for using some of your precious holidays to help." She turned to her mother. "Where are you staying, Mam?"

Valerie waved vaguely. "It's all right, I've got a room. It's only an hour away."

"Give me your address and I'll ring you. We could go out for a meal then I can show you the shop," she offered but Valerie shook her head.

"I won't be staying long. Just till I find your brother."

"I don't think we should tell her he was here," Gillian whispered. "He looked scruffy, didn't he? And not smelling exactly sweet. Sleeping rough, I suspect. I ran after him to persuade him to stay but as soon as I mentioned your mother he ran off."

258

Gillian's parents stayed to help clear up after the impromptu party and insisted on taking them out for a meal, taking the sleeping Little Lever with them.

"You haven't eaten a thing and you can't cook on your first day," Gillian's mother said. "Besides, it's all arranged."

They ate at a small restaurant but didn't stay long as Gillian's parents were driving back to Surrey. It wasn't more than two hours before they were back at the flat. There was music playing, Gillian having left the radio on, and lights shone.

"Go on up," Gillian said. "I'll push the bolt on the door." They shared the pleasant chore of bathing Little Lever and getting him ready for bed. He was an amiable baby and seemed unperturbed by his change of address. There were still a few boxes to unpack and Valentina filled the cupboards and looked at the surplus in dismay.

"I thought we'd have more room." She was pulling a box filled with books when Gillian held her arm and shook her head.

"There's all tomorrow to do this. I think we've done enough for today."

"I'm putting it off, aren't I?"

"Not any more you're not. I'm running a bath for you and then you're going to sleep."

Valentina lay for a long time in the strange room, reassured by the knowledge that her friend was only inches away in the next room and the phone was beside her bed. She woke once and thought she heard someone at the door. She went down to see a letter on the mat, a good luck card from one of the neighbouring shops.

"With all the good will we've been offered, we can't be anything else but happy here," Gillian said when she read it.

Gillian insisted they went for a walk the following day. It had been a long, hot summer which had shortened the flowering season on many blooms and scorched the grass in the parks. The ground shimmered in the heat. On their return she made sure Valentina went in first. Gillian knew she had to discourage her from enlarging her fears or she would never be happy spending the night there alone. Nothing untoward happened over the next few days, and although Valentina woke several times and had to go down and check the doors, she woke reasonably refreshed on the Monday morning, excited at the prospect of her first day as the proprietress of a London record shop.

She opened the doors of the shop at nine o'clock and at ten past was convinced she would never have a customer. By half past she had sold fifteen records and people were still coming. Danny came at ten and stayed to help serve the steady flow of people coming through the doors, some to buy, others to look. Peter called at lunchtime on his way to see a prospective buyer at a property nearby, bringing sandwiches and two bottles of Perrier in case she couldn't stop for lunch. She shared them with Danny while fussing over her stock like a hen with troublesome chicks.

At 2.30 the shop suddenly emptied and they became aware of a crowd gathering outside. She and Danny looked out curiously. "What are they waiting for?"

"Nothing to do with us, me darlin', so why worry?"

A news reporter came at three and asked when Tony Switch was due to arrive.

"Tony? I'm not expecting him." She looked at Danny, who shrugged.

"You must be! He's opening the shop, isn't he?"

Valentina looked again at Danny. "You haven't arranged this, have you?"

"Not me. What about Gillian?"

Remembering Gillian's feelings for Tony, she was vehement in her negative reply.

A ragged cheer was heard and she lowered the volume of the record that was playing and went to the door. The cheer increased in volume and enthusiasm as a car drew up and Tony Switch stepped out. He knocked ostentatiously at the door of the shop and walked in. Flashbulbs lit the interior and several cameras captured the scene as a startled Valentina was kissed by Tony.

"This time it'll be publicity for both of us, eh?" he whispered. He bought two records, one by Elton John and one by David Bowie. He kissed the fans, signed autographs and disappeared into the waiting car before Valentina had recovered.

Later, she and Danny wrote to thank him and it was delivered with a bottle of champagne. "Whatever his reason, he put us well and truly on the map," Valentina said.

"All in all, a very exciting first day," she told Gillian later.

"Did Charlie come?"

"No."

Valentina hadn't been to the cottage for several weeks. Besides the lack of a car, her weekends had been filled checking orders and accounts, cleaning, and shopping for food, and the cottage in the Welsh village seemed part of a previous life. Gillian had stayed with her; the usual pattern of five days at work then the weekends with her parents had been broken and Valentina was grateful.

"Do you mind if I go home this weekend?" Gillian asked. "It seems an age since Mum and Dad saw Dylan, and I don't want him to forget them."

"Of course I don't. I wish I could go away. I haven't seen Pink Cottage for weeks."

"Why don't you go after you close the shop on Saturday? You'd be there in a few hours and have the whole of Sunday, and — oh, the car," she remembered. "Isn't there someone you'd like to take? Someone with a car?"

Valentina shook her head; she still wanted the place to be for special friends only. "Perhaps I'll go by train and bus and taxi. But not yet."

Tony Switch called later that day and asked how business was progressing. Seeing him walk in, Valentina was afraid he was about to ask for his fee for his personal appearance. She still didn't know who arranged it.

262

"Whose idea was it that you officially opened the shop?" she asked as he browsed through the selection of records.

"Phil's, of course. Now you and I are friends I didn't need much persuading."

"Thank you. But Phil? I'm surprised. I didn't think he wanted me to succeed."

"He's proud of you. He tells everyone to come here to buy their records, and working at a record counter, he's risking the sack!"

In South Wales, Valentina's father, Dewi, sat staring at the television, not seeing, not hearing, as programme followed programme until the evening's offerings finished. He was so deep in thought, it took several minutes before it penetrated his mind that there was nothing more to see. After stretching over and switching off the set, he continued to sit until the chill of the early morning crept into his body and reminded him of the time. Still he didn't go to bed. Surely there must be something he could do to end this farce his life had become, bring Valerie back and return to how they were?

While Valerie was in London he had lost his job. Without her to wake him and set his breakfast on the table, his time-keeping had slid into disarray. The days had hung heavily and he wasn't even able to write or telephone to tell her about his dismissal. She hadn't given him an address.

Tomorrow he would find something to do to please her when she got home. Perhaps do some decorating?

Start on their bedroom and work his way through the whole house. He sat on the bed, which he hadn't changed since Valerie had left, and made a list of what he would need. He quickly decided there wasn't sufficient money. Valerie had taken what they had saved. With some relief, he gave up the idea.

Valerie Robbins, unaware of her husband's sleeplessness, lay awake in a cheap boarding house making plans of her own. She had found a trace of Moke and learned he was with a group of people who were following what was still called the Hippy Trail. West Country was all she knew but she would surely hear of him if she persevered. She wanted her son back. She wanted him near her, to blank out the loneliness of her existence.

If Dewi couldn't see that, it was time he did. Like her husband, more than 150 miles away, she sat on an unsavoury bed and made a list. She had enough money to travel by coach to Taunton, and it was there she would start her enquiries. She wouldn't give up on her son. She wouldn't. Dewi would have to accept that. She took out a pen and paper and began to write to him, pointing out that she had no intention of returning until she was able to bring Moke back with her.

CHAPTER
FIFTEEN

The record business took off in a way that made even the most optimistic of friends marvel. Valentina was kept so busy selling, reordering and trying to keep up with the latest artists that every night she fell into bed in sheer exhaustion. Her fears of living in the flat faded and even when Gillian returned to her usual pattern of spending weekends with her parents, nothing kept her from sleep.

Danny spent a lot of time helping and she admitted to Gillian that without him she wasn't sure she could have coped.

"He seems to know when I need him and he walks into the shop with that smile of his and starts dealing with customers, who melt at his approach. He never forgets to make notes of anything we need. Danny is an absolute marvel," she finished.

"Anything more than that?" Gillian asked.

"Nothing more," Valentina said sadly. "I don't think I'm capable of loving someone and having them love me back."

"I saw Bob today," Gillian said, equally sadly.

"Did you talk?"

"No. He was with a crowd of musicians organizing a concert in aid of some charity. At the Kingsway Hall, I believe."

"Get tickets and we'll go."

"I can't. There's the baby in case you've forgotten."

"Forget Little Lever? No way! Ring the babysitter and arrange it. Come on, Gillian. You and Bob have to talk."

"There's no point. There was this girl with them, hanging on to his arm like a shipwrecked sailor clinging to a rock."

"You know what it's like with these people; there's always a girl showing how willing she is. You never let that worry you before."

"Not when we were married, but we aren't any more. I'm here with someone else's baby and he's free to do what he wants."

"He hasn't asked for a divorce, has he?"

It was Danny who took them to the concert, and Danny who tracked down Bob and brought him to see the girls. Valentina watched her friend and Bob together and saw there was still that special spark between them. Something would have to be done.

Meanwhile, life was full and allowed little time for match-making. Besides the shop, Valentina gradually found other outlets for her stock. Buying records relevant to the big London shows, she delivered stock to the theatres, sometimes going along herself, to sell recordings from the performance. Some of these records had been deleted from the lists and bought very cheaply, resulting in a better profit for herself and the theatre management. This was so successful that after a time she didn't have to approach the theatres, they approached her. Life was very exciting and so busy she began to depend more and more on Danny to help her, which he did with obvious pleasure and enthusiasm.

"Don't thank me, me darlin'," he would say with a laugh when she tried to tell him how grateful she was. "Aren't I loving every minute? And knowing I'm helping you, well, it's grand."

She still tried at intervals to find Moke, asking about him whenever she saw someone who had once known him. The crowd changed, but a few regulars always remained, eddying around the periphery of her world. Members of Square Clock still turned up at gigs and she gave them her address and telephone number and asked that they get in touch if they had news of him. But she heard nothing.

She was also worried by the letters she had received from her father. Valerie was still in London searching for Moke and he, Dewi, was beginning to grow tired of living alone with only an occasional postcard.

"Your mother never gives an address," he told her on the phone one evening. "It's crazy, her wandering around looking for Michael. D'you know she's been as far as Gloucester? And Cornwall? It's madness. He knows how to find us — if and when he wants to be found! He only has to contact you or me. So, when you see your mother, tell her to get back home now before I give up on her completely, will you?"

"I can't, Dad. I don't know where she is either."

"She's in London, isn't she? It's easier for you than me."

"Dad, London isn't a village! And I'm building a business that keeps me occupied for twelve or more hours a day."

"You and your importance! Your mother was right about you!" He slammed down the phone.

Phil's record had been a mild success. Tony Switch played it and Marlene apparently liked it.

"She's very sweet but she has absolutely no taste," Tony told his audience.

Phil's personality lacked sufficient excitement for the song to develop into a performance, so the few bookings for personal appearances dribbled to a halt. Discussing a second record with Bob Lever had left him disappointed. The song and the record were a one-off. No exciting future was spread before him. He desperately needed to be someone special, still dreaming of showing Valentina that he was the more talented of them, that he could support her and give her an exciting life, but firmly in his shadow.

He smiled when he thought of the way Valentina's engagement to Charlie had ended. So far as he could discover, on his regular observations at the shop, there was no one to replace that boring restaurateur in her affections, apart from Danny Fortune, who wasn't her type at all. She was his and somehow he'd get her back.

One day he called on Bob to find him dressed in a waterproof jacket, hood up, ready to go out. It was bitterly cold and the rain poured down, darkening the sky and making everyone scurry along the pavements, heads down, anxious to get indoors.

"Sorry, Phil. I can't stop and talk, I'm meeting some of the boys for a rehearsal," Bob explained.

"I'll walk with you to the car," Phil said. "I have this idea for a song and I'd like your opinion." At the corner, Phil spotted a young woman pushing a smart pram, struggling to get it inside a food-store doorway. "Look," he said, pointing. "There's your Gillian's baby."

Bob looked for Gillian but couldn't see her. "Where?" he asked gruffly.

"The dark-haired woman with the pram. She's the baby-minder."

Bob said nothing more, but when he parted from Phil, promising to talk later about the lyrics, he went back and looked for the navy pram. He was in luck: seeing the girl coming out of the store, he ran to help. He waved away her thanks and looked down at Gillian's baby with pain in his heart.

As if he knew him, Dylan's blue eyes twinkled and he gave Bob a wide, knowing smile. Something inside Bob melted. The anger, hurt and bewilderment he had felt since learning about Gillian's pregnancy dissolved away and in its place came enchantment. The child was so beautiful and, in his eyes, so like Gillian. The fine hair was almost white, as were the lashes that framed the clear, blue eyes. The little mouth was soft and so willing to smile.

He stretched out a hand and the baby's tiny fingers clasped it at once. His own fingers looked coarse and dirty against the pale softness of the baby's skin.

"Do you like him?" the young woman asked.

"It's Gillian's baby, isn't it? Gillian Lever?"

"Yes, who are you?"

"Bob, her husband. Tell her he's — he's beautiful."

The young woman smiled. "I think she knows, but I'll tell her you agree."

His emotions were in turmoil. He didn't know whether to laugh, cry or kick something. Back at the flat, he did all three.

Dewi Robbins was finding it difficult to motivate himself. He was unreliable and had lost another job and was making little effort to find another. He still toyed with the idea of doing some decorating, but spent most of his time thinking about it without making a start. He was used to spending the day at the factory, coming home and eating the meal Valerie had prepared, then just sitting watching television. Now, with Valerie still absent, and only her brief messages to comfort him, and no job, there was no routine at all. There were too many hours in a day. He needed something to occupy his time, but repapering the bedroom didn't appeal. It would mean he'd go upstairs to the mess of a part-finished room every evening and his life was miserable enough without that. No, he decided, I'll work on the spare room; that won't be so depressing.

Instead, he sat contemplating his misfortune and waiting for each postal delivery to see if Valerie had

270

bothered to write. He knew he had to do something or he'd go crazy with boredom. Best he started on that wallpapering.

His first task was to empty the room as much as possible and moving the dressing table was first. To make it easier to lift he pulled out the drawers and as he did so, some envelopes and papers and photographs spilled out of the back. With no real enthusiasm for work, he used the excuse to delay and, sitting on the bed, he glanced through them. What he found angered him. She'd kept dozens of letters from that man!

Putting the drawers back in place with hands that trembled with rage, he went downstairs. What was he doing here, sitting around waiting for a woman as uncaring as Valerie? An idea entered and grew in his mind. He sat for three hours without moving, seeing the idea given form and strength, like a bud opening into a flower of many petals, all of them promising him a better life. Taking up pen and paper, he began to draw up a list of things to do. Tomorrow, some magazine had told him, is the first day of the rest of your life.

Having phoned via their neighbours, Valerie put down the phone on Dewi with a half smile. He was so lacking in understanding. She wondered why she had bothered to phone. Didn't he know how dangerous it was for her Michael to be on his own in London? Drugs and muggings, con merchants of all kinds. All watching for a victim, instinctively knowing who was vulnerable. Of course she couldn't go home. Not until she had found him, and persuaded him to go back with her.

She had travelled hundreds of miles in search of him and was now back in London, working in a food bar which offered tea and coffee, sausages and beefburgers in a bun, and she was living in a small room nearby. Having to share both kitchen and bathroom was distasteful. She hated the squalor of bedsit land where, at forty-three, she was out of place.

Many times she had been on the point of going back but always promised herself just one more day. She was determined that she would find Moke and take him home. Besides, she admitted, there was a certain thrill in the unlikely way her life had changed. How many of her friends would have been so daring? She would enjoy relating her adventures to them when she was back in the safety of her home and her marriage. Meanwhile, she went on looking for her son. Her last thoughts each night were of him, and of Valentina whom, she believed, had been the cause of him leaving home and therefore the instigator of all this worry.

"Boasting about her success, urging him to leave home and try his luck, she was," Valerie told anyone who would listen. "And there's that Phil Blackwood too, telling the boy how easy it would be to become a top musician." Valentina and Phil, they were the cause of her living in this horrible house so far away from home. Why couldn't Valentina have stayed at home and married Phil like everyone expected?

She put her thoughts in a long letter to Dewi and continued with the argument they'd had on the phone. She detailed the dangers and how vulnerable her son was. Surely he must understand? A mother couldn't abandon a child. Why couldn't he see that? After checking on her street map to plan her route for the following day, she slept.

By late November, Danny had become a fixture at the shop.

"I'm tired of record making and all the public appearances and the whole celebrity bit," he told Valentina. "And if that makes me ungrateful then it's ungrateful I am. I liked what I did before and I want to continue with that and step back from the rest."

"But you've been doing so well," Valentina protested. "Since you teamed up with Bob Lever, you've had two records that hit the lists. How can you give it all up?"

"With the greatest of ease, me darlin'. In fact, I'd like to work here, in the shop with you, for a while at least, until you get yourself organized with someone permanent. Will you let me do that?"

"I'm doing well and that's mostly because of you. But I don't think I'm ready to employ someone yet, Danny."

"Employ? Who said anything about employ? It isn't money I'm after. I'll help you until you can afford an expert assistant, how's that?"

She admitted it would be a great help. There were other ideas she wanted to try but with the shop taking so much of her time, she'd had to put them aside.

"Oh, Danny! If you would?" Her brown eyes glowed with excitement as the plans she had put on hold came forward to be considered.

"That I would, and the first thing I'll do is insist you go to the cottage for a long weekend, Saturday till Tuesday morning. Mondays aren't busy. You can take my car. You need a breather, someone to take over for a day, and I'm your man."

The cottage was tempting but she decided to leave that treat for a few more weeks. "Later," she said. "There are one or two things I need to try first."

"Such as?"

"I thought I'd contact a few hospitals and factories, places where there's a lunchtime canteen. If I bought some older records cheaply, I might make it pay, what d'you think?"

"You go while I look after the shop, you mean?"

"If you think it's worth a try."

"That I do and of course I'll help."

"Danny, thank you."

"But on condition you take that little holiday first."

She saw the determination in his eyes and nodded. "All right, I'll go and thank you. There won't be much chance later, with Christmas approaching, and I'd love to see the place again."

"Is someone keeping an eye on it for you?"

"Yes, Lillie, who's a part-time barmaid at the inn, goes there from time to time. It'll be lovely to stay there again. Now you've persuaded me, I can't wait."

"I'm glad you agree." He smiled and kissed her cheek. "And there was I thinking you'd be difficult."

"Don't tell anyone about the trip. I don't want a repeat of last time when we were run off the road. I'm asking Gillian and Little Lever to come with me."

274

At the shop door, she put her arms around him and reached up for a kiss. "Thank you, Danny. I don't know how I'd manage without you."

"Let's hope you'll never try," he said, holding her close. They stayed together for a long moment, and from across the road Phil watched and felt anger consume him.

It was time for another lesson. "A reminder that she belongs to me," he muttered. "My granny knew the best way to make someone behave."

Valentina had forgotten to phone to ask Lillie to turn on the heating, so it was surprising to walk into a warm house. The pleasure quickly turned to horror as she saw the mess. The couch had been slept on, pillows and blankets from the bedrooms were strewn over the floor as if the occupants had stood up, discarding the bedding wrapped around them, and just walked until it fell from their legs.

The once-neat living room was a mess of opened and abandoned tins and every utensil had been left used and unwashed. The coffee table was stained with an assortment of spills and broken glass filled a corner near the fireplace where bottles had been thrown.

The girls looked at each other in dismay.

"We can't stay here," Valentina sobbed.

Without touching anything, Valentina looked around the room, tears running down her cheeks. "Who could have done this?"

"Who has a key?" Gillian asked.

Valentina went again into the kitchen and saw that the lock on the back door had been forced, the wood splintered. "A key wasn't needed," she said sadly.

"We have to call the police straightaway," Gillian said. "They might be back and I don't feel happy about that, not with the baby to look after, do you?"

"Let's make a cup of coffee first." Stepping around the filth on the kitchen floor, Valentina managed to find coffee in the stores they had brought and thankfully unpacked some new mugs and a percolator, a present from Danny. They disinfected the tap and everything else they needed to use. There was no way they could touch anything before it had been thoroughly cleaned.

Gillian went upstairs while Valentina waited for the coffee to percolate, to see if the mess continued. As the coffee began to bubble, she came back down and said,

"It's as bad as the rest. You're right, we can't stay here. Best we find a room at the inn and come back tomorrow and arrange for someone to come and help clean up."

"We'll see if there's a spare room at the inn but let's drink this first. I can't stop shivering."

Gathering things they had brought from Danny's car, they were about to close the door on the devastation when a police car pulled up with two policemen. They were politely, but firmly, told to go back inside.

Valentina explained why they were there and what they had found. "No one else uses it," she assured them. "Only myself and a very few friends accompanied by me."

276

"You didn't agree to rent the property to anyone?"

"No, I did not."

"Does anyone else have a key?"

"You've seen the door — they managed well without one!"

Notes were taken and a room at the inn found for them.

Valentina telephoned Danny to tell him what had happened.

"Shall I come?" he said at once.

"We're leaving after breakfast tomorrow. The barmaid, Lillie, has agreed to deal with the clearing up once the police have given permission."

After another talk to the police, this time an inspector, they were allowed to leave. Apparently, their arrival had been noted by several people and no car had been seen there for several weeks. Whoever had stayed there had been on foot.

"Hippies, sure to be," Lillie said, after promising to arrange for professional cleaning. "There are still plenty of them wandering about pretending to have simple needs and living a free and harmless life. A lot of scroungers more like. Peace and love indeed! What a lot of ol' rubbish they talk!"

Valentina and Gillian hardly spoke on the return journey. Dylan slept peacefully for most of the way. They stopped for lunch at a small cafe and telephoned Danny to give him the time of their arrival.

Over the following days they heard little more. The intruders had been and gone without anyone being aware of their presence. Valentina decided to phone the inn every week and talk to Lillie and make sure they hadn't returned. Lillie had contacted a cleaning firm and assured her the cottage was back to its original neatness.

The run-up to Christmas was frantically busy, the shop already an important venue on the parade. Valentina enjoyed the hectic activity but dreaded the moment when the shop closed for the holiday. After their last visit, she didn't want to go to the cottage alone. She didn't want to go home either but felt she should. Her mother was certain to be there and perhaps Michael would decide that Christmas at home was better than Christmas on the street. She hadn't seen either of her parents since the shop opened and as far as she knew her mother had been still wandering the streets in search of her brother. She wrote to tell her parents that she would be travelling down late on Christmas Eve but to her surprise the letter was returned, marked "No longer at this address". She must have written it wrongly. She checked and frowned. The address was correct, so why wasn't it delivered? She threw it aside. She would phone the neighbour later.

With the increase in business brought on by the seasonal buying spree, it was several days before she remembered. On the 22nd, when she dialled Mrs Francis's number, there was no reply. Like a lot of people, she had obviously gone away for the holiday. Christmas, she thought sadly, was a time when most

278

families got together. Hating having to do it, she rang Phil.

"I'll find out for you and ring back," he promised. "But if you don't hear anything I'd just go if I were you. Even the Robbins family will want to be together at Christmas."

Bob called into the shop several times during the run up to Christmas. He asked about the baby and Valentina showed him some photographs Gillian had taken during the summer. He sometimes met the baby-minder out for a walk and talked to her about Dylan's progress. When Valentina suggested it, he refused to see Gillian, always calling when she was at work. Valentina wondered if he was trying, in his own way, to adjust to the idea of the baby before talking to her. If only there was some way she could help them.

Danny had become an indispensable part of her life, involved with the running of the business and occasionally taking her to the functions and meetings she attended, and to gigs where he performed. His car was a shared property; she used it whenever she needed to and if it inconvenienced Danny at all she was never aware of it.

Charlie called often and on occasions took Valentina out for a meal or to a dance. He was relaxed and affectionate but always respectful. She called to see Mary and Joe whenever she was near the cafe and was always welcomed like a dear friend. Danny's parents began to write to her from their home in Essex and Valentina began to wonder if her whole life would be spent on the periphery of other people's family life but she would never have one of her own.

Charlie bought her a beautiful necklace for Christmas and she wished he hadn't but couldn't hurt him by refusing it. She didn't love him and felt ashamed when she remembered how close she had come to marrying him.

Another letter had failed to reach her parents and she had heard nothing from either of them. She bought their gifts and wrapped them, in between decorating the flat, and wondered what would greet her when she eventually reached her home.

On Christmas Eve the shop was full all day and it was still packed out at six o'clock when she intended to close. She had packed her bag and a taxi had been booked to take her to the station at seven. Glancing at her watch and wondering whether she'd make it, she looked up and through the sea of faces she saw her mother enter. She looked thin and pale.

"Thank goodness, Mam! I've been wondering where you were. I haven't heard for ages and I couldn't get in touch. D'you want to travel down with me tonight? Dad's done the shopping, has he?"

"This is your fault, all of it," were Valerie's first words.

Valentina gave a sigh of exasperation. Surely her mother hadn't come just to blame her for her failure to find Moke? "Go upstairs, Mam, and make yourself a cup of tea. I'll come as soon as I can. You can see how busy I am."

280

"You're busy all right, my girl! Too busy for your own family," Valerie complained but she went up to the flat.

The shop finally closed at 6.30. Valentina cancelled the taxi and she and Danny went up to join Valerie. To their surprise, she was crying.

"Mam? What's happened? Is it Moke?"

"I went home and your father has gone."

"Gone? What d'you mean?"

"Gone! Don't you understand the word?"

"Gone where? He didn't have anywhere to go. Did he leave a note?"

"He's gone and the house is let to strangers."

"Come on, Mam, it's a council house, he couldn't sub-let."

"He didn't sub-let, you stupid girl! He gave the council notice and he's left me. I haven't got a home."

Gillian had gone to spend Christmas with her parents so Valentina decided to use her room on a temporary basis. Danny intended driving to Essex but he went out and bought an Italian takeaway, which her mother disliked, and a bottle of wine, of which she didn't approve, then, as he was leaving, Valentina asked him to stay.

"I know you have a long journey, but please could you delay just for an hour? I don't know what to do about this." When her mother had gone to bed, she said, "It's Christmas Day tomorrow and I haven't bought any food. But that's only a temporary problem. The real one is, what am I going to do with Mam? I can't have her living here. It's Gillian and Little Lever's home as well as mine and besides, I run a business from this place. There just isn't room. What shall I do?"

"There's Pink Cottage. Could you bear to let her use it until we find your father and get things sorted?"

"You've never seen it, have you, Danny?"

"No, but I've always hoped you'd show me one day."

"I love it. At least, I did."

"You'll get over the shock of finding it had been broken into and used so badly."

"I suppose I will, but if Mam sees it I'll never feel the same about it ever again. Where I see a beautiful place filled with the warmth and atmosphere of the many loving families it has protected over the hundreds of years of its existence, she'll see a ruin. She won't see the loveliness of its uneven walls, only the crumbling need of paint and repair. The thatch which I think so romantic will be a rotting monstrosity that should be replaced by decent Welsh slate." She looked at him sadly. "I suppose it's the only thing I can do, but I can't take her — she'll have to go on her own."

"I'll drive her there but it will be after Christmas. You can't dump her there without food and without warning. Don't worry, I'm your man. I'll take her as soon as we've sorted things out — if you can persuade her to go!"

"Thank you. It's a pity, though, I'd like to have shown it to you myself."

"I'll drive the last fifty yards with my eyes shut and you can take me when all this trouble is ancient history."

She smiled. "Danny, you're crazy."

He looked at her with a wry smile. "That I am. Over you." He arranged for them to eat at a hotel over the two days and regretfully left to drive to Essex and join his family.

Christmas was miserable. Apart from two splendid meals, the only food was what they could find in the cupboards. With only her morose mother for company and Danny far away, Valentina felt more lonely than at any other time of her life. All day her mother complained and demanded sympathy. All night she could be heard crying. It was with a sense of relief that Valentina opened her eyes three days later, aware that Danny would soon be back and they could reopen the shop.

Enquiries failed to find out where Dewi had gone and there had been no news of Moke. Valerie went to see Phil but came back without learning anything new.

"No one knows anything about Moke," she told her daughter, her voice filled with disbelief. "He seems to have vanished off the face of the earth."

Valentina suggested he might be in Wales and described the mess she had found at the cottage but Valerie refused to believe he had been involved. "Typical of you, always thinking the worst of him!" she complained.

"Could he have gone home?" Valentina suggested.

"Mrs Francis would have told me if he'd turned up there."

"Mrs Francis might be away for Christmas."

"I'd better go back." Valerie stood as though about to leave immediately.

"No, stay here for a few more days. Dad knows where to find me."

"But does Moke know? Has he been told about the shop?"

Valentina hadn't told her mother Moke had been there the day she and Gillian had moved in, or how he had run out when he heard his mother was there. It would not be politic to tell her now.

Valerie refused outright to go to the cottage, to Valentina's secret relief. She stayed at the flat, sleeping on a couch and helping by minding the baby when Valentina and Gillian had to go out in the evening. She even helped in the shop, cleaning, and learning where things went so she could tidy up at the end of each day.

Bob began calling every Saturday and he would buy a record or an album and casually ask how Gillian and Little Lever were getting on.

"Come any evening and you could see for yourself," Valentina told him, failing to hide her exasperation. "You know she goes home every weekend." But he never did.

Every Sunday, Gillian's first words were to ask if he'd been in.

"You're crazy, the pair of you!" Valentina snapped. "Forget your visit to your mother for one week. Be here when Bob calls. Surely you can bend that much?"

"What if he doesn't want to see me?"

"The door will be open. I won't lock him in!" The attempt at a joke reminded her of her own imprisonment in the bathroom and she gave an involuntary shiver.

The following Saturday, Valerie agreed to look after Little Lever for the day while Gillian helped in the shop. Valentina had had great trouble persuading Gillian to stay and see Bob and now Gillian was very nervous. She looked up every time the door opened. Bob came at three and she waited for him to see her, willing him to look up and come to her, talk to her. He went to the jazz section and fingered his way through the selection and, picking out a record, turned and handed it to Danny. Danny nodded and pointed to the counter. "And didn't you see our new assistant?"

At last he approached her. "I'll take this, Gilly," he said, and she took it from him, as speechless as a shy child. Collecting the record from stock, she handed him his choice then gave the empty sleeve in its master bag to Danny to replace on the shelf.

"You haven't given up your job, have you?" Bob asked.

"No, I'm just helping out for today."

"Where's the baby? Do you still call him Little Lever?"

"He's upstairs with Mrs Robbins and, yes, the name seems to have stuck. You don't mind, do you?" she asked anxiously.

"Do I have to wait all day?" an irate customer demanded, waving an empty sleeve. Startled, embarrassed, she turned to serve and when she looked back, Bob had gone.

That night Valerie went out, having heard that a group of young men were sleeping in an empty ex-railway yard a few miles away. It was a dangerous thing to do, wander in such places at night, but when Valentina realized what her mother was planning it was too late to stop her.

At ten o'clock there was a knock at the door and she flew down the stairs to answer, expecting it to be her mother returned. It was Bob.

"I — I wondered if Danny was here," he began. Valentina grabbed him by the shoulders and pulled him inside. "For goodness' sake, Bob, talk to her! I'll be in the shop." Taking no refusal, she pushed him up the stairs then sat on the bottom step waiting for her mother, giving Gillian and Bob privacy to talk. When her mother returned, she made her sit on the stairs too.

"I didn't find him," Valerie whispered when she had been told what was going on.

"He'll turn up. I doubt if he'll spend January and February out in the cold."

Bob didn't stay long but he came again during the week, and the following weekend Gillian again stayed in London.

"I'll have to tell him who Dylan's father is," Gillian told her friend. "I don't think he'll settle for not knowing."

"Then tell him. Get everything out in the open, make sure there are no dark secrets."

"I can't! He'll go away and never come back," Gillian said, her eyes reddening with anxiety.

"You haven't a future if you don't and you might have one if you do. Why throw away that chance?"

286

Sitting on the stairs in the flat one evening, with Valentina in bed and Valerie settled on the couch, Gillian told Bob about her brief and devastating affair. When she told him the man was Tony Switch, she saw pain cross his face and sat holding her breath, waiting for him to speak.

"If you promise me it's over, well, I can live with it," he said gruffly. "I sort of guessed it was him. I saw you once and caught the look you gave him. You were badly hurt, weren't you?"

"Anger for my stupidity was the stronger emotion."

"I love you, Gilly, and I've plenty to spare for Little Lever too."

She woke Valentina up to tell her after Bob had gone and while trying not to wake Valerie, whispering and giggling in their excitement, they opened a bottle of wine and drank to new beginnings.

After that evening, Bob became a regular visitor and on alternate weekends Gillian stayed in London and she and Bob took the baby to parks and to visit his parents, where he exhibited baby Dylan with great pride. In February, Gillian announced they were going to start again, with Little Lever a welcome part of Bob's family.

Valentina was ecstatic but amid her congratulations she selfishly wondered if, now there would be a spare room, she would ever be free of her mother.

CHAPTER
SIXTEEN

Valentina was told that Gillian was moving out at the beginning of April and she helped her friend to move into the flat owned by Bob with both pleasure and regret. She was thrilled that Gillian's future looked so good but knew that without her and the baby, her own life would be less fun.

"I'll miss you and Little Lever," she told her friend as they loaded the last of her possessions into Bob's car. "You'll have to come and see me often. I don't want him to forget his Auntie Valentina."

"I promise. I'll need to keep you up to date with the gossip from the office anyway," a happy Gillian replied. "There's Claire for a start — she's certain to turn up sometime, although there hasn't been a sign of her at the office since that disaster with her mother."

"No, in a strange way it was me she chose to be her confidante. I wish she'd get in touch. She must be desperate to talk over her problems."

It was a Sunday morning and Danny was away all weekend, doing a couple of gigs with a group of his friends. Her mother had also been away, this time searching not for Moke, but Dewi. Valerie still went off for days at a time in her desperate search for her son, wandering around his old haunts, showing photographs and asking questions, although Valentina told her repeatedly that she believed he had left London. If it had been he who had caused the mess in Pink Cottage, it was more likely that he was somewhere in Wales. But Valerie refused to believe her son had anything to do with the break-in and the resultant mess.

The last of Gillian's possessions were stowed away in the large car and Valentina watched as her smiling friend waved an excited goodbye. Behind her the flat was empty. Perhaps she would phone Charlie, see if he was free for lunch with Peter and John. She didn't think she could spend the whole day alone in the silence of the once overcrowded flat As the car pulled away, taking Gillian and her baby, she felt as if part of her was being tugged along with it.

She glanced up the dark stairs and wondered if the ghosts would return to haunt her now she was on her own. She wondered vaguely when her mother would return and hoped it would be before nightfall.

"Tonight," she loudly told her reflection in the mirror, "I'll face being alone, but I'll be a complete coward and leave all the lights on!"

She was about to ring Charlie when he rang her and invited her to dine with his parents. "So you won't be lonely and missing Gillian," he explained.

"Thank you. I'd like that very much. The time is already beginning to stretch out unendingly and it's only eleven o'clock in the morning!"

"I confess to being my usual thoughtless self," he admitted disarmingly. "It was my mother who reminded me you'd be alone in the flat tonight. I intended to ask you out for lunch."

"Either will be fine. The rest of the day will be spent delving into my books and accounts and other endlessly boring stuff, guaranteed to make me sleep."

"I'll stay if you want me to," he offered quietly.

Her heart leapt. It was so tempting, but unfair to give him hope of a future together. "I'll be all right, Charlie," she said, pretending not to understand the implication so clear in his voice. "I've promised myself I'll keep the lights on all night."

"Think of the expense," he joked. "I could prevent such extravagance."

She laughed and he didn't press the point.

The hallway and stairs were lit when she returned at eleven o'clock that night. She had deliberately left every light shining. But the staircase still looked dark and threatening.

"I'll come in with you, shall I?" Charlie said. He used his fingers and gently smoothed away the frown that wrinkled her brow. "Just for a minute or two, to frighten away the shadows?"

She wanted him to and knew that if he did, she'd want him to stay. This wasn't about loving him or not loving him, this was pure funk and she had to fight it. From now on, and far into the future, she would have to face the emptiness and cope with the frightening memories of being locked in the bathroom.

"Thank you, I do appreciate it, love you for it, but the nonsense has to stop right here. I'll have to manage on my own sometime and now is the best time to accept that small fact." She kissed him affectionately and was aware of him clinging until the very last moment, unwilling to let her go, hoping for a change of heart.

She leaned against the door and listened as he walked away, and heard the car engine until it blended with the rest of the traffic, then she slowly walked up the stairs. This was her life from now on, and on, and on, she thought, swamped in melancholy.

Phil watched from across the road. He had seen Charlie pick her up and had driven after them until he had seen where they were heading. So Charlie was in the picture again, he fumed. Wouldn't she ever learn?

He had left his job on the record counter of the store and spent his days watching the shop from his car or from a nearby cafe, or just standing in shop doorways, watching, noting and analyzing her movements. He would have to find a way to make her listen to him. She had to come back to him, then he'd get his life back on track and she'd understand what it was like to be truly loved. Charlie and Danny were a joke compared to how he felt about her. He had to make her understand.

Because her mother called on Phil so often to ask if he had news of Moke, he had become a fairly regular visitor to the flat above the shop, confident of a welcome as long as Valerie was at home. At first Valentina had made it clear he wasn't welcome but when she saw how much her mother valued his apparent concern, she accepted his visits with a little more grace. He talked to Valerie about their neighbours and what was happening at home, gossip passed on by his landlady, with whom he still stayed on his rare visits home, and he always patiently allowed her to repeat time and again her worries about the stupid Moke.

With Valentina he discussed music and musicians, making her laugh at times at the events that were startling or amusing or horrifying but which hadn't reached the media. She was careful not to ask questions about anyone or make strong comments, afraid her remarks would be twisted and passed on. He could be disarmingly pleasant, but she didn't trust him not to make trouble if he could.

She was thankful when midnight passed on that Sunday night without him making an appearance. She lived further away from him now but he still seemed to know exactly where she was and what she was doing. Mainly due, she surmised, to her mother's chattering tongue. She had half expected his knock ever since Charlie had driven off. She slept fitfully, waking frequently to listen for sounds that threatened danger. Twice she got up and made a hot drink and at five o'clock she got up and tried to concentrate on her accounts.

Valerie returned mid morning and Valentina was blasé about her uneventful night. "I was fine," she told her. "Although it will be a long time before I stop missing Gillian and the baby."

"Lonely, were you?"

"Yes, I was."

"Don't take me for a fool!" Valerie said, glaring at her. "I know you had someone staying here. Who was it? Charlie? Or that Tony Switch?"

"What?"

"Phil told me he came by to see that you were all right and when he saw Tony making for your door he turned away. Hurt he is. How could you have discarded him and had secret affairs?"

"This is rubbish! Nothing more than Phil's overactive imagination. A secret affair? Fat chance with him watching my every move! But Tony?" She frowned. "What was he doing near the shop?"

"Ask Phil. He saw him."

"Mam, I doubt that Phil saw him — but either way, I didn't!"

Being alone in the flat while her mother was away continued to be a worry for her. She had the impression, based on nothing at all, that she was being watched. One evening, when Valerie was out, she heard tapping on the window and, afraid to investigate, she rang Charlie. He said not to worry but he would come as soon as he could get away. Danny answered on the first ring and left immediately.

He came within minutes and found a button tied to a piece of string that was attached to the window frame, so every breath of wind made it tap against the glass. "An innocent bit of fun, me darlin'. Children, for sure. Didn't I do silly things like that when I was little?"

But she thought the pressure on her nerves was intentional and by someone who wanted to remind her he was still out there, and watching. She rang Charlie, who still hadn't left the restaurant, and explained what Danny had found.

He was quite jovial and said, "There, didn't I tell you it would be nothing to worry about?" She put the phone down feeling silly and immature.

"From now on I'll give you a telephone number of where I'm playing so you can always reach me," Danny promised. Then he added, "Supposing Charlie can't come, of course." He looked at her quizzically but she didn't reply. "I'll always be there, whatever happens in the future. Always." He ordered her to take a long relaxing bath and actually ran the water for her to make sure she did, before he left with a brief and brotherly kiss.

Danny knew from casual remarks from Valentina and Valerie that Charlie was becoming a more frequent visitor, stopping sometimes to help Valentina sort out a query in her book-keeping and sometimes taking her out when they were both free. Running a busy restaurant, it was often late when he arrived but he never stayed all night so far as he could tell. Although he wasn't there every day, Danny almost always arrived early to open the shop and let her know of any arrangements he had to fulfil that day. Before they opened, he had coffee with her. There was never anyone else in the flat, except Valerie.

Danny loved Valentina. The realization had been slow to mature but now she filled his every thought. However, he was convinced Charlie was the man she'd marry. Being a successful and increasingly wealthy woman, she would want someone ambitious and successful too. With a couple of records to his name, his own ambition had quickly blossomed and died. Now all he wanted was a quiet life with the woman he loved, doing something he enjoyed. Every time he saw Charlie or heard his name, that simple dream faded further away. Tonight, he had been encouraged by the fact that Charlie hadn't bothered to go when she called him, and he had.

Valentina didn't go back to bed after Danny left. Sleep was far away and the dark morning, clouds heavy with imminent rain, added to the unfriendly atmosphere in the silent rooms. She turned on all the lights and sat looking at the walls until Danny returned, freshly bathed and dressed, to open the shop. She was still in her dressing gown, the bath water cold and unused. He made coffee and opened up while she got ready.

"I'm supposed to be meeting Charlie at lunchtime," she told him later. "He's coming with me to a record company's preview."

"Supposed to be?"

"I don't want to go."

"Then don't. Tell Charlie his services aren't required and I'll go instead. I'm more involved than he is anyway." He was staring at her as he spoke.

"D'you know, Danny, you work here almost full time and I've forgotten you aren't even on the payroll!"

He looked at her quizzically. "Forget payroll. Make me a partner."

Valerie had asked all the neighbours in the street where she and Dewi had lived but no one knew where her husband had gone after he had vacated their rented house. Or, she suspected, they weren't telling. It was several weeks before she found him. She walked past the factory where he had once worked and from where, she had been told, he had been sacked. The factory was now a wholesale store selling children's toys. It only employed about five men and as the group came out at midday one Saturday, she saw to her disbelief that Dewi was one of them.

She didn't know how to handle it; couldn't find suitable words with which to greet him. Should she say a casual hello or ask him what on earth he thought he was doing? It didn't occur to her to smile and tell him she was glad to have found him. Walking slowly towards him, she stood and said nothing while the men who accompanied him fanned out and went their separate ways.

"My big adventure didn't get much mileage, did it?" he said. "I'm living in a bedsit a few yards down the road. Want a cup of tea?" He gestured with an arm and she followed him silently.

"I don't want you back," he said when they were sitting drinking unwanted tea in his sparsely furnished room. "I know about that Italian being Michael's father. Careless you are, Valerie, leaving letters about. I found the one he wrote after you'd told him. No wonder you're obsessed with the boy."

"Dewi, I'm sorry. I wanted to tell you but I couldn't."

"I wouldn't have stayed if you had," he told her calmly. "I understood why you disliked our daughter, her being the cause of us getting married, I knew about you and this Ernesto, but I never dreamed that Michael wasn't ours."

He took her cup and saucer and washed them at the sink in the corner of his room, then turned to her and said, "I'm not having you back. I wouldn't. Not if you begged."

"I don't want to come back," she replied sadly. "I have to go on looking for Michael."

Telling Valentina she had found her father was surprisingly hard. She and Dewi had talked for hours and what had come out was his strongly held opinion that she had used him to pile on her resentment about the way her life had turned out. "When really," she admitted, "we're architects of our own destiny, Dewi as well as me. He knew I didn't love him when he married me, that I was only doing so because our families insisted."

"Is he all right, Mam?" Valentina asked. "Will he want to see me?"

"Love to see you, he would. I'm the one he doesn't want to see, and who can blame him? I *had* to marry him and that phrase means I was expecting you and my parents insisted, even though we didn't love each other. I was in love with someone else, you see."

Valentina remembered the story Phil had told her but she wasn't certain it was the truth, so she pretended to know nothing and encouraged her mother to talk.

"Tell me about it, Mam."

"This other man, he was from Italy, an ex-prisoner of war. He went home for a visit but said he'd be back and when I realized after a year that he wouldn't, well, I sought comfort with your father. Then he did come back and by that time I was pregnant with you and married to your father and I had to let him go. I think I've been punishing you and your father ever since." She was speaking so quietly Valentina could hardly hear her. It must be agony for her to talk about such things with me, she thought with compassion.

"And you've never seen the man again?"

Valerie turned away, hiding her face in her hands, and Valentina guessed there was more. What Phil had told her had been the truth. "Tell me, Mam, I want to understand."

"Ernesto he was called, but I called him Ernie." She smiled then, remembering. "I left you and your father for a few days, but I knew where my duty lay and I told him goodbye. And, he and I —" Her voice sharpened, became harsh and she forced herself to speak. "Nine months later Michel was born! There! Now you have it all! Satisfied?" Tears slid down her cheeks and Valentina hugged her until they stopped.

So much became clear to Valentina after her mother's confession. Valerie's devotion to Michael, who had been given the epithet "Love Child". The love her mother had wanted to give to Michael's father had been transferred to their son and had become distorted into an obsession. Poor Michael. Perhaps now she would be better able to help him. If only he could be found.

298

There was a knock at the door soon after Valerie had gone out and Valentina opened it to see Claire and her ex-boss Ray Everett standing there.

"Claire! Ray! What a lovely surprise. Come in!" She led them up the stairs, her mind dancing about in wild guesses, wondering about the reason for their visit. It must be important for them to come together.

"You've tried to be my friend," Claire said as they found seats, "even though I couldn't tell you everything. I appreciate it more than you know."

"You believe me when I said I didn't know who Myfanwy Mayhew was, when I arranged that interview?"

"We believe you," Ray said.

"The reason we called is to tell you that our story is now in the open and we wanted to tell you first. Tomorrow the newspapers will run the story and we're glad it's out in the open at last. It will probably be unpleasant for a while but we're prepared for that and we'll just face it until it all dies a natural death."

"Why now?" Valentina asked. "What has changed?"

"My mother has agreed to a divorce," Claire told her.

"We'll marry as soon as I'm free," a smiling Ray added.

The news was cause for celebration and Valentina opened a bottle of wine and sorted through her rather sparsely filled cupboards for nibbles. "This meagre feast doesn't express my delight. I wish you every good fortune and much happiness."

The story about Ray and Claire filled the front of many newspapers and when Phil went to have lunch at The Bull that Sunday, knowing Valentina would be there, he was the only one who didn't rejoice. Unfortunately the occasion wasn't a happy one for him. Danny was there and it was obvious to his obsessively jealous mind that he was too friendly with Valentina. His Valentina. It seemed life was rewarding everyone, even those who broke the rules, while he was still waiting for Valentina to come to her senses and admit she loved him.

To aggravate his sense of outrage further, John and Peter told Valentina that Peter's family had accepted their son's relationship with John. They had visited Peter's family and told them that they were a couple. Instead of anger, dismay and embarrassment, Peter's mother had explained that she had guessed and, aware of how well suited they were, couldn't be anything but happy for them.

Later, when that bit of excitement had calmed down, Valentina told the others that she and Danny were now partners in the record shop. Phil felt anger rising like the build-up to an explosion.

The celebrations lasted for longer than the lunch hour and when they all went for a walk and found somewhere to sit and discuss their plans, later finding somewhere to order tea and sandwiches, Phil tagged along with them. No one seemed to notice him but he watched Danny with his arm around Valentina and the way she hugged him occasionally.

When he finally left them no one said goodbye; no one had seemed aware he had been with them. He drove back to his flat too fast and sat up all night staring into the darkness, imagining Valentina and Danny together. Remembering how his gran had made him obey. His heart raced as he remembered those first few times being locked in a dark and terrifying place, afraid no one would come to let him out, how the hours had seemed like eternity. After that, the threat had been enough to make him promise anything his gran demanded. Then it all became clear. Valentina did love him, but pride was stopping her admitting it. Foolish girl. All she needed was time, a quiet time, to accept her true feelings.

Valerie couldn't give up on her search for Michael. She half promised herself that once she had him safely back with her, they would go together and talk to Dewi, see if something could be done to bring them all back together again. News of him came, as usual, from Phil.

"He phoned to tell me he's at your cottage and he's hurt," Phil told Valentina. "I don't know any details but he asks that you tell no one, specially not your mam. He begged me to make you promise to keep it to yourself. Don't let him down, Valentina."

Valentina arranged for Danny to stay at the shop, borrowed his car and set off at once, telling him only that she was meeting Michael but not saying where.

"The car's playing up a little," Danny warned her. "If you're going far I'd rather you didn't use it. It keeps stopping, then if you wait it recovers and starts again.

It's booked into the garage for tomorrow. Will you be going far?" he asked.

Keeping the promise to Michael, she shook her head. "Not far. I'll be all right."

The car faded out a few miles after leaving the motorway and as she pulled into the side of the road she was overtaken by a long, sleek Jaguar. She recognized the driver at once. It was Tony Switch. He got out of his car and walked across with his friendly smile.

"Can I help?" he asked. "Give you a lift somewhere? To the nearest garage at least."

She was afraid. Was this planned? Had he somehow persuaded her to take this road at this particular time? Perhaps Michael wasn't in trouble at all. With trembling hands, she tried the engine and this time it fired and she moved off. "It's all right, thanks, I'm fine," she shouted as she moved off. She stayed in second, allowing the powerful car to overtake, and waited until it was well out of sight before she picked up speed. A few miles further on the car stopped again. Frightened, with empty fields either side of her and no one to help if Tony returned, she sat, watching the clock, giving the engine time to recover from whatever was troubling it. Again it started but she decided that whatever the delay, she would call at the next garage and find out what was wrong. Michael would have to wait.

"Capacitor possibly," the mechanic said, rubbing his chin thoughtfully. "Or something blocking the fuel pipe? Best you leave it for me to have a look. I can arrange a taxi to take you to the next town?" he offered.

"I can't spare the time," she explained. "Will it get me there if I persevere?"

"No telling."

"I think I'll risk it," she said. "Thanks for your help." Filling up with petrol, she went on.

The third time it stopped, a car pulled up in front of her and it was with relief she saw it was not Tony, but Phil.

"Thank goodness," she said. "Tony Switch followed me. He stopped and offered me a lift and I was afraid he'd be back."

They discussed the problem with Danny's car and decided to abandon it and arrange for its repair later. She didn't question Phil's presence on that particular road at that particular time — she presumed he was on his way to see Michael too, although why he hadn't offered to travel with her was odd. There was little time to worry about it though. Leaving the car in a layby near a small village, they went on in Phil's car. During the journey she told him her mother had confirmed what he had told her about her affair with the Italian she had so loved. To her surprise he became very angry.

"Marriage should be for life!" he said. "She should have honoured the promises she gave your father and put aside others like the marriage vows say."

Remembering his disturbed childhood, being moved from family to family around unwilling relatives and uncaring strangers, she didn't argue too strongly in her mother's defence.

"Life isn't that orderly, Phil. We don't chose who we love."

"Honour and loyalty don't come into it, then? Is that what you're saying? That it was all right for her to cheat on your father? She'd have been justified in leaving you to go off with this other man because he was better in bed?"

She turned away from the image of her mother in bed with a stranger, but answered honestly. "It happens, Phil, as you well know. And it always will."

"Like you, you mean? Abandoning me as you did when better things were offered?"

She was alarmed at the fury in his voice and the wild anger on his face. "That's rubbish, Phil. We weren't a married couple and there's no chance we ever will be."

"Not married but we belonged together, we both know that."

She was honest enough to admit that. "For a while I imagined marrying you but it was simply a habit. We grew together as very young children and I stayed, helping with the band and all the other dreams you dreamed. Nothing more than that. Remember when you dreamed of being a wrestler? I used to go and watch as you trained."

"I looked after you."

"You were a good reliable friend, Phil, but nothing more, although it took my leaving home for the truth to emerge. It would have been a terrible mistake for us to marry."

"You used me."

"All right, we used each other. We were both unhappy with our lives, my mother treating me like an irritation, showing no love or affection or even liking, and you left by your parents and living on the periphery of other people's lives, taking what scraps of kindness they could spare. It isn't surprising we were drawn to each other."

"You love me. How can you deny it?"

"I loved you but in the same way I love other friends, not the love that leads to marriage."

"So my kisses were a substitute while you waited for the real thing."

"No, Phil. I just knew they weren't a promise of a future together."

"I protected you, fought your battles for you, while you were playing with my affection, my love." He began to rant alarmingly about fidelity and truth and women who lied. She began to feel afraid and searched in her handbag, pretending to look at details in her diary. She had never seen Phil like this and wondered if the brief affair with Penelope had unhinged him in some way. She remembered the expression on his face as he watched her with Tony Switch. She couldn't walk away. She had to hope he would calm down and return to the person she knew — or thought she knew.

His anger had dissipated by the time they reached the cottage, where all looked quiet. She unlocked the door and saw to her surprise that Phil hadn't got out but had driven the car through a field gate further down the lane. Panic made her heart race. Why was he was hiding it? But no, of course he wasn't putting it out of sight, he was just making sure he didn't block the lane. She didn't manage to convince herself fully, though, and she was tense when she stepped inside the cottage, which no longer felt a safe haven.

The house was cleared of the previous chaos. Lillie had done a good job cleaning up. The heating wasn't on and she went to press the switch when Phil's hand covered hers and stopped her.

"No need for that, love. I can keep you warm." He leaned closer to her, his lips seeking hers.

She pushed him aside. "Let me pass, Phil, I want to see Michael."

"He isn't here," he said triumphantly. "There's no one here. We're alone. Just as you wanted it. Now you can be honest."

"Stop talking nonsense and move away from me."

"It's what you want, you might as well admit it. Don't pretend any longer, my lovely Valentina."

Something in the way the words were spoken frightened her and she turned sharply to look at his face. His dark eyes were wide open, showing the whites and giving him a malevolent look. His mouth was a rictus of a smile but there was no humour in the half-open lips. She stepped back and pressed against the wall.

"Come on, Phil, if he isn't here we might as well get a garage to look at the car."

"We haven't looked upstairs yet."

"Michael isn't here and I don't know what you're playing at but I don't find it funny. Now get out of my way. Please, Phil. Stop this." Her voice faltered as he held her arms and pulled her away from the wall. Still smiling that awful parody of a smile, he began to pull her towards the stairs.

"Stop this, Phil. Stop it at once!" She struggled but found it impossible to prevent herself being forced towards the staircase. She grabbed furniture and the door edge and the newel post but each time she found anchorage he used the side of his hand to slice a sharp blow and make her release her grip.

Phil, thinking she would leave without the talk which he believed would put everything right between them, knew he had to make her stay. Valentina was remembering his stories of how his grandmother made him submit to her demands and was afraid he intended to lock her in until she made the promises he wanted to hear.

She didn't grasp what he was saying, only picking up the occasional word, as, screaming and struggling, and being slapped until she fell silent, she was pulled inexorably up the stairs. Her wrists hurt and had no strength; the way he had hit her had bruised the muscles. There was only a step landing at the top and she knew that once she was in one of the rooms she could be locked in and then escape would be impossible. Thoughts of being locked in made her scream again, the noise unexpected and making him release his tight hold for a moment. She tried once more to break free but he caught her and shook her until she felt dizzy then pushed her into the back room which overlooked fields. He was holding her with his arms around her, his cheek against hers. He was panting slightly and she was afraid to move. She stood trembling while he rambled on about his own sad experiences, hardly hearing the words as her mind envisaged Danny. He knew when she was locked in the bathroom above the flat when no one else did. But what chance of him turning up here when no one knew where she was? She relaxed a little as the realization overwhelmed her. There was no possibility of anyone coming. She was on her own with only her wits to help her and they seemed to have deserted her.

"You're going to lock me in, Phil? Make me obey?"

"I always gave in when Gran locked me in the coal shed. I remember that so clearly and I relive it in nightmares time and again. It was completely dark and cobwebs touched me every time I moved. Spiders and beetles walked across my face as I tried to sleep, and mice wandered around searching for food. Oh yes, I remember how that felt and I'd have promised anything to get out of there."

"Let me go, Phil, we can forget this happened. Please. You shouldn't be doing this, you know you shouldn't."

"I'm not going to lock you in, Valentina! How could you think that I would? I love you, we love each other. I'd never do anything to hurt you."

"But why did you trick me into coming here?" she asked, her voice quivering with fear.

"I know that if we sit and talk, like we used to do, face how much we loved each other, everything will be all right. I need you, you are my good luck charm as well as being my one true love. I'll be a success, bring you all the luxury Charlie offered — that was the real reason you were getting engaged to him, wasn't it? I've always understood you, my love. Trust me, I'll give you all you need and want. Once we're together everything will work out."

"Phil, listen to me." He seemed not to hear.

"You belong to me and I won't give up on a love affair, not like my father did. My mother told me all men are fickle but I'm not. And you won't be either. You'll learn to be loyal. You won't get away with cheating on me like your mam cheated on your poor father, so don't think it."

"It isn't your place to make me behave. We aren't married, we're not a couple, and never will be whatever you think!"

He was standing in front of the low oak chest in which she kept spare bedding. It was a few feet away from the wall and level with the back of his knees. If she could suddenly run towards him, push him, he might take long enough to recover for her to open the door and get away. But there was little chance of succeeding and she almost gave up before trying.

He had relaxed his hold and she began to move away but he grabbed her close to him and began pulling at her clothes, smothering her mouth with his so she couldn't speak. When he talked, his hand covered her mouth and he brought his face close to her as if trying to mesmerize her into listening.

"You love me."

"I don't love you. I can't love you."

"You might have forgotten, but you do. Love doesn't change and you can't be disloyal. Come on, Valentina, show me how much you still love me."

Struggling with him was exhausting her and doing no good. She relaxed suddenly and seemed to submit to his kiss and he smiled. "I was right, wasn't I? This is what you want."

Desperately she shook her head. "Not like this," she managed to say before his mouth came down on hers, hard, punishing.

He was gradually forcing her to the floor and she knew that once there she would be helpless. In one final effort she kicked his shin and as he was off balance, she twisted her foot behind his legs and pressed against his body, sending him crashing backwards until he reached the chest and fell heavily, his head hitting the wall. He gave a roar of anger. She began to sob.

"You bitch!"

"I'm sorry I hurt you but you know this isn't right. We'll forget it happened, get help for you. I'll drive us to hospital. We'll say you tripped when you were helping me search for Moke."

He came towards her again, anger glistening in his dark eyes, and she grabbed a bedside lamp and raised it above her head. "I'll use this! Don't think I won't! Now, get out of my way!"

Speaking calmly now, he said. "I'll leave you for an hour or so to consider where we go from here."

"There's nothing *to* consider. I don't love you and you can't love to order, whatever you think."

310

He went to the door and she stood near, watching him warily, then she squeezed past him. He grabbed her and pushed her, trying to get her back into the room. She fell down the stairs, grabbing the banister to slow her fall, and lay there, her ankle twisted beneath her and trapped across the other foot, where her weight had pressed on it. But she felt no pain; she was stunned with the shock of the fall and frightened by what she saw as Phil's part in it.

In a cold silent rage he hauled her to her feet and dragged her back up again, stair by stair. She became aware of a pain in her ankle and pleaded with him to stop. "My ankle, I hurt it when you pushed . . . when I fell." In the bedroom he threw her on the bed and glared at her. Her ankle was beginning to throb painfully. She felt it with her hands and wondered if she'd be able to walk. "Phil, I've really hurt myself."

"I'll be back in two hours. You have two hours to think about our future."

"Phil, I've hurt my ankle. Take me to a hospital, please."

"Rubbish, you're bluffing, trying to make a fool of me."

She called and pleaded and promised to talk about things, but she heard him leave the cottage and reverse the car out of the field and drive slowly back to the road. He'll stop and come back, she thought. She moved and cried out in pain. She had to get out before he came back. His anger had got completely out of hand.

Danny was worried when he hadn't heard from Valentina by six o'clock. Because the car was giving him trouble he had made her promise to phone him. She should have called before now; she had told him she wasn't going far. When the shop closed he rang Charlie to ask if he knew where she had gone, then contacted everyone he could think of. No one had any idea where she could be. Moke, he decided. It must be something to do with that brother of hers.

"We can't call the police — they won't be interested in someone missing for such a short time," he told Valerie. "What can we do? We can't just sit here and hope she'll turn up safe and sound. Isn't there anyone else we could try?"

"You could try the hospitals to make sure she hasn't been in an accident," Valerie suggested, a twinge of fear crossing her face.

Danny did try the police, but as he guessed, they weren't worried. "There could be a dozen reasons why she hasn't phoned, sir," the desk sergeant told him reassuringly. "Perhaps she met a friend and got talking. People do forget the time when they stop for a chat. Or she might have decided to see a film?"

"She'd have let me know," Danny protested. "My car wasn't behaving, you see."

"She'll be back, sir. Missing people aren't often really missing. If she hasn't been in touch by morning call us again."

Danny gave him the registration number of the car and the policeman rang off, after offering more comforting remarks, but Danny was far from content.

Charlie arrived and said firmly, "This time I'm listening. If Valentina's in trouble I want to be the one to find her. Where can we look?" His jaw was tight with tension, sounding determined, but he was looking at Danny, waiting to be told what to do.

"She didn't intend to go far, or so she told me. But I keep thinking of that cottage. I have a feeling that she was going to meet Moke. He's been to the cottage before, when he and his friends left that terrible mess." He glanced at Valerie, expecting her to argue, but she did not.

"If that was where she was going, why didn't she say?" Charlie asked.

"I don't know. I'm guessing like the rest of us." Danny found the calm attitude of Charlie more irritating than Valerie who, in her anxiety, said repeatedly that she was worried and should she make more tea.

Phil's anger didn't abate, it grew with every passing mile. A small voice told him she was telling the truth and they would never get back together, yet a louder voice insisted that she loved him but was too proud to admit he was right. She owed him love and loyalty. Hadn't he given her the experience that had led to her success?

His head ached. Every unexpected bump in the road was painful. He felt sweat running down his forehead.

He had managed to reach a cushion from the back seat and propped it behind his shoulder and neck.

The ache in his head increased as he thought of Valentina. A couple of hours would calm her down, make her see he hadn't intended her any harm. They would talk and settle things between them then he would drive her home and tell everyone they were back together. During that crazy drive, he believed it. In his mind now, the fight had been sexual. She loved him and was only fighting him because she was finding it hard to admit. His Valentina, proud and successful and in love with him.

He managed to obey the speed limit for twelve miles then became impatient. He reminded himself that she had fallen down the stairs. She might have been hurt more than he realized. Ashamed that he hadn't believed her, he knew that he had to get back to her, make sure she was all right. She was his love and he should have shown her how much he cared, even if she had been exaggerating. He'd been very thoughtless.

Then visions of the way he'd behaved came back to him and it shocked him. It was like looking at the behaviour of someone else. She had made him like that, with her treating him like so much rubbish, using him then discarding him. He'd never lost his temper like that before. It was moving away from everything familiar. London wasn't for them. They had to get back home, then everything would fall into place. She'd understand when he explained that to her. He frowned. But she might have been telling the truth about her ankle . . .

314

His foot was pressing harder on the accelerator and the speedometer surged around the dial. He couldn't make her wait two hours, she'd be so afraid. In his confused mind the cottage had changed to become the dark place of his childhood, a nightmare of spider webs and scurrying beetles. How could he have left her there? Calmer now, he imagined the loving welcome she'd give him when he rescued her.

He stopped the car, imagining her smile, just like he'd smiled at Gran when she came to let him out. He turned the car around and pressed the accelerator further and further as he drove through the narrow country lanes, dreaming of their reunion.

On a corner he met a tractor trundling along and in his anxiety to get back to Valentina and the wonderful welcome that awaited him, he sounded the horn impatiently and tried to overtake it. He swerved across the tractor's path and into a ditch. The tractor came to a stop after crushing the back of the car, which slid hard against the tractor.

Phil was shaken but unhurt but the door was tight against the other vehicle and he couldn't get out. Leaning over, he tried the passenger door and after a few squeals, groans and kicks it opened and he got out. His arms were shaking and his legs trembled as he tried to walk. The driver of the tractor was standing in the road, obviously unharmed, swearing at him. Gathering his strength, Phil staggered, walked, then ran away.

After removing her shoe, Valentina strapped her ankle with a pillow case. Then she slowly and painfully began to move. She wrapped herself in the blanket. She didn't know how long she would be there and warmth was always a comfort. Comfort she would certainly need — and persuasive words. There was no way to fight her way out of this.

Supporting her injured leg on a pillow, moving it with care, she edged closer to the front door. Then she tried to stand and found she couldn't. The movement was too painful. Even with the other leg sound, she didn't have the strength to struggle up and reach the door handle, the ankle was too painful. Phil hadn't locked her in the cellar but because he hadn't believed her when she told him her ankle was injured, he had left her a prisoner just the same. Her arms ached and her face hurt where she had knocked it as she had fallen.

Sitting on the bare, polished floor, she thought of Phil's childhood when the slightest misdemeanour resulted in him being locked in a small, dark cupboard and left to cry until he was exhausted. Surely he wasn't punishing her in the same way? For what? A misdemeanour only imagined in his unhappy, confused mind.

Why hadn't she accepted a lift from Tony? Phil had convinced her that the man was full of hate towards her but was that more of his confused thoughts? Phil, she decided, had manipulated her ever since they left home.

Time passed slowly as she began to believe she would be left there all night. She gathered the bedcover around her and resigned herself to a long, lonely night. She put the bedside light where she could reach it. It was the only weapon she had and she was angry enough to use it. He wouldn't find a frightened prisoner prepared to say anything he wanted to hear, but a furiously angry one.

She should have told Danny. Even if his car was found, it was a long way from where she now sat.

At 8.30 she heard a sound and, expecting it to be Phil, she reached for the lamp. But the sounds weren't right. There was more than one voice. "Danny?" she whispered, but the sounds died away before she could begin to bang on the door and shout for help. Whoever it was had gone, but she called anyway. Night had fallen and outside there were only the sounds of birds settling to roost. She closed her eyes and tried to pass some time in sleep but she couldn't stop listening, hoping for someone to come.

In the darkness she could no longer see her watch but guessed it must be about ten o'clock. She was hungry but no one died of starvation after one night and even in his strange angry mood Phil wouldn't leave her for longer than that. She wondered what to do when he did come. She hoped he would have calmed down and would take her to a hospital. Her ankle needed attention and he would surely do that before anything else.

She was woken out of that half dreaming state between wakefulness and sleep by voices. Not Phil. There were several voices, people laughing. This time she reacted fast. At the top of her voice she shouted, "Help me! Please! Help! I'm in the cottage and can't get out. Help, somebody! Help, it's Valentina! Please, find Lillie, she has a key."

The voices had stopped. Had they passed without hearing her? Then they began to talk again, this time to her.

"Valentina? Is that you? It's Lillie."

"It's me. Thank goodness you came. Let me out, please. I'm hurt and . . ." She began to sob.

Within just a few minutes, Lillie was kneeling down beside her and listening to her story. "It's my ankle," she explained. "I hurt it when Phil — when I fell down the stairs."

"And your poor face, it's a pretty sight you'll look by morning. All the colours of the rainbow you'll be." Lillie sent one of her friends back to the pub to call an ambulance. "And bring the makings of a hot drink," she instructed.

Phil managed to get a lift but when he reached the cottage he saw the activity outside and turned and walked away.

He arrived back at the flat in the middle of the following day and as he approached, pulling out his key in readiness, he saw a policeman standing near. Turning again, he went to a cafe and sat, wondering about the mess he had made for himself and wondering how it would end.

He drank several cups of tea in several cafes and thought about his life. He reluctantly faced the fact that his dream of a career in music was over. He felt the pain of realization that he didn't have the talent. Then he caught a train back to South Wales. As the miles passed beneath the wheels, he planned his story.

He would explain to his friends that being at the top was exhausting, with all the personal appearances. He would tell them he was on the very edge of a breakdown and on his doctor's advice had come home to rest and recover. As the train reached Cardiff, he almost believed it.

Within the hour Valentina had been rescued and taken to hospital and Danny and her mother had been informed. The following morning, Danny, her mother and Charlie were at her bedside.

"Danny was convinced you were at the cottage," Valerie told her, when Danny went to talk to the nurse. "He couldn't get through to the inn for them to check, so he borrowed a car and was here before us. He sat here waiting for you to wake. He really loves you, doesn't he?" Valerie made the remark as if she found the idea of someone loving her daughter surprising. "Frantic he was, wondering how to find you. He would have gone to the cottage ages ago but wouldn't leave the flat in case you came back."

Sitting up in bed wearing the unattractive hospital gown, with no make-up, her hair pulled back from the bruises and swellings on her face, Valentina wished Danny hadn't seen her until she had recovered. He came back, ignoring the nurse's demands that they now must leave, leaned over her and said with a frown, "If there was only an inch that wasn't covered with sticking plaster or blue with bruises, I'd kiss you."

She pointed to her lips. "Try here."

"That'll be grand."

She looked into his eyes, breathless with the thought that this kiss was important. It would put a seal on her realization that she loved him.

During the official visiting time later that day, Valerie told her they were staying at the inn. "The doctors say you can leave this afternoon and you must come home with me." Then her face twisted with dismay. "I don't have a home, do I? At a time like this I should be taking you there, looking after you, fussing over you till you're better. Mr and Mrs Francis said we can stay there. Will that do?"

"I should be getting back to the shop."

"Not yet," Danny said firmly. "Gillian is taking a week off. Ray has willingly given her time to help you. So we'll manage just fine."

Charlie had said very little. "If there's anything I can do?" he asked sadly.

"Charlie, thanks, but I'll be all right. There's nothing seriously wrong with me, thank goodness, just a sprained and bruised ankle and a face that looks like the work of a maniacal artist. I'll enjoy a bit of *maldod* for a while, though," she said, smiling at her mother as she used the Welsh word for pampering.

"Then I'll get back. Oh, I did think of something useful. Danny's car has been fixed and will be delivered to the cottage later today."

"That was so kind. Thank you."

He shrugged deprecatingly and kissed her goodbye.

With the ankle strapped, Valentina felt able to travel without too much discomfort. She and Valerie waved goodbye to Danny, then locked the cottage before starting on their journey back to South Wales.

As they headed west, a very subdued Phil was travelling in the other direction, on his way back to London with a police escort to face charges of dangerous driving and leaving the scene of an accident.

Moke was thumbing lifts without any interest in the destination. One day he'd have to go home, but not yet.

Once Valentina felt a bit more comfortable, she and her mother went to the council and explained that Dewi had vacated the house while, she, his wife, had been in London searching for their missing son. The official promised to do what he could to find her a flat. Meanwhile they were comfortable in the home of Mr and Mrs Francis.

With nothing to do and feeling they should stay out of the house for at least a few hours each day, Valentina and her mother went to places they had visited regularly when Valentina and Michael were children. They sat in parks and on beaches and talked, as they had never talked before. At the end of the week, only two days before Valentina was to go back to the shop, Valerie tried to explain about her affair with Ernesto.

"We met in a shed on the farm where he worked. It was only used for storing tools, and hay when there was a surplus. It was old then and unsuitable for anything valuable, but I wonder if it's still there?" she mused. At once Valentina insisted they went to look. This might be an opportunity to lay a few ghosts.

The actual farmhouse was gone, demolished to make way for an estate of prefabricated houses and a few self-build bungalows. There was a stream running past where the farm gate had once stood and they followed it, with Valerie describing how it had been when she was young.

On Saturday morning they went again to look for the barn and found it. It was in a dangerous condition, the wooden walls gaping as rotting wood had collapsed and fallen, to be hidden by the grass growing in and around the ruined building. The double doors had been tied ineffectually with string, which had been pulled apart with ease, leaving one door standing drunkenly ajar.

"Not much of a love nest," Valerie said sadly. "But then, it was secure from bad weather and warm. It always smelled sweetly of hay."

"I doubt if even a tramp would use it now. It looks in danger of immediate collapse. Yet young love must have made it a wonderful haven."

"When you feel so alive, glowing with happiness, and believe you must be the first to feel that way. Such precious moments when you are young. And when you're old, the memories can be so childish when seen in others; you're convinced they couldn't know love as you had."

At Victoria station, Valentina gathered her few possessions and went towards the exit. A taxi was justified, she decided. She was giving her destination to a driver when a voice called her. Danny came running towards her.

"Valentina, it's been forever! Are you all right? Oh, just look at your poor face, still battered and bruised."

"Danny, I'm fine. Even better seeing you."

"Are you? Are you really?"

"Danny, I don't want to go anywhere without you again." She smiled, knowing she meant it.

During the drive he brought her up to date with news of the shop. "I even managed to keep the appointments you'd made. One to the electric factory one lunchtime and I sold all the middle-of-the-road and oldies you'd bought. What about that then?"

Gillian was in the flat with Little Lever and Bob. The lights were on, there were flowers everywhere and the room looked bright and welcoming, free from any thoughts of danger. With the news of Phil's arrest and certain he was now out of her life, the ghosts had fled.

During the next week there were several phone calls from friends bringing news; including Claire and Ray, who were living together openly now their relationship had been revealed and the publicity had faded. John and Peter were also relaxed about their relationship now Peter's family had accepted their situation. Tony Switch sent flowers and Valentina rang to thank him, any animosity over between them.

Charlie called at the shop three or four times during those first days and Valentina noticed that when he came, Danny always went into the back room on the pretext of making tea or checking the stock.

"Why are you avoiding Charlie?" she asked as they closed the shop on Saturday evening.

"Me? Avoiding the man? Why should I be doing that?"

"Why, Danny?" she insisted. "Don't tell me you and he have quarrelled!"

"We have not. I didn't want to eavesdrop on the pair of you, that's all."

"There's nothing I say to Charlie that I wouldn't want you to hear."

"Not 'I love you' or anything like that?" He was smiling.

"I was an idiot to think I could marry Charlie."

"And so you were, entirely. And through it all there was me, loving you enough for two lifetimes."

"Only two?" she teased.

"Marry me."

She went to him, knowing it was absolutely right. With Danny as her partner she would be allowed to be herself but at the same time safe and secure. Together they would grow and not be stifled by resentments or past regrets. She looked into his eyes and nodded, her answer as brief but as binding as his question.

"Come with me to the cottage this weekend, Danny. I want to show it to you properly."

They set off an hour later and reached the village about 11.30, having stopped on the way to eat. Danny had appeared to be guiding her towards a rather expensive restaurant and she followed, feeling a slight disappointment. Did he think she needed spoiling with extravagant gestures and expensive food, a celebration of their commitment? If so, he didn't know her as well as she hoped. But no, he stopped a few doors further

324

on at a small corner cafe, where he ordered sausages and mash with onion gravy for the two of them.

"This is very good," she said as they began to eat.

"I'm not the man for fancy food with a little bit of this and a small scraping of that and la-di-da savoury sauces. Hunger is the best sauce, don't you think?" Then he looked alarmed. "But we can always eat somewhere special whenever you fancy. Be sure of that, me darlin'."

She smiled and shook her head. It was no wonder Danny had abandoned the trappings of success; he simply didn't need them. She took another forkful of the simple food, chewed appreciatively then said, "This is perfect."

They switched on all the lights in the cottage and if there were any lingering fears they were immediately bleached away. Making coffee with dried milk, she laughed, remembering the weeks she and Gillian were without a fridge. She told Danny about the green margarine and sour milk. "So much has happened since then."

"Disappointments and sorrows, mistakes and disasters, frights and dangers, and through it all there was this precious moment waiting to happen." He kissed her gently. "Isn't it grand?"

Also available in ISIS Large Print:

Nothing is Forever

Grace Thompson

Ruth has looked after her brothers for ten years since the death of their parents and believes that her role as head of the family will continue for the rest of her life. With two of her brothers already married and living away she has only her youngest brothers to care for. The arrival of a new, very determined sister-in-law makes change inevitable and Ruth struggles to maintain her superior role. Troubled by problems in her own relationship with the ever-patient Henry, she must recognize her priorities in time to salvage her own chance of love and happiness.

ISBN 978-0-7531-9112-5 (hb)
ISBN 978-0-7531-9113-2 (pb)

Goodbye to Dreams

Grace Thompson

In a small seaside town popular with summer visitors, Cecily and Ada run their father's grocery shop. Since their mother left them, they have lived above the shop with Myfanwy, a six-year-old they adopted when her parents died. The business is successful with the assistance of friends and Willie, their hardworking stable boy, and their deliveries extend to the stalls and cafes on the beach, where one stall handler, Peter, becomes a close friend. Love for the sisters brings only heartache. Cecily's wedding is cancelled and a secret revealed changes her life forever. Ada is happily married to Phil until disappointment touches her too. Is the growing business the only part of their life to offer them happiness?

ISBN 978-0-7531-8906-1 **(hb)**
ISBN 978-0-7531-8907-8 **(pb)**

Paint on the Smiles

Grace Thompson

Cecily and Ada Owens' shop is very successful. Their reliable deliveries and service is valued by cafes, tea stalls and shops on the Pleasure Beach during the summer months. However, things turn sour when Ada's husband, Phil Spencer, comes out of prison a very strange and dangerous man. And Myfanwy, Cecily's daughter, denied for too long is planning a cruel revenge. Unaware, Cecily and Ada hand over most of their business to Myfanwy during the difficult years of World War II. Is it too late for the Owens sisters to survive or can they celebrate the end of the war with hope in their hearts?

ISBN 978-0-7531-9058-6 (hb)
ISBN 978-0-7531-9059-3 (pb)

Gull Island

Grace Thompson

The year is 1917, and Barbara Jones is shocked to be told that she is carrying a child. Her boyfriend is a soldier and there is no one to whom she can turn for support. Indeed, her horrified father sends her away in disgrace when he learns of her condition. Fortunately, the generous Carey family give Barbara a home in a derelict house on a beach near Gull Island and it is there that her daughter Rosita is born.

Gull Island traces the lives of Barbara, Rosita and the Carey family over many years — through wars, hurt, hope and betrayal. When Rosita grows up, she must cope with more than her share of deceit and disappointment — but when she faces danger on Gull Island, those around her find that they are stronger than they ever imagined.

ISBN 978-0-7531-8786-9 (hb)
ISBN 978-0-7531-8787-6 (pb)

Facing the World

Grace Thompson

Sally Travis appeared to have been badly let down by Rhys Martin, who had gone away when under suspicion of burglary. Sally knew he was at college and secretly supported him. She had faced the gossips alone when their baby was born, and ignored the worrying rumours about him.

Rhys's father, Gwilym Martin, had lost a leg in an accident but whereas Sally held her head high under difficulties, Gwilym, who had been a popular sportsman and athlete, hid away, unable to face being seen in a wheelchair. But Sally ignored unkind remarks and helped others, especially Jimmy, a young boy put in danger by his parents' neglect during their marital difficulties.

But doubts about Rhys begin to grow. When Rhys finally returned, would she still be waiting? Or had too much happened for things to be the same?

ISBN 978-0-7531-8586-5 (hb)
ISBN 978-0-7531-8587-2 (pb)

ISIS publish a wide range of books in large print, from fiction to biography. Any suggestions for books you would like to see in large print or audio are always welcome. Please send to the Editorial Department at:

ISIS Publishing Limited
7 Centremead
Osney Mead
Oxford OX2 0ES

A full list of titles is available free of charge from:

Ulverscroft Large Print Books Limited

(UK)
The Green
Bradgate Road, Anstey
Leicester LE7 7FU
Tel: (0116) 236 4325

(Australia)
P.O. Box 314
St Leonards
NSW 1590
Tel: (02) 9436 2622

(USA)
P.O. Box 1230
West Seneca
N.Y. 14224-1230
Tel: (716) 674 4270

(Canada)
P.O. Box 80038
Burlington
Ontario L7L 6B1
Tel: (905) 637 8734

(New Zealand)
P.O. Box 456
Feilding
Tel: (06) 323 6828

Details of **ISIS** complete and unabridged audio books are also available from these offices. Alternatively, contact your local library for details of their collection of **ISIS** large print and unabridged audio books.